Praise for

EVERYTHING LEFT UNDONE

"Georgina's story was such an emotional one and took me on a rollercoaster ride."

"Wow! So much emotion packed into this read!"

"A gripping heartwarming and heart-wrenching read."

"The fascinating, complicated characters are worth getting to know and you'll be glad you went on this journey with them."

"This is an amazingly powerful story that will have you laughing, crying and feeling so many things."

"This story will have you in its grip where you may laugh one minute and cry the next."

"I have laughed out loud and sobbed (so hard I couldn't see my kindle), but one constant is, I could not put it down!"

THE BUCKET LIST, THE FOREVER LIST, AND THE EVER AFTER LIST IN ONE COMPLETE EDITION

Published by Lena Fox

© April 2018 All rights reserved.

Published in parts as The Bucket List, Forever List, and Ever After List by Lena Fox

Everything left undone

LENA FOX

Chapter One

GEORGINA

I have very few memories of my mother. Few good ones at least. I mostly remember the days when she was dying.

Before that, she was a fulltime career woman. Dad was the one who was home the most, who took care of me and did all the playing and cooking and teaching. But he was terrible at keeping the house clean. So, once a week, on my mom's day off, she would put on her favorite music loud enough to make the neighbors complain, and we'd have a cleaning party. Just the two of us, dancing and giggling as we wiped and scrubbed and swept the house clean. I was probably only four years old, but that was one memory that I still held. The memory of her carrying me on her hip as she twirled around, singing into the broomstick like it was a microphone, came with such painful clarity it brought the sting of tears to my eyes.

The music pounding through the club now was a newer song, a hit from a couple of years back that everyone knew the words to. The room was filled with competing voices shouting out of tune.

Let us live forever,

Or let us die together,

Without you, what is life for?

It was not without irony that the teen popstar who sang that tune had died young from an overdose.

I shuddered and gave myself a mental slap.

Stop thinking about death.

I probably should be more focused on the man kissing me.

He leant into me, and my back rubbed against the wall. Grimy posters scraped my skin and from them I could smell decades old cigarette smoke, feel it sinking into my hair and flesh.

The man's lips were firm, demanding. My mouth opened under them, and he delved in. I wrapped my tongue around his, tasting bourbon and a tangy, smoky flavor from the barbecue crisps he'd been eating. My heartbeat tap-danced in my throat. Nerves made me question my every action, but my mouth seemed to know what to do, as though it was made for kissing and had been waiting for this moment.

The sensations of his lips against mine made my scalp tingle and I wrapped my hands around his neck as I relaxed, embracing the experience, letting it go on and on.

I wanted to explore those sensations, hold on to the moment for as long as possible, but eventually I had to come up for air.

When I did, I got a proper look at his face for the first time. He was a nice-looking guy, with a mess of curly black hair, and hooded eyes. He wore a pair of ultra-skinny jeans, a well-tailored shirt, and a smart black tie that contrasted against his roughed up old skate shoes.

The way he gazed at me, eyes wide and lips curled into a sweet and confused smile, made me wish I hadn't looked. My imagination started playing out dreams of more romantic encounters with him, dates we could go on, kisses we could share. A future.

I shut it down fast. None of those things could happen. He was just an item on *The List*. I could never even know his name.

I turned and walked away.

He yelled after me. The music swallowed his voice, but I heard the slur of alcohol, confusion, even anger. Fair enough. I'd used him. Although the thing he seemed upset about was that I had *stopped* using him. I wasn't going to let his disappointment change my plan. *He* didn't get to decide what part of my list he ticked off—*I* did.

My lips were pulped and bruised from that long kiss, and I wore them like a badge of honor. Tonight was a test, and it proved I could do it. I could muster up the courage I was going to need.

I squeezed past a group of girls surely using fake IDs and stepped out of the club. The air outside felt fresh and clean in my lungs and I drew it in, standing for a long moment under the golden-orange glow of the flickering streetlight before getting into my car. I stared at the sky, starless above the glare of the city. A dense, unforgiving void. I blinked eyes that felt gritty and heavy. The night had become a long blur. I was exhausted and still had to drive half an hour back to my house.

My feet, unaccustomed to wearing high heels, ached like someone had run over them with a monster truck. I slipped the shoes off and threw them over my shoulder into the back of the car.

A pile of textbooks sat on the passenger seat, delivering a message of guilt. I had always studied hard. Ever since I was accepted into university, I had worked my butt off to make sure I made good grades but right then, none of that mattered.

Nothing mattered anymore.

Anger took over and I shoved the books onto the floor. They landed with a dismal thud that echoed inside the confines of my hatchback.

I dug through my purse and pulled out a tiny black notebook. Snatching a pen into my hand like clutching a dagger, I scratched away the first item on the list in violent thrusts.

~~Make out with a stranger~~
Get to second base
Lose virginity
Sex on a beach
Bondage sex
Make love with a woman
Sex in a public place
Sex with two men

My fingers shook, and I dropped the pen and the notebook.

Mom, what on earth am I doing?

Tears filled my eyes in a sudden, unexpected rush. I stuck my palms into them to hold them back. *Don't think about death. Just think about The List.* I had no time for tears.

I only hoped I had enough time to finish The List.

Chapter Two

GEORGINA

"You missed a whole day of classes." Julie, my roommate, stood in the kitchen staring at me as I fumbled around on my shelf of the pantry.

I winced and continued rummaging for something to eat that would take little effort. "Yeah, I know."

"Are you sick? You look sick." She managed to sound both condescending and concerned. I could never get a clear reading on Julie. She was a strange, mousy thing with the kind of big brown eyes that made the rest of her features insignificant. She looked so vulnerable and childlike, but spoke in the same monotone, dry voice whether she was wishing you a good day or telling you her grandmother had died.

Julie had seemed the obvious choice for a roommate. She was as serious about her classes as I was, as bereft of a social life and boyfriend, as well as a clear grip on how much we both liked our privacy. We never spent much time in the shared living room or kitchen together. Julie never ate the food on my shelves in the refrigerator, and I never used her bathroom products. It was a good arrangement.

Just yesterday, I had wished there was more between us. Wondered if we could be friends. We'd always been too busy, our class times always misaligned, her work hours too long, and plenty of other excuses about why we weren't close. The truth was that I'd never tried. It would have been nice to have a friend to talk to right then, to confide in.

Now it was too late to try.

Julie tilted her head. "You should get a doctor's note or something. If you don't, you might lose your scholarship."

I grumbled under my breath. "That would be a tragedy."

Julie may be twenty-going-on-eighty, but there was nothing at all wrong with her hearing. "It would be. Do you know how important it is to start out debt-free? My parents say that it's the best start to a strong future. Don't you care about your future?"

What future? "Sure. Yes. Very important."

With one blink of those big, brown eyes, Julie shrugged and walked out of the kitchen.

I rested my forehead on the cabinets, closed my eyes, and took long, slow breaths. Even though I'd only had one drink the night before, I had a nasty, weak feeling in my belly. I knew it had nothing to do with alcohol consumption, and everything to do with the future that I really did care about. That I was already grieving.

I heated up some ramen and ate it standing in the kitchen, trying not to think about tomorrow or the day after or the day after that. All I wanted was a full belly and to sleep the rest of these feelings away.

I stared at the peeling paint on the ceiling above the oven. I'd missed out on getting into student housing, but Dad had managed to find this place for me, right around the corner from the campus. One of his favorite customers at his restaurant, an old lady who still ate like a fourteen-year-old, had been looking for a tenant. It was a small townhouse that hadn't been renovated for thirty years, but I loved it, from its peeling mint-green paint to its potted geraniums. It stood defiant in the face of inevitable entropy and decay. I was jealous.

I shuffled into the bathroom and winced away from the cabinet mirror above the sink, but not fast enough to avoid a glimpse of myself. Matted hair swirled down over my shoulders in stringy clumps. I'd developed a nasty set of raccoon eyes, having neglected to wash off my makeup before I crashed.

What a mess.

I popped a couple of aspirin from the cabinet and shambled back to bed.

My purse lay on the bedside table, dumped there the night before, half its contents spilling out, including that little black book. I pulled the covers up over my head to hide from it.

The best thing would be to give up on The List and get back to my life. I should blow it off, just forget the whole deal. It was stupid, and I was crazy for even writing it out. I was a squeaky-clean twenty-year-old virgin. *Who am I kidding? I have zero experience with men and even less with women. How am I going to make those things happen?*

The answer was obvious.

I can't.

Across the room, my work desk was a mess of papers, markers, and paints. An artwork lay half-finished taped to some board, a palette and brushes laying around it. The assignment it was for would be due soon. My heart was nowhere near in it.

I can't do anything.

I could only curl myself into a ball and wish for sleep to take everything away.

I was woken by the front door shutting. Julie had gone to class. *Where I should be.* I groaned away my guilt and rolled over.

When I peeked out from under the bedspread, the clock said it was four in the afternoon and I stared at it, wondering how it had gotten so late. If I cleaned up quick, I could maybe make it to my evening class. I could get notes from the classes I'd missed. I could catch up.

A surge of adrenaline got me to my feet. I could forget all this insanity and be normal and *forget …*

I made it all the way into the bathroom.

Then I remembered the kiss from the night before.

That kiss.

I made that happen. And it was so real, so exciting, and so immediate. It wasn't something that was right, or something that had tomorrows. Debt-free futures, studying hard, and doing the right thing seemed so distant now. All I wanted was the daring, sexy thrill of warm bodies in contact with each other, to cling to life and let that energy make me forget everything else.

I forced myself to look in the mirror and say out loud,

"Georgina Stone, you can do this."

The body in the mirror was a body I had not yet made peace with. Since age fifteen I had gone from being a medium to an extra-extra-large and back to a large. I had spent so long trying to be invisible, it was hard to shift my perspective to wanting people to see me, wanting them to find me attractive. Last night was my proving ground. I'd dressed up and acted the part, and men had watched me with desire. The first item on my list was successful. I'd made out with a guy I had never seen before, one who I couldn't pick out of a crowd if my life depended on it.

I could be the daring, seductive woman who completed The List in that little black book. I could be, and I would be. There was no way I was backing down.

Chapter Three

GEORGINA

The club was packed again. After spending the week alternating between guilt-ridden study panic, morbid sleep-in-past-midday depression, and excited list-preparation shopping, I ventured back to the same place I'd gone last weekend. I teetered on my high heels as I stared at the crowd, holding a drink in each hand. *Why did I order two drinks?* I'd caught a handsome guy giving me a long look when I first came in, and had bought the second drink, planning to take it to him. But by the time I had the drinks in hand, he was neck-deep in a tall slim blonde. I was left standing there like an awkward, alcoholic wallflower.

I had to get over my freeze-up and find a partner for the next item on my list. *Get to second base.* It seemed like the logical next step for The List before hitting the big leagues, so to speak. On paper it sounded easy enough, but how the heck was I supposed to get there?

A free-spirited dancing girl bumped my elbow, and one of the drinks sloshed over the rim of the glass and down my hand. I cursed, mentally counting the cost of the lost alcohol. I gulped from what remained of the half-spilled cup.

The music died away just to pump back up again. The lights switched from dull and pulsing colors to full, bright white and the magic of the room was lost. The dancing crowd went from music-video cool to a mess of limbs. Maybe my own awkwardness wasn't as big of a deal as I thought. Maybe everyone here was as odd and out of place as each other. The idea made me laugh, despite knowing that laughing on my own for no apparent reason probably made me seem even weirder.

A deep voice chuckled from behind me. "It's lucky I don't dance. Would've hated to be caught in that harsh, bright light of reality."

I laughed again, and when I turned to see who my partner in weirdness was, my heart almost jumped out of my mouth.

The man was like something out of Nordic legend. All

I could do was stare at his wide shoulders and the imposing height of him and think *he's just so damn big*. His caramel hair was sun-streaked with blond and just a hint too long to be anything other than wildly sexy. It fell around the back of his shirt and I wanted to touch that hair, lift it away from his collar and kiss his neck … I wondered if he'd let me.

His smile was wide and sly, his face almost boyish except for the strong jaw and high cheekbones. Bright blue eyes shone between thick lashes, flashing with humor and something dark and dangerous. Like he knew exactly how attractive he was, and he knew how to use it. I hoped he was planning to use it on me.

I should say something. That would be the not-weird thing to do right now.

All I could do was gawk. My mind looped through another round of *sooooo* biiig, and the lights switched to strobing. I almost had a word out when that dancing girl crashed into me again. She ran into my back, the contents of my second glass splashed up as though in slow-motion, forming a perfect little mini-tsunami of rum and mint leaves that hovered in the air between me and the man, before my chest mashed into his, and the liquid drenched the both of us.

"I'm so sorry!" I squealed. I tried to brush the droplets of drink off his white shirt with my hands, but all I did was saturate the fabric more, turning it transparent and making me blush from my cheekbones to my knees.

He picked a mint leaf off my shoulder. "No problem. I think you came off worst from that little scuffle. You're proper wet."

Interesting wording. He had a low husky timbre to his words that made some very pleasant feelings arise within me. I'd been turned on before. I knew what was going on, but never so much, so easily. And that accent …

"You're English?" I asked, hoping I didn't sound too dumb, or that he was actually from Australia.

"What gave me away?" Thor-man's grin widened, revealing a tiny dimple in one cheek. A very kissable dimple. He wiped the alcohol off his hand, then extended it to shake mine. "I'm Blake."

"Georgina." *Darn it. Mouth faster than brain.* I should have said something else, made up some awesome exotic name. A fake name would have been a good idea, especially if Blake was going to be an item on my list, which I was hoping he could be.

I wasn't sure how someone as beautiful as this man could exist, or be there talking to me, but somehow, I had to keep him talking, and turn that talking into more. I wanted to go into flirt mode but I'd never acquired that particular skill-set. "So … What are you doing here?"

"Staring at the pretty girl holding two drinks and hoping one isn't for your very jealous boyfriend."

Pretty? I felt a stutter coming on. "I meant in this country, not in this club specifically."

He assessed me with furrowed brows. "Are you avoiding the topic of your very jealous boyfriend?"

I narrowed my eyes back. "Are you avoiding answering why you're in this country?"

He made shifty eyes and whispered, "Is he standing behind me right now?"

I cracked. A bashful grin stretched my lips. "No, there's no very jealous boyfriend."

Without warning, Blake threw an arm around me and dragged me between him and the wall. The sheer mass of his bicep pressed against my shoulder, but I managed to see past it to the dancer girl from before, who twirled around where I'd been standing a moment ago.

He saved me.

"Someone should revoke her dancing license," I muttered.

Blake smiled at me. "So, your boyfriend isn't very jealous?"

I liked that Blake had a one-track mind, but I didn't like

the line of questioning. My smile faded. "There's no boyfriend."

There never had been. Ever.

Remember why you're here. It's not to make friends or boyfriends. It's to get through The List.

Blake loomed over me, a solid wall of man-flesh between me and the dance floor. "That's good then. Otherwise I would've felt like a tool for wanting to kiss you."

His lips were already so close to mine. I got so hot so fast it was a wonder I didn't faint dead away. "You want to kiss me?"

"I would have asked first. It's only polite—"

My lips were on his. I didn't want polite. I wanted a man to get me to second base. That was all. And if it could be this gorgeous specimen, *hells yes please.*

His kiss was nothing like the guy's from the week before. His lips felt soft and full, his tongue thick and warm as it filled my mouth. He ran his fingers up the sides of my neck and held my face, and an ache started in my belly. I felt hungry in a way I had never been hungry before.

Everything but that kiss, those physical sensations faded from my mind. Just as I wanted.

I pressed into him, pushing my body into his as he bent over me. My breasts flattened between us and his arms came down behind my arched back, bringing me into him even more.

The only problem with the situation was that I still had the remains of a drink in each hand. When Blake ducked his face away from mine and kissed my neck, a shockwave ran through me and the fullest cup slipped right through my fingers and landed on the ground. It landed with a splash and I stared at his black boots in horror. They were covered with ice and liquid.

Looking down at himself, wet from shoulder to toes, Blake sighed. "I'm not normally the type to get cold feet—"

"I am *so* sorry."

"—but I think I ought to go home and change."

I could see the moment slipping through my fingers the same way the glass had. If I couldn't do this, if I failed tonight, I wasn't sure I'd be strong enough to try again. Dark thoughts already invading my mind. I needed more, more touch, more physical closeness, to drown them away. *Be brave.*

"Can I come with you?" It didn't sound sexy like I wanted, but at least I'd said it.

A wide grin split Blake's mouth. "Would I say no to a gorgeous woman drenched in alcohol?"

He extended his hand to me, an invitation and a dare. *Am I really following this god-like man out of a club? To go home with him? Did he really just call me gorgeous?*

Yes.

Everything was unfamiliar, surreal. My heart beat so fast. The crowd was shoulder-to-shoulder, blocking our escape, but Blake took the lead, clearing a path before him like one of those icebreaking ships, pulling me behind him by the hand.

Outside, reality seemed much closer than it had in the colored-light world of the club.

I froze in the middle of the parking lot. "How do I know you're not some serial killer or something?" *An incredibly sexy serial killer.*

Blake turned around, and narrowed his eyes at me again. "How do I know *you* aren't? You're the one bringing it up."

"It's very rare for a woman to be a serial killer. I mean, there are documented cases of it, sure, but the odds are far better that you're the serial killer. And on the unlikely chance we both are killers, you're like, twice as big as I am. I think you've got the upper hand here."

He looked like he wanted to laugh. "You're a very interesting woman, Georgina. If you're worried, stay here. But life is what it is, and it doesn't last long."

Ice spread in my chest.

He continued, "I'm all for taking chances. So how about this—I'll take my chances with you being a serial killer if you take your chances with me. Deal?"

I could imagine all kinds of terrible outcomes that could, and did, happen to women all the time from situations like this. But inside of me there was a part that was already cold and dead. He didn't know how right he was about life not lasting long. What did I have to lose? *The List Georgina is brave Georgina. The List Georgina says yes.*

"Deal."

He smiled. "My bike is over here."

"I love motorbikes." *Well, that is an outright lie.* I had a thing for them when I was a kid and didn't know better, but now they just seemed unnecessarily dangerous and impractical.

When he led me to the gleaming chrome and steel beast, I almost called the whole thing off. He gave me his helmet.

"What about you?" I asked, as he helped me push the thing down over my head.

"The helmet goes to the prettiest person on the bike."

I would have thought him prettiest, but I wasn't going to argue. I couldn't figure out how to climb on, and he was no help. He just sat there astride the huge thing, gunning the motor so it roared.

Taking a shot at it, I swung my leg over like he had and slid into the space behind him. My dress was too short and too tight to be sitting astride the wide seat of the bike, and it scrunched right up to my hips. I tugged at the fabric, desperate to cover myself, but just had to be satisfied that I was mostly hidden behind Blake.

The breeze picked up and the door of the country-western club across the parking lot swung open. A snatch of a song blew out; a guy was wailing about living like you were dying, and my heart dropped into my belly, surrounded by butterflies.

"Let's go," I said, unsure whether Blake could hear me.

The rumble of the bike mixed with the nervous hum in my chest. Blake took off and I wrapped my arms around his waist and waited to end up as a smear along the highway.

Cool air rushed over my bare legs and streetlights flashed by as fast as the strobe light at the club. The cars in the other lanes all seemed too close. Strangely, I didn't feel scared. I felt alive.

I could smell the leather of Blake's jacket and feel the smooth muscles of his back tensing as he drove us into the night. Soon I relaxed into it, bending as we went around corners, the two of us moving together as one. When he paused at a traffic light, he reached one hand back and ran it down my bare thigh. Heat zinged through me. The whole experience felt so intimate I was almost ready to tick some items off The List right there and then.

Ten minutes later, Blake pulled up in front of an old, two-story bungalow that crouched between what looked like a closed-down kennel and a row of equally run-down homes. The wood paneling had more paint peeled off it than paint remaining, if you didn't count graffiti tags. It made my place look downright fancy.

I managed to get off the bike and remove the helmet without killing myself—literally or with embarrassment. I stood there, the feel of the bike still imprinted between my thighs and my face flushed from more than the wind. "Your place?"

Blake winced dramatically, sucking a breath in between his teeth. "I know it's dodgy. But rent is cheap, and the neighborhood is pretty good, really."

Looking around, I had to disagree. Weeds grew up through the sidewalk, half of the streetlights were out, and the other houses on the street looked just as broken and worn-out as the one we stood in front of. I was ready to place bets on whether I was more likely to die here in a mugging or a drive-by.

Luckily, Blake led me inside before any street crime could occur. The interior wasn't a whole lot better, filled with mismatched furniture that looked like it had been collected from sidewalk garbage pick-ups. Milk crates with a street sign on top made a coffee table, and a long brown sofa of cracked leather was covered with newspapers, textbooks, and an empty pizza box. From the corner of my eye I was sure I saw Blake snatch some underwear off the floor and throw it behind the kitchen counter. It didn't look like men's underwear.

I thought this had been easy, and realized I probably wasn't the first girl he'd brought home like this. There I was feeling proud of my catch, when I was the one who'd been hooked. How many other girls had Blake caught? And what had he caught from them?

My mind was spiraling, looking for excuses to leave. I needed a breather, so I asked for the bathroom. He pointed up the stairs.

His bathroom wasn't a total sty, but it was obvious he was a guy who lived alone. His clothes were on the floor. Damp towels hung off the back of the door, and the toilet seat was up.

I sat my purse down on the bathroom sink and opened it, digging around for gloss and a hairbrush. My hands shook and the tiny make-up tube kept slipping through my fingers, so I dumped everything out. I swiped the blueberry-scented lip gloss over my pout, and dragged the brush through my dark hair. I no longer looked like I had just gotten caught in a windstorm, and packed the contents of my purse away again. Fixing myself up was enough of a confidence boost to keep going. I took a slow breath.

To second base only. That's not too hard. I can do it. And Blake … Blake is gorgeous. When will I get a chance like this again?

Back in the living room, Blake shuffled stuff around so that the sofa was cleared off while I stood there watching, awkwardly.

Since the kissing had stopped, I wasn't sure how to get it started again. Just going and throwing myself at him didn't seem right this time. Especially since he was the kind of guy who asked first.

He vanished into the kitchen before I could decide either way.

"So, what do you do?" I asked, trying to break the silence.

"A bunch of things," he called back. "I like building motorcycles."

"Like the one we rode tonight? You built that?" I could barely grasp how one person could build something as complicated as a motorbike.

I heard him rummaging around in drawers. "Yeah, just a hobby really. What do you do?"

What did I do? Moving forward, all I had was The List. All-consuming. My only goal. But that wasn't a normal answer.

"I used to go to university."

"You're too young to be finished. You drop out or something?"

"Or something."

Blake returned, holding two bottles of beer.

This could be good. Liquid courage.

He handed me one, then kicked off his wet shoes, and peeled off his jacket and shirt. He gave them a flick to shake away some mint leaves, then threw them over the mountain of books on the coffee table.

I gawped at him standing there topless. He didn't seem to be making any move to replace the shirt he'd just removed. He was *godly*. I took a long scull of my beer.

"You still wet?" he asked.

I choked. "Uh, no, the ride back dried me off."

Blake sat down on the lounge, sipping his beer. He patted the cushion next to him.

The old, cracked leather sagged and a small puff of dust came out of it. So what if he was a slob? Other than that, he seemed perfect. Perfect for the next item on The List, that was. The last thing I wanted was to get too close to anyone.

I took another swig, then sat down next to him. I intended to sit *juuuuust* touching against him, but the lounge slumped unexpectedly to the side, and I ended up practically on his lap.

Our noses brushed each other. Our lips moved in as though drawn together by a magnetic force. Blake paused, and chuckled a soft, throaty chuckle that sent a shiver down my back. "How about we put our drinks down first, this time?"

"Good idea," I whispered back, my voice refusing to work fully.

There was no space on the coffee table, so I reached down and placed my bottle carefully on the floor beside the sofa. I could see Blake stare at my breasts as I bent forward, at how they almost spilled from my tight minidress. He didn't hide that look, that smolder of animal lust. With a playful growl, he flung his nearly full bottle across the room and pounced on me. I squealed, half in fun and half in genuine shock. The beer bottle thunked against a wall.

The squeal turned into a giggle as Blake nuzzled into my neck, and then a gasp as he brought his lips closed around my earlobe. Just my earlobe, oh god, and how it felt. No wonder people liked this sex business so much. I suddenly started getting excited about the rest of my list. This was why I wrote it. To feel … *this*. Only this. And forget everything else.

I leaned back, and he leaned over me until we were both lying down. His weight was comforting, and I could tell he was holding most of it up off me. His hair was soft under my fingers, and his hands were warm when he ran them down my body. I enjoyed the way he kissed me almost too much. Like I could float there in the warm sea of his kisses forever. But I didn't have forever. I had to keep my eyes on the goal.

The dress I had bought specifically for tonight had corset-like clasps that ran right down the center of the bodice, and I guided his hands to them. I could feel the tug and twist of the fabric as they opened under his fingers.

I wore no bra, and as my flesh bared to the cool air, fear ripped through me. Nobody except nurses and doctors had ever seen me naked—not since my childhood, anyway. As my dress peeled away, I felt so vulnerable, visible, and judged.

Blake pulled back for a moment and looked at me, taking me all in. I was ready to run, but the way he groaned at the sight of me made me ache, made me feel so wanted. The air whispered across my nipples, and they grew taut. When Blake put his mouth on one, all my fears left me. It was like he lit a match and my whole body went up in wildfire. I couldn't think of anything at all except for how incredible it felt, how incredible *I* felt. *Earlobes, schmearlobes.*

His mouth tugged at my nipple and his fingers squeezed the other then slid along the flesh of my breast.

Every movement of his mouth stole my breath. Every touch made me shiver. *Let's do the whole list right now, please?*

I could tell when he found the scar. His fingers stilled, and he backed up.

"What's this?" he asked, sounding out of breath.

I sat up. The tingling sensations his mouth had started in me died out abruptly. "I … had a breast reduction." It wasn't a very convincing lie, when the scar was only on one side.

His hands ran over the slopes of my chest, feeling the fullness there. "Wow, you have plenty left. How big were you?"

I shied away from his touch, covering myself with folded arms. His focus on my breasts made my skin crawl with buried fears, trying to dig their way to the surface. I couldn't face them. I couldn't do this. "I have to go."

"Shit, I'm being insensitive. You don't have to go. I'll stop asking questions. Unless you want me to, and then I have plenty of questions. Or we don't have to talk at all, of course." He gave me that sly smile again.

I pulled my dress back up from where it was crumpled around my waist and turned my back on Blake while I did up the clasps. I could only repeat, "I have to go."

I expected him to argue but he just said he would take me back to my car. When we got there, he tried to ask for my number. I fumbled my keys and pretended not to hear, pretended not to remember I'd been drinking as I started the car and pulled away, leaving him alone in the night.

I finally arrived home, tired and confused. Dying for some water, I trudged into the kitchen. It had been cleaned, even though I knew it had been my turn to clean it, not Julie's. Another part of life I'd neglected. She'd even left a bag on the counter of the garlic fries from her work that I liked. They wouldn't reheat well, but I doubt she was expecting me to be out so late. I ate a few anyway, cold, soggy, and delicious.

There was a faint rim of light coming from around Julie's door. I could hear the low drone of barely audible music and voices. Probably Julie binge-watching some sci-fi series like she often did after work. I wanted to knock, to ask if she wanted to hang out, to tell her about Blake and how hot he was, and giggle like two schoolgirls into the night. But all I did was look at that closed door of hers for a few more minutes before grabbing some water and returning to the garlic fries.

I was on my second glass of water when I heard a theme song play, then click off.

Julie came into the kitchen, put an empty plate in the sink, gave me a polite nod, and asked, "Do you know if the lab is going to be open for all students this weekend?"

Julie was a physics student and I wasn't, so I had no idea. Just as I opened my mouth to say so she tapped her ear to draw attention to the headset there, gave me a half-wave, and left the room.

It wasn't the first time we'd managed to not have a conversation, so why was I crying?

I wiped the tears away angrily with my arm, stumbled to my bedroom, and closed the door. I didn't need a girlfriend to gossip to about Blake. I'd probably never see Blake again. I didn't need anyone.

At least I'd completed another item on The List.

I opened my purse and reached in, looking for the journal to cross *second base* off The List.

It wasn't there. Not The List or the book. I dumped the purse out on the bed, sure that it was in there and I had just missed it somehow, but amongst all the makeup, loose coins, pens, tampons, and old receipts, it wasn't present.

I panicked. Where had I seen it last? I had moved it to one side to get to my hairbrush … while I was in Blake's bathroom.

No, no, no, no, no!

Chapter Four

BLAKE

I'd seen her at the bar the weekend before. I'd almost walked out of the place when Seyvia's song started playing, then Georgina had caught my eye. I'd gone back hoping she would show up again, and she did, wearing a dress that was even tighter than the first one, showing off her incredible curves. Her face held such a vulnerable and innocent beauty, but she had these wide, impossibly full lips that I couldn't get out of my mind. Her long dark hair hung down past her waist. It was sexy, in a ragged kind of way. Everything about her was sexy in a ragged kind of way that first night—from the little tears in the material of her dress to how she grabbed a punker-wannabe out of nowhere and made out with him for the sheer hell of it. It turned me on like nothing else. She seemed so wild and uninhibited. The kind of girl I needed. Someone who liked to have a bit of fun, with no commitments.

When I got the chance to talk to her, I said something dumb about not dancing and thought I'd ballsed the whole thing up. Everyone knew ladies liked guys who could dance. I knew that too well. It was half the reason I didn't dance anymore. The other half of the reason was too painful to think about

But Georgina had just laughed with me, and I suddenly had no idea what kind of girl I was dealing with. When she joked with me, and went home with me, I figured she was a goer after all. Then everything changed again, and she was gone.

And now this. This list.

I stared at the items written out in the little black book. *Make love with another woman.* Wow, that sounded good. The arousal I'd been fighting since Georgina let me play with her gorgeous breasts came back again with a vengeance.

It wasn't hard to picture Georgina on her back with her legs spread open, her eyes closed and her hair flung out all across the pillows as another woman licked her thighs, starting low, working her way higher, higher. I could see myself in that encounter too …

"Bloody hell." Even as a fantasy it was almost too much to bear.

I shook the vision off and splashed my face with cold water in the sink. The journal was personal. I'd only looked inside to identify what it was and why it had appeared on my bathroom floor. It wasn't right to snoop on her like that.

I closed the book, but that didn't shut off my thoughts.

I had to wonder why she was doing it. From the list, I understood that she was a virgin and that she wanted to drop that like a lead balloon, but what about the rest of it? The list was new, that was obvious—she'd only gotten to the first item.

Scratch that. Top two items now. Second base was made tonight. She just hadn't had a chance to cross it off. Bloody Americans and their baseball metaphors.

Second base. I put the journal on top of my dresser and lay down on the bed, staring up at the ceiling and thinking about her breasts, how soft they had been in my hands, how her nipples had gotten so hard they'd felt like tiny pebbles between my lips. The way she'd gasped, it was like she'd never felt that way before. Why had she never gotten to second base? She was so sexy I was still hard and aching for her. Surely she'd had other opportunities.

My hand was reaching for my fly, but I groaned and

stood up again. I had to go and get that damn sexy list out of my house or I'd be spending the whole next week tossing off. I had dropped her back at the club where her car was, but someone there had to know where she lived.

I grabbed my bike helmet, and opened the front door.

And there she stood.

A light drizzle of rain created a halo of mist around her. The small smile on her face didn't hide the fear in her eyes. "Sorry, I know it's really late. I think … I left … *something* here. I hope you don't mind me dropping back in but it's … very important to me."

I held the journal out to her.

Her face went pale. She reached for the notebook but before she could put her hand on it I asked, "Did you think I was too hot to resist, or did you just grab the first guy interested in tits?"

I had meant it as a joke, but for some reason it came out wrong. It sounded like I was angry. *Am I?* I'd been used before, and I'd used others before, but never for this, like this. Never as an item on a list. I had no idea how to feel.

Georgina took a long breath. "You read my list?"

She looked so shell-shocked I tried harder to be jovial. "Not that any guy would mind being used by a girl like you."

She flinched at the word '*used*'. "It's not like that. Not

really. I just … I want to do those things on the list, and you seemed to want to do that thing as well, and you're pretty much the hottest guy I have ever seen …" Her voice cut off and her cheeks turned an adorable shade of pink.

I wished I could say I was confused, but I wasn't. I knew how the world worked, just like everyone else. And when I went to the club hoping to see Georgina again, I'd have been lying if I'd said I wasn't just thinking about sex.

I held the journal back out and she took it. She tucked it under her arm and said thank you so softly I almost missed it.

"I could help you with that list, if you want." I said it quickly. My brain was still stuck on the idea of watching her and another woman making love.

"How?" she asked.

How? Well, shit. I hadn't really thought it through before I just blurted that out. Now I realized I'd basically just offered to be her sex toy. What was a good way to say, 'Hey, I would love to be between you and another woman'? I sure didn't know how. I just knew it sounded like a bloody good time.

The awkward silence drew on. She just stood there, soaking wet, staring at me, waiting for an answer. Sweat broke out on my forehead.

Soaking wet …? It struck me then that the rain that had started out as a light drizzle had turned into a full-on gusher. Her black hair was plastered to her face, and beads of water had collected on her long eyelashes. No wonder she was looking at me like I was the world's biggest jerk. I was too busy trying to lay her to see that she was inches away from drowning.

"Damn. It's pouring out there. Come inside?"

She glanced at her tiny, bright green hatchback that was sitting in my driveway. I half-expected her to tell me to sod off and be gone again, but instead she took one long step inside the house. I could smell the faded ghost of her light perfume, making me think of blueberries and caramel.

She must have gotten home and changed before coming back. Her pale pink T-shirt was wet and her bra showed clearly against the fabric of it. I stared at it, at the cups and the flesh rising above them, for a full minute before I remembered my manners. Feeling even more like a tool, I ran down the hall for a towel but all the ones I owned were on the bathroom floor. I did the sniff test on a few of the cleanest dirty towels before deciding that none of them were any good. I had been meaning to get to the laundry for two weeks now, but I'd never been good at keeping chores and housework under control. I caught sight of my unmade bed in the other room. I grabbed a sheet off it, plus one of my old football shirts, and headed back to the living room.

The jeans she had on were as soaked as her T-shirt. They clung to her thighs and hugged the curves of her heart-shaped ass. I paused for a second, staring at her bottom, at the uplifted cheeks neatly bisected by the seam of her jeans. That body … that list … if she agreed to my offer it would be like an open pass, and I imagined ticking the items off. I grew so hard so fast I considered going back the other way, but she turned around and saw me so I lost my chance to hide. I held the sheet out in front of me so she wouldn't see my bulge and I wanted to laugh at the whole situation. This was like being back in high school and dealing with a perma-erection all over again.

I started to dry her off, hoping to give myself time to calm down but touching her, even through the dingy sheet and her wet clothes, was not the best idea. My jeans just got tighter. Out of sheer desperation, I tossed the sheet over her head and let her handle it. If I touched her again I was going to have jeans wetter than hers.

"You never answered my question," she said as she dragged the sheet off and started drying her hair with it. She was standing in a puddle of water that was getting bigger with each second and not realizing in the slightest how bloody delicious she looked, demanding to know how I was offering to help with her sex list.

"Well," I started, trying to be delicate. "You'll need a man for some of your list, and I'm … a man …"

Fuck.

Chapter Five

GEORGINA

He really surprised me by saying he could help me with my list. I didn't know how to reply, so I said the first thing that came into my head: "How?"

I was expecting him to say some lame line like 'come on in here and I'll bang you silly' or something like that, which of course I imagined in his cute British accent. Instead, he just asked me to come in because I was getting soaked on his doorstep.

I kind of hoped he'd say the lame line. I wanted his offer to be an offer for nothing but sex, not an offer of *help*. That was the last thing on earth I needed—a nice guy who wanted to help me. I'd had enough of nice people who wanted to help me. Some things couldn't be helped.

After a failed effort to dry me off—sheets aren't the most absorbent material—he threw the sheet over my head, making me look like the world's least ambitious ghost. He'd seemed so confident before. Then he developed a very cute stutter when trying to offer to be the man I have sex with.

I couldn't help but smile. It was sweet, but I didn't need sweet right now. I did need a man though, and my faux bravado was sighing in relief at the thought of not having to pick up someone new all over again. Plus, Blake was mind-blowingly handsome. Big bonus there.

I was toweled off a bit and started to pull up my shirt so I could put the dry one on. Blake saw what I was doing and turned his back. For a guy who had just offered to help me do some raunchy stuff, he sure was shy. Or a gentleman. I wasn't interested in either of those kinds of guys.

I should just leave. Using a nice guy for my list was going to feel a hell of a lot worse than using some jerk.

I undressed quickly, relieved to be out of my wet things, and pulled the shirt over my head. It wasn't as clean as it could have been but that was okay. I smelled Blake as the sleeves and neck passed by my nose. The earthy yet sweet scent clung in my throat and warmed my chest.

I folded up my wet shirt and dumped it on top of Blake's clothes, still on top of the other mess on the street sign coffee table. I felt frumpy. The oversized man's shirt draped like a tent across my breasts. I could see how uneven they were, the surgery having removed just enough from one side that there was a noticeable difference. I hoped it was only noticeable to me. I folded my arms across my middle.

Blake was still looking the other way. I cleared my throat, feeling even more at a loss. "You can turn around."

Blake turned and looked at me, then quickly sat on the couch like someone had knocked his legs out from under him. He cleared his throat too, and gestured for me to sit as well.

I was wary of the couch this time and sat carefully so I didn't end up on his lap again. Our knees touched, and a little thrill ran down my spine.

"Can I ask why you made a list like that?" he said.

"Just stuff I want to do. That's all."

"But why now?"

"Why does it matter?" I sounded too defensive. I needed to relax and just make it seem like some playful thing I wanted.

"I'm not sure. Maybe it doesn't. I'm just trying to get to know you. Make sure it wasn't in response to being treated bad by that very jealous boyfriend I still worry you have hiding behind me."

He peeked over his shoulder and I cracked a smile.

He had the nicest eyes. They looked out at me from between that thick border of lashes, and my heart gave a squeeze. He would have been perfect, if things were different. But my life was what it was, and The List was important to me for my own reasons. Getting to know each other more was a temptation I had to resist. I had a super-secret invisible armor hidden under my skin, and I bolted it into place. I could almost hear the clicking.

"Do you need to get to know me to do the things on my list?"

"Not really. I'm just curious, is all. I'm not asking because I'm looking for ways to dissuade you."

Dissuade? Who used words like dissuade in a conversation? Maybe he was doing that thing where you used a new word every day. Like that mature-age student in one of my classes who used the word minutiae four times in a conversation once.

"I'd prefer to keep things casual."

"Sounds perfect to me." He grinned as if I'd just taken a load off his mind. Maybe I'd judged him wrong, and he wasn't the nice guy trying to get to know me. Maybe he was the one-night stand guy who was fishing around to make sure *I* wasn't going to be the clingy one. I sure hoped so.

He clapped his hands together once. "Okay, let's stick to the basics. You want to do the list, and I want to help you. Now, let's suppose the best place to start would be with you losing your virginity."

I tensed. I didn't really expect him to leap across the couch at me, but you could never tell. He just sat there looking at me, smiling, but with a small wrinkle of concern near his eyes.

I tried to act blasé. "Doing pretty much any item off my list would cross that one off as well. Two birds, one cherry, and all."

"You really want to lose your virginity and try out bondage all in one hit? No pun intended. I mean, haven't you thought about how you want to lose your virginity?"

Not since I was a tween and had all kinds of romantic ideas about what that first time would be like.

It was going to be with Bobby Vaughn, in a room filled with candles, rose petals, and the piano he'd serenade me on before we made love on white satin sheets.

I didn't have such impractical dreams anymore.

"I was just going to wing it." I made it sound so matter of fact.

"That doesn't give me a lot to work with. There's a really wide margin of error here. I mean, what if I went the sex-under-the-stadium-seats-at-a-football-game route and you were really more of a surrounded-by-candles kind of girl. It would totally ruin the experience for you."

I could see Blake reading my face and knew my inner tween was putting out traitorous signals at the sound of his words.

"I'm really not that fussy," I said.

"You should be. It's your first time. We should try and make it special, as much as possible. I've got a few ideas already." I swore his cheeks turned a little pink when he said that. "But you've got to give me something to go by. Like, what kind of music do you like?"

"I don't really know. I mean, I never listened to it much after the summer I turned fifteen and … I've just been too busy studying …" I had almost said something I shouldn't. I buttoned my lips tightly together and stared at the floor between my bare feet.

Insecurity and doubt came back to haunt me. Did he really like me or did he just see me as a chubby girl he could have sex with in all sorts of interesting ways? Did he see me as just the person who was wild enough to write The List?

Why did I care what he thought? He was supposed to

be just one more black line across the words on The List.

"Is there really nothing you would like for the big event? I just feel as though you haven't thought this through. The whole list, sorry, but it's kind of a noobs idea of a sex list. I mean, it doesn't even include having an orgasm. That seems like a bit of an oversight."

"Oh, well, I just thought …" I didn't know what I thought. I hadn't even thought of it. I really was in over my head.

"You could get all the way through that list of yours without having a single orgasm. In the wrong hands, of course. Which would be a true shame."

I raised my eyebrows. "And how are your hands?"

Blake blew out a breath and met my gaze. "I won't lie. Well-practiced."

Was he trying to play sex-chicken with me? If he was well practiced, all the better. I didn't care how many partners he'd had or would have after I was gone. "Okay. I'll let you help me with my list."

"I'd be honored to be your guide through uncharted sexual territory."

"Look, I'm not asking you to wine and dine me. I'm not asking for a friend or a boyfriend. The goal is to mark off all the things on my list—that's all."

He paused, assessing me with a confused stare. "But in an enjoyable way though, right?"

The soft, teasing tone in his voice made a pleasant sensation curl from my tailbone into my spine.

"When do we start?" I asked, my voice rough.

Blake reached to the coffee table and checked his phone. "Damn, it's late. I mean, not that I wanted to start anything now … I have to work in the morning. How about tomorrow night?"

So soon? Setting a date for the big event made my heart flop against my ribcage. *The List Georgina is brave Georgina. The List Georgina says yes*, I reminded myself. "Sure, sounds good."

He gestured to the phone in his hand. "Could I grab your number?"

I hesitated, but figured he might need it while helping me get through my list.

As he typed it in, I stood up and gathered my wet clothes.

Blake stood beside me. "You're welcome to stay here."

The temptation to stay was very strong. I could imagine what it would be like to wake up next to him, feeling his body pressed against mine under crisp morning sunlight. "No," I said hastily. "Thanks."

Sleeping next to him implied a level of commitment I didn't want in my life, that I couldn't have even if I wanted it. I couldn't afford to let my feelings get all tangled up in this arrangement. I was doing this for a reason.

Chapter Six

GEORGINA

I woke up in my own bed. I barely remembered getting home in the early hours of the morning, and the night before felt so dreamlike. But Blake was real, and The List was real, and the two of those things were going to be getting very intimate with each other real soon.

My sheets were cold, and I groaned as I slid out of them. I hated the cold. I really did. I wrapped myself up in a fluffy robe and put on an extra pair of socks before shuffling out to the kitchen.

Julie was already gone for the day. A sprinkle of toast

crumbs and a cold cup of coffee sat on the counter. When she was up before me she had a habit of making instant coffee, then not drinking it. She only really seemed to drink coffee when I brewed it. Those were some of the few times we spent together, sipping our coffees at the kitchen counter, smiling together as the rich warmth of it woke us for the day.

I put my vintage percolator on the stove, and while the smell of coffee filled the kitchen I simmered some oatmeal with an obscene amount of honey, blueberries, and cream, which I refused to feel guilty about.

I had stopped eating foods that were fatty, carb-loaded or sugary two years ago when I got serious about losing weight. I saved those things for special occasions, but I didn't see the point in 'special occasion' food now. Every day could be Special Occasion Food Day from now on and really, if there was ever a special occasion, this was it. Later tonight, I would be having sex for the first time.

The full implications of that thought caught me off-guard. I stopped eating with the spoon halfway to my mouth, and a big glob of oatmeal dripped onto the counter. I was going to have sex. With Blake. Tonight. Sex. With a man. His-parts-in-my-parts sex. Tonight. My thoughts looped, short-circuiting.

Calm down. It's just sex. Everybody does it. I mean, I

knew about sex. Who didn't?

Theoretically, anyway. Everything I knew was from television, or movies, sex ed lessons, or stories from other kids. Even before high school, everyone was talking about it. None of us were doing it, not that I knew of, but there were plenty of whispers about it. Back then I thought a blowjob was something to do with blowing on someone. I mean, the word usage more than implied blowing, when it was more about the opposite. Why be so pointlessly confusing? Not that I really knew exactly how to do it. *What if I need to know by tonight? What if Blake expects that to be part of the sex?*

The oatmeal had gone cold. I shoved it aside. Blake knew I was a virgin but he didn't know just how much of one. Would he be gentle with me? Would it hurt? I started wondering how big he was in the pants region. Crap. Maybe I should have hooked up with someone of smaller stature. Because he sure was big everywhere else. *Sooo ... biiig ...* My vision glazed over as I thought of his body.

Feeling desperately unprepared, I rushed into my bedroom, closed the door tightly, and opened my laptop. YouTube provided me with a wealth of information from some perky pro-sex feminist vlogger who went to great lengths to explain every aspect of sex and how women shouldn't feel ashamed for wanting it. I suddenly realized how much I had been slut-shaming myself for making The List. Like wanting those things was as much self-punishment as it was about new experiences and experiencing pleasure, about using this body before it was gone. But between my research and having Blake be part of my plans, I was starting to get excited by what was ahead.

Feeling all empowered, I ventured into parts of the internet I'd never been tempted by before. After a few searches, I came across some websites with free videos and managed to end up in one for people who really enjoy fellatio. I stared at it, fascinated, as clip after clip of dicks and lips flashed before my eyes.

Every few seconds I would get paranoid, and become positive that Julie had come home, and I would turn the speaker volume back down to silent even though I had my headphones on. Once or twice, I even got up and went to see if she was back, but she wasn't.

I kept taking mental notes, trying to treat it purely as research, but soon found I was getting really turned on. I started imagining myself with Blake, how his mouth had felt on my breast, and whether the rest of sex would feel that good. *Or better.* I angled my hips so my crotch pressed firmly into the seat below me. I was getting so turned on I could barely stand the wait until tonight.

I'd never felt like this. Sex hadn't really interested me or been on my mind for the last few years. I'd shut those parts of my body down, too scared to even try for a relationship, too hateful of my own body. These feelings though, this was just the awakening I yearned for when I wrote The List. I licked my lips. Now seemed as good a time as any for some preparatory self-exploration. A brief glance to triple-check again that my door was closed, and I slipped my fingertips down through the elastic band of my pajama pants.

Bang, bang, bang.

Someone pounded on the front door. I jerked my hand back out again. Panic filled me and I slammed the laptop closed. Too paranoid to leave it there in case someone was to open it and find the webpage still there, I flung the laptop under my bed.

"Georgina?"

The last person I wanted to see right now—my dad.

"Just a minute!" I shed my pajamas, grabbed jeans, and yanked them on, ran a brush through my hair, and tugged a clean shirt on over my head. I opened the door, forcing a smile onto my face that quickly became a real one.

I loved my dad. He was a darker-skinned man with a head filled with curly black hair, and bushy eyebrows like a Muppet. Dad was an inch shorter than I was—although he'd say it was the other way around—and he had grown cuddly and round from the amazing food he cooked.

Apart from his lovely olive skin, I think I inherited most of my genes from Dad, but he always told me I looked just like my mom. She had been dead for so long I couldn't really remember what she looked like, but from the photos of her, I didn't see it. In those photos she looked so glamorous, exotic and gorgeous. Of course, we only kept photos of her from before her cancer treatments. Sometimes Dad looked at me and smiled, and I knew he was thinking about her.

Dad had never forgotten her, or remarried. But he did date sometimes. He thought I didn't know about that, though.

"Hi, Dad." I hugged him, and he hugged me back. He smelled like roasted garlic and oregano.

"How's the restaurant?" I asked, trying to sound casual.

"Packed. Got a TV network sniffing around, trying to get me to do some reality cooking show."

"Again? I thought you'd scared the TV execs off for good last time," I said, smiling.

He chuckled. "That was before being an asshole on television was the in thing. Is that fresh coffee I smell?"

I stood to one side so he could come in. "I made some about an hour ago. But I could whip up a fresh pot if you want some."

"Thanks."

"Tell me more about this show they want you to do," I said, trying to keep the focus on him.

My attempt was futile. Dad shook his head and grumbled under his thick moustache, "I came to talk to you about school."

My heart dropped and I turned away, pretending to be busy making a fresh pot of coffee. "What about it?"

"You haven't been going."

"How do you know that?" I asked. "I mean, maybe, sure, I missed a class or two, but I can always catch up."

"Not when you're on a scholarship you can't. And I know it's been more than a couple. Sherrie in the admissions office called me. You've missed classes for nearly a week. You're about to get placed on probation."

"It's really not that bad. Sherrie probably only rang because she's trying to hit on you. She's always had her eye on you. You really don't have to worry about me." Fussing with the percolator, I dropped the entire contents of old coffee grounds on the floor and cursed.

Dad came and stood next to me, putting his hands on mine, stilling them. "Is there something wrong?"

Yes, everything. "Nothing. I just had a cold and got a bit overwhelmed." There—simple but convincing, and not too far from the truth.

"You know you can talk to me."

"I know." Tears welled up, but I held them back. *Click. Armor on.*

"I want you to come over tomorrow for Sunday dinner. No excuses, do you hear me?"

Sunday dinner was our tradition. I had blown it off last week. Looking at him, I could see how worried he was. If there was a list anywhere that had the things that I did *not* want to do on it, upsetting Dad was at the top of it. But I knew the moment was coming when I broke his heart forever.

"No excuses," I said, and he gave me another warm hug.

Dad helped me clean up the coffee, then left. I stood there in the middle of my kitchen, my arms wrapped around my middle, and tried not to cry.

I failed.

Chapter Seven

BLAKE

I put the champagne down and picked up the six-pack of beer for the fifth time. The motherly woman with a super-model hairstyle at the bottle shop counter watched me, clearly amused.

Just buy something. It doesn't matter.

I kept telling myself that, but clearly it did matter or I wouldn't still be there.

This was going to be Georgina's first time. If she was just some other girl, just having normal, done-it-before sex, this would have been a lot easier. It *was* a lot easier. I knew from experience. But first times should be … something. Good, memorable—not a complete disaster, like most were in reality. Georgina was coming late to the party, and given the situation, she had a chance at a good one. I had the chance to give her a good first time. That seemed worth a little effort.

But I didn't want things to seem too serious, and maybe champagne was too serious. I didn't want to seem too cheap or uncaring, and maybe the beer would give that impression. Wine introduced way too many questions: white, red, rosé, sparkling, dessert? Would craft beer be a good in-between or just seem too wanky? *Yep, definitely overthinking this.*

I went and stared at the wall of wine bottles for a while anyway, avoiding the issue. The bottle shop smelled of cardboard cartons and stale alcohol. I wondered how many bottles had been dropped and smashed on this floor in the past. I imagined red wine seeped down between the floorboards, the kind of stain that would never leave. Like the stain of loss on a heart.

Life was short. Cruel. Unexpectedly tragic. Or expectedly tragic. It was even worse when the tragedy was your fault. When you saw it coming and didn't stop it happening.

The champagne it is.

No point overthinking it. Always choose the option of most enjoyment for the here and now. My bank account was running low, and the next check of royalties wouldn't be through for another month but screw it. I had to live for the moment, or what was the point? The past was too painful to bear, and the future could easily be the same. Now was all that mattered.

I grabbed a mid-priced bottle of champagne and thumped it down on the counter. The woman clicked her huge, elaborately painted and bejeweled nails over it as she scanned it through. She eyed me, still amused. "Doing something special?"

Was I doing something special? Or someone special? Did it even matter? The future wasn't in my mind at all. It went only as far as tonight and no more. *One day at a time.*

I tapped my credit card to pay and grabbed the brown-paper-bagged bottle. "Just getting laid."

Chapter Eight

GEORGINA

"Hi," I said, standing on Blake's doorstep. I was cool, calm, confident, and hadn't just rushed over here with my heart pounding so hard that I almost forgot how to drive. Nope, tonight I was List Georgina, and List Georgina was Brave Georgina.

"Hi," he replied.

A moment of silence stretched out, then Blake stepped aside and ushered me in.

There was a bottle of champagne, two mismatched wineglasses, and a bouquet of roses on the coffee table. The lights were dimmed, and he had cleaned up.

"I understand the alcohol. Good call. But why the roses?"

"I know you said you didn't want anything special, but I just thought this might help the whole ... procedure." Blake cringed and ran his hand through his hair. "We'll take it easy on the alcohol. Just enough to calm nerves."

"You've really thought this through, haven't you?"

He chuckled softly. "Don't think I'm not nervous, too. There's a lot of pressure and expectation. I haven't been someone's first since I was sixteen. And also, there's all of this hotness to deal with," he said, gesturing to my body while biting his bottom lip. "I just want you to enjoy this. I don't want to hurt you at all."

"You know, the whole hymen-popping thing is a myth, really. Hymens don't work that way." What was I saying? Blake looked highly amused. "Shut up. I've just been reading up. Fine. Watching YouTube videos. Whatever."

Blake looked even more amused. "Videos, hey?"

I flushed red all over. "So, alcohol?"

With a leering grin that made me giggle, Blake poured a drink for each of us. Pressing one glass into my hand, he clinked his own against it. "To first times."

Blake wore a plain black T-shirt that fit tight against his

body, and large, baggy jeans. I was already thinking ahead to if I was meant to undress him and how I was meant to do that, and what he looked like under those clothes. I'd seen the top half. I was nervously excited about the bottom half.

I downed my first glass of champagne in three huge gulps. It was good, and left a warm trail from my throat to my belly. Before I had time for it to absorb, Blake leaned in and kissed the last drip of champagne off my lips.

I kissed him back, and we stood there like that for minutes, exchanging slow, burning kisses that left me breathless and flushed. His fingers slid up my neck, caressing it and then my earlobes before moving up to my scalp. He tugged at the comb holding my hair and it tumbled down onto my shoulders. He brushed the strands away from my neck. His tongue flickered over my throat, resting on the point of my pulse.

I could feel it, my life, resting there against his flesh. His tongue withdrew and his full and sensual mouth laid a trail of butterfly-soft kisses from that pulse point to the valley between my breasts. Blake was practically kneeling before me with our height difference, and when he stood up again, he wrapped an arm around my legs and shoulders and scooped me up with him. He lifted me like I weighed nothing and carried me up the stairs to his bedroom.

Tiny points of light flickered around us. LED candles

were spread across every flat surface. The room was tidy and the bed made, a handful of red rose petals thrown on the covers. On the nightstand sat a single condom. I smiled a little, grateful Blake had the insight to not put a whole box out there.

Blake laid me down on the bed, then knelt next to me, leaning across my body. The sheets weren't satin, or white, but I was already so blown away by the effort he'd made. I couldn't expect him to be a mind reader too. And I didn't want him to be.

I had worn a halter dress without a bra, and he kissed the exposed flesh of my cleavage. Blake followed the line of the dress straps, then hesitated. "May I?"

I didn't reply, just reached around and tugged the ties loose.

I lay still while he pulled my dress away, down over my legs. It made a whispering rustle as it dropped to the floor. I wished I hadn't chosen a halter dress. Just one item of clothing gone and there I was in nothing but high heels and black lace panties. Blake still had so many clothes on. It seemed unfair. I brought my hands up and covered my nipples.

Blake's hands still rested near my ankles, and he gently slipped my shoes off.

My glassful of champagne was kicking in, and everything got fuzzy. I felt like I should do something. Should I be taking off his clothes? Should I be helping him take off my clothes? Do I look okay without my clothes? *I can't believe I'm doing this.* This wasn't the first time I'd dreamt about. Our bodies, this room, our actions, it looked and felt the part, but it was just window dressing, fake. *Is this a mistake?* Then Blake kissed a soft spot on my thigh, and all doubts left me. It was all I could do to keep breathing.

He moved back up my body and grabbed both of my wrists, bringing my hands away from my breasts and forcing them down on the bed on either side of my head. He wasn't rough, but he was so strong I knew if he wanted to be forceful with me, I'd be helpless. That thought scared me, but before I could react, Blake had let go, trailing his fingers along my arms and down my sides. His hands cupped my breasts, and his tongue and teeth played against my nipples until I arched my back, crying out as heat grew and spread between my legs.

Blake seemed to be moving slowly, caressing one part of my body at a time, but a fire rushed through me and I no longer wanted slow. I clutched the hem of his T-shirt and pulled it up his chest. He grabbed it as well, lifting it over his head.

His chest gleamed and rippled with muscle. He wasn't sharply chiseled, just thick and strong. My eyes wanted to trace every single inch of him and they did. "Sooo … biiig …"

"Sorry?" he asked.

"Nothing!" *I can't believe I said that out loud.*

A soft, grunting noise came from somewhere deep in Blake's throat as he looked down at me, and his fingers slid between the waistband of my black silk panties and my skin. I gasped as his fingers tickled and stroked at the sensitive spot there, and a powerful feeling built inside me.

So that's what the clitoris is all about. I'd felt around down there before—who hadn't? But I'd never really succeeded in anything. I guess it turned out that bud needed a bit of love to blossom.

My panties slid down. I closed my eyes, allowing Blake to take them away from me. When they were gone, I pulled my legs together, scared of being so visible.

Blake slid his hands up my legs, easing them open again. "Don't worry. You don't have to do anything except relax. If you ever want to stop, just tell me."

His fingertips reached the tops of my legs, the join between them, tickling against me. "I don't want to stop," I gasped.

Dipping his head, Blake's lips grazed my navel, and then his tongue licked my most sensitive area. It created intense bursts of craving in me. I could feel him bring a hand close and then he slid one finger inside me. *Inside me.* It felt so strange, yet so good. I could feel it when he added another, stretching me softly. Preparing me. His tongue kept moving against my clitoris and I began to shake, my inner thighs quivering.

Blake slid his belt buckle free, and his baggy jeans dropped on the floor with a thud.

His manhood jutted out at an angle from his body, so hard. I took in every detail, amazed at how he looked, how his body responded to mine. I could see it all in the low light of the candles, and I kept my eyes open as he knelt between my legs and unrolled the condom down his thick shaft.

He bent and kissed my neck, and whispered, "Are you ready?"

The lucid parts of my brain had melted away. My heart pounded, and my body throbbed. I looked up at his face, my sight hazed with pleasure. This was everything I wanted to be experiencing—the pleasure, the terror, and the pure, naked, powerful mess of life.

"I'm ready."

He entered me slowly. I cried out, not from pain, but the intensity of the feeling. My back curled and my fingernails raked across the bed. He waited, forehead pressed into mine, panting, letting me adjust before pushing in farther.

The presence of him inside me, the pressure and heat as he eased in and out of me in slow, deliberate movements, could drive me insane. It was such a delicious violation, such intimate torment, I wanted to beg for him to stop, and scream for him to go faster all in the same breath. I opened my mouth, but nothing came out, my lips quivering. Blake stared at them, then pressed his mouth against mine, hot and hungry.

I could feel his deliberate slowness, how he held himself back, in the shake of his body, and see it in the clench of his teeth. Sweat beaded on both our bodies, sparkling in the candlelight. Blake's body was firm in a way so unfamiliar when compared to my own soft flesh. My hands had taken on a life of their own, exploring every muscle they could reach.

We eased into a rhythm together, and my body met his movements with its own. My hips lifted, pushing against his, experimenting with tilting back or rolling forward, enjoying how the changing angles made him feel different inside me. Everything was wet and smooth, sliding easily yet pushing firmly, filling me, pressing inside of me. I wanted to stay like this forever. I wanted this feeling to last forever. I didn't know how anything could feel better than this.

Then Blake brought his hand down again and rubbed his thumb against my clitoris. An intense pressure, an even greater pleasure ran through me. His thumb rolled against me as my eyes rolled back, lend I hung there in that exquisite feeling, almost in tears at the strength of the sensations running through me. Blake's thrusts became sharper, hammering into me, making my whole body lift and shake. His fingers and thumb moved faster, flicking and pressing, and my body jolted, uncontrolled, terrifyingly. Every part of me went rigid and white-hot pleasure burned through my mind. My muscles went tight then loose, and my high-pitched, breathy scream filled the room. Blake slammed into me, any effort to be gentle or in control lost, crying out as well, and each thrust drove my pleasure on longer. He collapsed onto me, both of us panting and breathless.

We lay there, neither of us speaking. His weight was comforting, solid, and so very alive. I closed my eyes and went to sleep in his arms.

Chapter Nine

GEORGINA

I slipped out of bed and into my clothes as quietly as possible. Stupid halter dress. Why didn't I bring another outfit with me? Why had I refused to accept the idea I'd be sleeping the night? Did I really think I'd just have sex with the guy, then shake hands and head off home to bed?

Sunlight highlighted the edges of thick, closed curtains. It was hard to tell what the time really was, but I was pretty sure we'd slept in.

"Morning," Blake said from behind me. His voice was

soft and gravely from sleep.

"What time is it?" I asked, unwilling to turn around and look at him. I'd bet he looked gorgeous in the morning, his blond hair tussled and—*stop it, damn it. Don't look.*

I heard him rattle around things on the bedside table. "Eleven. You need to be somewhere?"

"I have to go to my dad's for dinner."

"You've got plenty of time then." Blake shifted across the bed and looped an arm around my waist.

Slipping on my second shoe, I stood up out of his reach.

"We start at noon, and I help him cook. It's sort of a tradition. Sunday is the one day he doesn't work at the restaurant and instead makes dinner just for us."

"He's a cook?"

"He's a chef. He owns the restaurant Stone Soup."

"I've been there. It's pretty good."

"It's the best." I walked out of his room and clip-clopped down the stairs in my heels. I could hear Blake scrambling behind me.

He came running after me with his bedsheet wrapped around his waist, toga-like, his chest bare and rippling. *Oh mercy. I shouldn't have looked.*

"You can't stay for breakfast? Or a shower?" he said.

I tore my gaze away from his god-like form in an almost painful effort and marched out the front door. "We did what needed to be done, and now I have to go. If you still want to help me with the rest of my list, that's cool, but I never asked for anything more."

Blake chased after me onto his weed-encrusted lawn. An old man next door looked up at us as he collected his newspaper, and Blake adjusted his toga with one hand and waved casually to him with the other. The old man rolled his eyes like this happened every morning.

"I know that," Blake said. "It's just the list. But can't you at least tell me if you enjoyed last night? That it wasn't the most terrible thing you've ever experienced?"

I stopped and looked down at my feet. "It wasn't the most terrible thing I've ever experienced."

"Sorry, what was that? I couldn't hear you."

"I enjoyed it, very much." I spoke louder and turned to face Blake. He was grinning widely.

He kissed me quickly on the forehead. "Me too."

That would have been a nice place to leave things, but when I swung into my car seat and turned the keys, the car made no sound. Not even a small lurch.

"No, no, no! Jiminy, don't do this to me now," I begged the steering wheel.

"You call your car Jiminy?" Blake laughed. "No wonder she's not starting for you."

"Jiminy is a *he*. And he loves me. But I think I left my lights on."

"I might have some old batteries and jumpers in the garage that can probably get *him* going again, but I'd have to dig around. I mostly have bike parts."

"I don't have time."

"Let me take you then," Blake offered. He was already backing toward his house. "I'll be dressed and ready to go in thirty seconds, trust me!"

I was already going to be late by the time I got home, cleaned up, changed, and headed out to Dad's. Maybe Blake's motorbike could cut some time off that.

"Thirty, twenty-nine, twenty-eight ..."

Blake was off at a run. Through the open front door, I saw his sheet flutter to the ground behind him as he ran up the stairs.

Chapter Ten

GEORGINA

I have to be out of my mind. I have to be. I have a brain tumor. That must be it—there's no other explanation. I can't believe I let Blake take me to my dad's house.

As soon as he came to a stop, I got off Blake's motorbike as fast as if it were made of molten lava. "Okay, thanks, bye. See you later."

Blake took my helmet and then took his time strapping it to the rack at the back of the bike.

"Georgina?"

I cringed, then spun around with a big smile on my

face. "Hi, Daddy."

"Is that a friend of yours?"

Blake was taking off his helmet. *Don't take off your helmet! Go, go! Fly, you fool!*

I fluffed out the innocent flowery dress I wore and tried to somehow hide Blake and his bike behind me. We'd stopped at my place on the way and I'd showered and changed in record time. Julie was making toast in the kitchen when we'd gone through, and I saw her give Blake a surreptitious onceover as her face turned red. *Damn straight he's gorgeous,* I'd thought.

I'd left them talking about some sci-fi show they both watched and took a moment to do my makeup. I knew it seemed odd to put on makeup for my dad, but I had to look good for him. I had to look *healthy.* There was no way I was going to beat Blake's thirty-second dressing record though. I was impressed he'd managed that.

Then it struck me that that meant he hadn't showered since we had sex. And now he was here. Talking to my dad.

Blake extended a hand from where he still sat on his bike. "I'm Blake. It's great to meet you."

"Mr Stone." Dad brought his hands up in front of him, holding them as a surgeon would when keeping them sterile. Only Dad's hands were covered in red gore and slime.

Dad shook his head at me. "Honey, I'm still disposing

of the last boy who took you on such a dangerous vehicle."

Blake leaned closer to me. "Is he serious?"

I sighed a long, exasperated sigh. "He's been peeling beetroot."

"Come on in then," Dad said, turning and leading the way into his house. "I want to get to know the man that my daughter would put her life in the hands of."

I turned to Blake, deadly serious. "Go, go now. Save yourself."

Blake swung himself off the bike. "What are you talking about? I like him already."

"You are seriously not walking in there. We do not have a meet-the-parents type of relationship. Don't. You. Dare!"

Blake's grin turned truly mischievous.

He followed my dad inside, and all I could do was chase after them.

Dad's house was a strange combination of a Greek-style exterior and a Canadian lodge-like interior. It was low and sprawling with whitewashed walls and decorative wrought-iron bars on the windows outside, and inside, it was dark and lush with wooden paneling and the scent of smoked foods. It was almost as much of a mess as Blake's house had been. Dad never had gotten any better at cleaning. Only the kitchen was kept immaculate.

Dad led us in there through the saloon doors, and we got to work. It was big enough for all of us, even given Blake's size. The granite counter tops were already laid out with fresh produce, mixing bowls and chopping boards in use, and my stomach started grumbling at the smell of baking pastry. Dad gave Blake what I knew to be a blunt, old knife, and asked him to finely dice some tomatoes. *I warned you.*

"Interesting ride you arrived on," Dad said.

"Blake built it himself," I jumped in, trying for some reason to defend him. Blake shouldn't even be here.

"Quite poetic," Dad said, his knife working easily to slice neat rounds from the beetroot, "to build the thing that will ultimately kill you."

"They really are safer than most people think," Blake said.

"That's what every bike rider says before they lose an arm." Dad pointed his knife at Blake to make a point. "I trust my daughter to make her own decisions in her life, but I'm telling the both of you right now she's too precious to lose like that." He turned directly to me. "You're too precious."

My whole body froze for a second while I did everything in my power not to burst into tears. I forced myself to brush it off and let out a weak, whining, "Daaaad, stop it."

"Sorry, honey. Your life. Your decisions."

Blake's brow was furrowed, beaded with sweat, and his

knife slipped as he failed to slice the tomatoes. I wondered why he was even trying, and how long he'd persist before giving up. It was such a small thing, but conniving in its simplicity—to give a person who was trying to make a good impression in front of a professional chef a tool he could only fail with. Dad once promised me he'd never be the kind of father who would do things to scare away any boyfriends I brought home. That he would always trust me to follow my heart and make the right decisions. Not that I ever brought any home. But I guessed bringing one home on a motorbike was going to test that promise. Not that Blake was my boyfriend.

I grabbed a real knife from the block and slipped it to Blake, a move Dad watched with interest. I turned away quickly to busy myself with crumbing the lamb cutlets.

While stacking marinated goat's cheese between the beetroot slices, Dad said, "Bike building—is it your profession or pastime?"

"Hobby mostly, although I sell a few to get new parts to make more. I just love the process of putting together broken pieces into something new. But I mostly work as a roofer since I left university."

"Since you left?" Dad's eyes went to mine, and I knew what he was thinking. Here was the reason I was skipping classes. It would have been easier to let that go on than tell the truth. I never got a chance to toss Blake under the bus though because Dad added, "So you two didn't meet on campus?"

"I thought she wasn't—" Blake's face contorted as my foot met his shin.

"Yeah, he was working on one of the older buildings." I talked right over Blake. His face was one big question mark that I ignored. I was standing there, outright lying to my dad with very unconvincing lies, and Blake knew it. But I'd had to come up with something quick.

A subject change was the only way to go now. I picked a spoon up and tasted the tomato sauce simmering on the stove. "This is great, Dad. Have you been using that smoked garlic again?"

He looked up from where he'd been carefully rolling the beetroot and cheese stacks in crushed walnuts. "Smoked salt." He grinned, always proud when I picked a flavor in his dishes.

"Yum. Should I start taking things out to the table?"

"I just have to fry the cutlets and mac and cheese, then we're ready to go."

I took the finished dish off him and headed to the door. "Blake, can you come help me set the table?"

He dropped the knife next to the mangled tomatoes with clear relief. He hadn't had much luck even with the better blade. "Sure."

As he followed me out, I whispered, "You know he doesn't need those tomatoes for anything we're eating today, right?"

"Your dad is awesome," he said, without a hint of sarcasm. "So, why are you lying to him?"

Reaching the dining room, I pointed to the cabinet. "Grab any plates and cutlery, we're not fussy."

Blake stood, ignoring the directions, giving me a no-nonsense look.

I rambled, "Just wait until you try Dad's mac and cheese. It's the creamiest, most delicious mac and cheese in the world, and when it's done, he sticks it in the refrigerator overnight to set and gel. The next day he slices it thinly, breads it and drops it into a deep fryer. He covers it with a rich, slow-simmered tomato sauce to serve. I swear once you eat his version you will be ruined for life. Nothing else ever comes close to it."

Blake didn't break. "He doesn't know you dropped out?" he hissed.

"Shut up! He's got ears like a fox!" I hissed back.

"Georgie, can you come into the kitchen please?"

Kill me now. There was no use arguing, so I put the plate down in the middle of the table and went.

Dad stood over the stove, deep-frying the pasta in a

wok as the lamb chops fried in a cast-iron pan beside them at the same time. "He seems nice. Is this a serious thing?"

I shot a look at the swinging saloon doors that separated the kitchen from the dining room. "Shh, no! He's not my boyfriend. We're just friends. Barely acquaintances. He just gave me a ride because my car battery was dead. You're the one who invited him in—don't forget that."

"You could have invited him. I'm happy for you to bring boys home."

I smiled at how he said *boys*, but didn't like the frown that stayed on his face.

Then he asked, "Does he know?"

"*No.* Don't you tell him, either." I rested my hip against the kitchen bench. "Dad, do you know how bad it sucked to wonder if guys were looking at me because they thought I was cute or because they were staring at my wig?'

His fingers touched my hair. "The wig is gone."

"Do you want me to take anything else out?" Blake stood behind the kitchen doors, peeking over them. He looked uncomfortable, but also determined. It was obvious that he had come to rescue me, and Dad chuckled under his breath as he said, "Yeah, let's get this food out. Dessert is coming up well. I hope you like fruit tart and ice wine."

"Ice wine from Canada?" Blake asked with a grin.

"Is there another kind?" Dad raised one bushy black eyebrow—a skill I didn't inherit, or I would have, too. Blake didn't seem like an ice wine guy.

"No, sir."

Blake opened the door for me as I walked through carrying a bowl of salad. We headed back for the dining table, but Blake stopped in front of the wall where Dad had my childhood artworks and school photos framed.

A pit of nausea opened up in my chest.

He smiled as my photos progressed through infancy, childhood, teens, and then he paused when he reached my fifteenth year.

I stared at my fifteen-year-old self, at the wig that was always slightly askew on my head, and the pasty skin of my swollen face. I looked so different there to how I did when I was younger, my hair color and style at odds with before and after, dark shadows under my eyes aging my young face.

Blake didn't say anything, but his expression said it all.

"Bad flu. Bad hair day." Lying had become my go-to. I walked past him, past the hateful reminders of my teenage years, but he didn't follow me. I turned around and snapped, "Please stop staring at that thing!"

Dad came in then, his arms loaded with plates of food, and we all sat at the table.

We ate, and talked, and Dad seemed to be warming to Blake—a turn of events I was not sure I liked very much. I didn't need the two of them ganging up on me.

I had hoped that the conversation would stay out of dangerous waters but it headed back that way as soon as we had dessert on our plates when Dad asked, "Why did you leave university?"

At first I thought he was talking to me, and I nearly choked on my wine.

Blake replied, "I thought that some physical labor would help me put things in perspective."

"That's an interesting reason to drop out."

"Dad, this is personal!" I protested.

"It's all right," Blake replied. "But I didn't drop out."

Dad frowned. "You said you left."

"Sorry, I should have said finished. But I'm considering going back to do my master's, so I guess it still feels temporary."

"What subject?" I blurted, curiosity overcoming me. I knew so little about Blake. *Which is how it's meant to be. He's not my boyfriend. Don't get attached.*

"Economics."

I sucked the last of the wine out of my glass and reached for the bottle. *Blake is smart.*

"I almost went that direction," Dad said. "I love how

numbers play together. Good options for careers there too, especially with a master's."

My world was spinning. *Blake has career options.*

"There's a certain science in cooking which I love too, but with cooking you get something to eat as well." Dad patted his belly. "Got to watch how much you eat, though, when you're no longer young and fit like you."

Blake is good-looking. Blake is healthy.

I stared at my plate, the tart there with its flaky and perfect crust cradling the rich ripe berries, and wanted to scream. Blake had so many options ahead of him.

Blake has a future.

And I was here, selfishly stealing time from him. All I had was The List. I had to finish it. As fast as possible. I didn't have a future. I didn't have time, and I couldn't sit here a second longer pretending I did with someone who had so much to live for.

I pushed my chair back and grabbed Blake's plate off him while he was still eating.

"We have to go," I announced. "We have that thing."

"What thing?" Blake asked, trying to grab the plate back and missing.

Dad passed the whole remaining tart dish to Blake, and damn, if the traitor didn't grab it, sink his fork into the sweet dessert, and keep right on eating, with a sly wink to my dad.

"*That thing*," I said through tightly clenched teeth.

"Is it so important that he can't finish some dessert?"

"Yes!" God, Dad was practically doting on him now. He did love people who appreciated his cooking.

Blake shoveled one last chunk into his mouth, stood, and said, "Thanks for dinner, Mr. Stone."

"Call me Tom."

They stood there, giving each other a tender bromance look, so I grabbed Blake by the arm and propelled him to the front door.

Dad walked us out, giving me a kiss on the cheek, tickling me with his beard. "I like him. Be safe."

I bit my lip, then kissed him back. The door closed, and I caught up with Blake out on the sidewalk.

"Are you okay?" he asked.

"Fine. I just want to do the next thing on my list." I was out of breath and had to lean against the motorbike for a minute. "Right now."

"Don't you think that would be a bit awkward in your father's driveway?"

"You know what I mean."

"We're nowhere near a beach. It would take ages—"

"The one after that then!" I snapped. I couldn't wait. I

had to cross something off. I had to do something.

His eyes were soft, and he leaned close to me. I flinched away. I could see the curtain moving in my Dad's living room, in the house where I had grown up, where my mother had died. My dad was watching. Watching what he thought was a new relationship. Imagining what might be a future I would never have.

"You don't have to do this, you know," Blake said. His breath touched my cheek when he spoke those words.

I wanted to believe him. Death doesn't give you many options though. You live well for the time you have or you die with things undone.

Blake twined a finger around a strand of my hair. "Why is this so important to you?"

His question made me angry. My reasons were none of his business. I closed my eyes and it all hit home …

Chapter Eleven

GEORGINA

No. No. This is not happening.

Only it was.

My worst nightmare. The fear that had haunted me for years ever since my living nightmare had ended.

I stared at my reflection in the mirror and if things had been different, I might have laughed. The sight of myself standing naked in front of the mirror, one hand grabbing at my breast, open-mouthed shock on my face, was almost funny.

But there was nothing funny about the lump under my fingers. I'd never wanted to feel that feeling again, but there it was, a hard little harbinger of death under the pliant skin of my right breast.

Breathe dammit … inhale … exhale … inhale …

My mom's face swam in my mind. Pale, flaky skin, fleshy, red eyelids with no lashes, a scarf wrapped around her head that didn't quite cover her hairline, or the lack of it. Cancer had spread its poison throughout her body, taking her from us too soon, and she had passed that gene onto me. We knew that for sure when breast cancer came for me at fifteen. I fought it, desperate not to die, not even really understanding that possibility with my youthful view of mortality.

I could see the aftermath of that battle even now. My hair had fallen out in chunks. It finally grew out and had gotten long since I'd refused to ever have it cut again. But it had never really regained the thickness and sheen it once had. I had gained weight due to the treatments that had cured me. The steroids were supposed to help combat the nausea brought on by the chemo, but they also threw the pounds onto me. The foods that I could keep down were not only comforting, but fattening: ice cream, Dad's mac and cheese, mashed potatoes with more butter than potato. Food was one of the ways Dad showed he loved me, how he cared for me through that hard time.

Dad … this is going to break his heart. It's going to break all of him. My reflected face collapsed, fell like a ruined soufflé, scrunched into wrinkles as though that could hold the stinging tears at bay.

Could I have imagined it?

I pressed my fingers into my flesh again. The lump was still there. The world and life and all it encompassed felt like it had narrowed down to a tiny little growth the size of a marble.

I'm going to die this time. That thought made my belly feel cold.

I hated the cold. I couldn't stand it. I drank my sodas out of bottles that never saw the inside of the refrigerator, kept a space heater in my bedroom so I could heat it up when Julie ran the air-conditioning too high, and had a vast collection of oversized sweaters to hide inside. Anything to avoid cold.

Cold reminded me of hospitals and chemo rooms, of the frigid, prying fingers of doctors, of beds that were never warm no matter how many blankets were laid out, how many flowers or cards were up on the walls around them. Cold made me think of the chilled chemo fluids pumping into my veins, of chewing crushed ice so my gums didn't bleed, of a scalp so bare that no number of beanies could keep it warm. Cold made me think of death, the iciness and finality of it. Cold reminded me of my mother's hands, the hands I touched for the last time as she lay in her coffin, when Dad lifted me up to say goodbye.

I turned away from the mirror, unable and unwilling to look at myself any longer. The long scar on my left breast had always bothered me, always reminded me of the cancer, but now it seemed precious. It reminded me that I had survived … *once.*

I wouldn't again. I just felt it. I couldn't make myself believe that I would, no matter how much I wanted to.

Someone gave me a plaque once that read 'Live like you are dying.' I threw it away. I was trying not to die back then. Now, I could see very clearly that I'd never learned how to live. The cancer had stopped me in my tracks at fifteen. I'd fallen behind my peers, lost my friends, had to work so hard to catch up on the schoolwork I'd missed. I'd all but given up on my passion for drawing and painting. My body had survived, but my spirit had been broken. I could barely look at myself, and wanted no one else to look at me. All I had was studying, and waiting for my next check-up, and the next, to see when cancer would grow in me again. To get the six-month all clear, the one-year, the five-year, as though they would mean something. All they did was give me a way to waste those years in waiting until it really did come back again. I hadn't lived, and now I wouldn't have the chance.

That made me angry as hell. It also made me so sad I couldn't breathe.

My gaze flicked to the photo of Mom on my bedside table. *Mom. What am I going to do?*

That year of fighting against the cancer had been hard, but that five-year all clear had given me false hope. Maybe it was a one-time thing for me. I had been so sure I had enrolled in university, begun to think about the rest of my life: love, children, the great works of art I would create, the books I would illustrate, the adventures I would have.

You haven't even started dating yet.

I wished I could turn off that nasty little voice inside my head. It was always talking and, worse, it was usually right. I hadn't started dating yet. I had been unable to date through my teen years due to the cancer. Most guys didn't mind a girl that puked because she'd had too many beers, but none of the guys in my high school had been even slightly interested in dating the bald-headed blob that was prone to bouts of projectile vomiting at the drop of a hat. Literally at the drop of a hat too; even hats triggered nausea. I couldn't wear them anymore. They reminded me too much of that time spent covering my baldness with hats and wigs. My pale skin took a beating because of it, and a light spattering of freckles had developed across my cheekbones. Cheekbones no man had kissed. A body that had done so little.

I got dressed in whatever clothes I could reach first,

and went to the drawer of my desk where I had a stash of blank journals. I'd been given so many over recent years, mostly from Dad since he knew my counsellors recommended journaling as a way for me to deal. I pushed away the pink glittery and rainbow ones and found a small, black, leather-bound one. It seemed fitting—black was the color of death, of mourning.

I did need an outlet now, to write all the feelings that overwhelmed me. Maybe I could make a will or write my own eulogy in that journal. There was nothing to give away. Nobody would fight for my meager six-hundred-dollar bank account or my frumpy clothes. I squeezed the pen hard in my fist, angry at myself for not having anything of value, having left no mark on this world.

Friends—ex-friends—sometimes asked what I would do if I knew today was my last day on earth. What *was* I going to do? I had more than a day, but how long I couldn't know. I had to treat every day from now on like it was my last.

So why am I sitting here staring at a blank page instead of going out and doing something amazing and enriching and ...?

Was there anything that I even really wanted to do anyway? I probably didn't have time for the kind of grand items on the bucket lists of people with a whole life to fulfill them in. I hadn't even done the basics.

I'd never been kissed.

Not really. Not romantically.

Never been touched.

Never known physical pleasure.

Those simple, primal, human desires had been denied to me. By illness. By *myself.*

Rage shook me. My hand scrawled words out into the journal. Black ink spilled onto white paper as I wrote out my

Make out with a stranger
Get to second base
Lose virginity
Sex on a beach
Bondage sex
Make love with a woman
Sex in a public place
Sex with two men

bucket list.

I stared down at those words, still shaking from shock and adrenaline, at the discovery and also at what I'd dared to write. I slammed the journal closed. *This is crazy. This list is crazy.* Did I honestly want to do those things I'd just written?

Yes. I did. Some wild, vital part of me wanted to pour the last days of my life away into lust and mindless, physical indulgence. My body was mine only for a limited time, and it might be all I would ever have in this existence. Any thoughts, feelings, actions, creations … what would they really matter in the grand scheme of this infinite universe? Nothing would. Only here, now, this body, these experiences. I wanted to do all of it. I wanted pleasure, untouched flesh knowing touch, life knowing life.

I had never told anyone that I had promised myself that if the cancer came back I wouldn't go through treatment again.

I just couldn't.

I knew how that would sound to other people, like I was too pitiful to deal with the necessary evil of getting well again. I knew damn well the people who would think that were the same ones who had never had to spend a night curled up on the cold floor of the bathroom, trying not to make too much noise while vomiting because someone you loved was sleeping down the hall and you didn't want to wake them up. Because you didn't want them to see you like that.

I wouldn't go through treatment again. Not just to prolong an unused life for another few years until cancer came again, and again. And if that meant I was going to die faster, then I would have to get my list done fast.

I opened the journal and stared at the list again. The first few things were simple. I could do them. It would be like testing the waters. I could do those easier things and build up my self-esteem enough to do the rest of them.

But how could I actually do them? Where would I even start?

A club seemed the obvious place, but I had never been to a club. And then I'd have to actually pick up a guy, or hope one would pick up me. Would anyone even find me attractive? Desirable enough to do those things with? Should I just be using a hook-up app?

No. I kind of wanted to do it the traditional way. It was something else to experience. And I wanted to do it right now. The only other option was to sit here alone and cry myself to sleep.

I got up and went to my closet, rooting through it for something sexy to wear. No luck—all I had were the same jeans and T-shirts, sweaters, and childish dresses that always hung there.

In the very back hung a dress I had never gotten to wear, one I kept for some reason I could never really explain. It was a short black dress with a sparkly little bow on the waist and a tiny ruffle of tulle around the hem. How I'd longed to wear that dress to the school dance. I'd begged and begged Dad to buy it for me, and he did. Three days before I discovered the cancer for the first time.

I pulled it out, shed my baggy sweats and T-shirt, and tried it on. It barely fit, much tighter than it was meant to be worn when I got it five years before. I couldn't even zip it up all the way, only enough that I was fairly sure it wouldn't fall down again. The bow and ruffle looked silly and dated and I took the dress off, ready to put it back in the closet.

I can't give up so easily.

I took my scissors and cut the bow off the dress. Then I cut the frilly little flounce off the bottom hem. It left ragged hems and loose threads, but I didn't care. I cut a short slit down the middle front of the bodice to provide more chest room and put the dress back on.

The dress looked a thousand times better. The cuts and roughness looked almost intentional, fashionable. It was still tight, but it clung to my plump curves like it was meant to. The pale skin of my cleavage glimmering in stark contrast to the dark material, and my waist looked smaller thanks to the tight cut of the dress.

I rummaged around again, coming up with a pair of black pumps I had worn to an aunt's wedding. The heels were scuffed so I colored them in with markers before putting them on.

I dug around in my drawers for the one pair of silky little black panties I owned, and when I stepped into them I felt like a different woman.

I had no idea how women wore their hair when going out, so just put a little leave-in conditioner into it and left it out. I ran a kohl pencil around my eyes until they were rimmed in heavy black, as though applying war paint. I smudged that eyeliner like I would charcoal on paper, then dabbed a dark maroon lipstick across my lips.

Not bad, I decided. *I might be able to do this.*

I grabbed my purse and marched out of my room, knowing any hesitation would stop me forever.

When I walked past the kitchen, Julie looked up from the grilled cheese sandwich she was eating. Her physics textbook was open on the counter, and her big brown eyes skipped right over me at first, then widened, came back, and outright stared.

"I thought you had a late class tonight." Her eyes narrowed as they got to my feet, then made their way back up. "What kind of class are you taking?"

"I'm going out. To a club." The words started out strong then faded away to a bare breath. It sounded so ridiculous. Me, at a club, and on my own. I scuffed one toe into the worn linoleum. "You want to go with me?"

"I'd have to shower for half an hour to get the fryer grease out of my hair, but—"

"Never mind." I cut her off, angered by her refusal, and how much I'd hoped she'd say yes. How much I needed someone to come on this adventure with me. I clutched my purse a little tighter under my arm and headed out the door.

Halfway to the club, I lost my nerve. I pulled over into a breakdown lane, fighting tears and the beginnings of a full-blown anxiety attack. It was too scary, too hard, too crazy. I could stop this now. I couldn't make it home, change, and make it to class on time, but I could spend the hours studying.

Or I could find some guts and go to the club. What was the point in studying when I'd never be there to graduate? I had to do the List. *The List Georgina is Brave Georgina.*

My tires squealed out of there as I headed for the nightclub.

Dusk had smudged the sky with heavy purple shadows, hovering above the buildings surrounding the club. The entry door was a glossy red, like a beacon, a dare.

I ran my hands over my face, angry and scared and torn. I was sweaty, and my makeup had smudged. I was looking for every possible excuse to not get up and walk into the club, so I had to just do it.

And I did.

The club's interior was grainy black and white. I stood there, feeling like I had somehow gotten caught up in an old photograph, one that continuously moved around me. Bodies filled the small dance floor, limbs flailed, and laser lights cut through the darkness. It was as if the crowd was a huge sea and the music provided the tides that it followed.

The smell was pungent: spilled beer and liquor, perfume and cologne, sweat and something else—something that smelled like life.

I was jostled inwards by more people entering the club, and wound up close to the bar. I grabbed an empty stool and clambered up, my legs shaking from nerves.

The bartender slapped a napkin down in front of me. Some suspicious-looking liquid immediately soaked through the thin paper. "What do you want?"

I tore my eyes off the spreading brown stain and glanced in panic at the little stand-up pamphlet on the counter advertising the night's cocktail specials. "That one," I said, pointing at what I only found out later was a mojito.

He moved away, and I let out a long breath. The music became more frenetic and louder. I wanted to cover my ears but didn't. My purse was too heavy, and I sat it down on the bar just as the bartender reappeared with a squat glass full of liquid and leaves.

The first sip stung my mouth and puckered my lips. Fire ran into my belly. It burned my doubts away.

I took the rest of the drink down in long steady gulps. I pivoted on the stool to observe the other people in the club, a little calmer this time.

A guy with curly hair and a thin black tie looked at me. He saw me catch him, held my gaze, and smiled.

This is it. Just go for it.

My belly tightened with fear, then I did it. I slammed down the rest of my drink, got off the bar stool, walked straight over, and kissed him.

I expected him to freak out but instead he kissed me back, hard and rough. Everything spun away from me—the lump, the terror I felt, death and the emptiness beyond it. It all vanished.

I was alive right then. I could feel that, feel life running through my veins. It was as vital and hot as his tongue beside mine.

I knew then that I'd do anything to have this feeling again, and again. I wanted to feel alive until the very moment of my death.

Chapter Twelve

GEORGINA

"Georgie?" Blake's hand on my arm brought me out of my reverie. "Are you okay?"

"I'm great." I shut the tears from my eyes with one hard blink. I locked my invisible armor back on. "Do you want to do this or not?"

Blake's gaze searched my face, as though he could see that armor, as though trying to find chinks. Something changed in his expression, concern shifting to blankness with just the hint of a smirk. "I just want to know this isn't getting complicated."

"If you want out, that's fine, but I'm completing my list no matter what," I said, yanking my helmet on over my head.

With a shrug, he joined me at the bike, climbing on and putting his helmet on too. "Let's get kinky then."

I hopped on the back behind him. "Now, what do we need for this … bondage stuff?"

He just patted me on the knee, and we were off.

It was after dark when we pulled into the parking lot of the strip mall, and I stared at the building. The exterior was dirty-white and hot-pink. A neon sign overhead announced it as "your premiere destination for excitement!"

From the outside, it didn't look very exciting. Only one car, plus Blake's bike, sat in the lot, and there were no X-rated signs or anything. I was a little disappointed. It looked like any other storefront—not at all what I had expected.

I got off the bike and removed my helmet, shooting an uneasy glance at the street that ran past, but there was no traffic at all, not a single car on the long gray ribbon of four lane.

Once inside the shop, I didn't know which way to look. No matter where I turned my head, something lurid assaulted my eyes—racks full of videos, magazines, and a whole section of things that looked more like strange, bright-colored kid's toys than something used for sex. On another wall, there was a dildo as long and thick as my forearm. Surely that was just for display. Nobody could use that. Could they? How? Could I? I started picturing how big Blake was, trying to compare, and heat rushed up my cheeks and down my belly.

The surprisingly cheery and gorgeous girl with pink hair behind the counter gave me a nod. I retreated, half-afraid that she would open a cabinet, pull out one of those huge fleshy vibrators, and start her sales pitch. I turned to find Blake and freaked out when he wasn't next to me anymore.

I heard him call out, "Why, hello there, pretty eyes."

Blake was behind a life-sized, realistic sex doll, puppetting her arm so she blew kisses at me. Her lips, opened in a pucker I was sure was meant to be cute, were painted a scarlet red, and her legs were open to show the advertised 'smooth, tight tunnel of love!' nestled there.

"Quit mucking around. Can we just hurry up?"

Blake stepped away from the embodiment of uncanny valley, and I scooted over beside him. The shop was tightly packed with narrow aisles, and I almost knocked down a display of flavored condoms. I was already in panic mode, the little time bomb inside me ticking away audibly. The sheer overwhelm of this shop wasn't helping.

"Do we really need to be here?"

"You want to do this bondage thing. I thought you'd want some supplies." Blake shrugged.

I just want to get it done. Only I wasn't entirely sure how.

He seemed to know where he was going when he led me to some shelves that held all sorts of crazy-looking contraptions. There was brightly colored bondage tape—guaranteed not to leave marks or stick to hair, which was a relief, I supposed— bottles of heating lube, packages of silk rope in various colors, and handcuffs lined with hot pink feathers or fur. Those looked ridiculous, really, like a joke toy.

I wanted something real.

A little farther along that row, things shifted from colorful to black-leather serious. Straps, gags, masks, harnesses—I didn't know if these were what I'd imagined when I added bondage to The List, but I had to get something and get out of here.

"Just what kind of bondage are you thinking? Just a bit of blindfold fun or getting more into S&M territory? Because these floggers are pretty good." Blake pointed. They dangled from hooks, their colorful tails swinging as I reached out and touched them.

"You know this, how?"

Blake half-smiled. "I had a girl once who was really into this stuff. A little too into it for me, to be honest. I drew the line at some of the things she wanted to do so we stopped hooking up."

Jealousy erupted in my heart. Blake had already done this with someone else?

I knew I was being irrational. He was gorgeous, and he'd already said he was experienced. I wasn't his girlfriend, and I didn't want to be. I didn't have *time* to be.

Urgency drove me onwards and I grabbed one of the small, flail-like whips. I didn't really want to try it. I guessed I had just been imagining some "blindfold fun", as Blake had put it. Probably extremely lame to a seasoned fetishist.

Blake smiled. "Nice choice. That one is leather; they give a nice thud. Those cheap ones over there are plastic. They'll cut if you get hit too hard."

I repeated my mantra of *The List Georgina is Brave Georgina,* but I was faltering.

"You're trying to freak me out on purpose, aren't you?"

"That depends. Is it working?"

"No." That lasted about three seconds. "Yes."

His lips went up at the corners, but he didn't laugh. If he had, I might have kicked him in the shin and run away as fast as I could. The whole day had been awful, and I needed to get rid of that feeling that was sitting on me, that feeling that time was running out.

I closed my eyes for a second, but there was this low

steady *tick-tock* sound there in the darkness that terrified me. I opened my eyes again and Blake was poking around in the aisle where more of those giant dicks sat displayed in boxes. He picked up a long thick black one that looked weirdly glossy. "You know, I am a little surprised that you didn't put sex with a black man on your list. It's pretty high up there in some women's fantasies."

I'd never considered that racist cliché, but the time this was taking made me irritable. "Maybe that's what should be next on my list."

I grabbed for my purse, yanked my journal out, and started to write it down. His hand came down on mine and my pen scribbled a big black line across the page.

~~Make out with a stranger~~
~~Get to second base~~
~~Lose virginity~~ ✓ *+ bonus orgasm, wow*
Sex on a beach
Bondage sex
Make love with a woman
Sex in a public place
Sex with two men
Sex with a ~~B~~

I slipped my small hand out of his and tried again, grinning defiantly.

"You can't go adding stuff in." Blake laughed at my efforts, easily snatching the pen from my hand.

"Says who?" I plunged my hand back into my purse to bring out one of the many other pens it held.

Blake wrapped his arms around me from behind, grabbing both my wrists and pinning them against my body. My back pressed tight into his chest, and I could feel him chuckling silently.

"Are we starting already?" I joked.

"Not in the shop!" yelled the pink-haired girl at the counter.

I wonder how often a day she yells that out.

Blake's breath tickled my ear when he spoke. "I'll let you go as long as you leave that off your list. For now. Look, that is a pretty long list of sexual adventures. It's more than most people ever get around to doing. Maybe you should get through that first, then consider if you want to add something more."

"Fine. Spoilsport."

He was right though. It *was* a long list. I did *not* need to add in anything else. If I did, and didn't get to do those added things I might regret it throughout all eternity. If that was a thing. Why take that chance? This was already taking too long.

I stared down at my list, at the black line running across the paper. Did I really want to do all that stuff? Still?

The answer was yes. I *had* to do it, and I had to do it now. There might never be another chance for me to do the items on The List, or anything else I wanted to do—like ride carnival rides all night, see Niagra falls, swim in the ocean, or have a family …

So many things. Simple things. Things some people took for granted. Tears pricked my eyes. I wanted to live. There was so much to do and not enough time to do it in.

"Are you okay? You look a bit off. Come on, let's get out of here. Honestly, this place makes me a bit green in the gills too." Blake took me by the arm and started leading me back out of the shop.

"But we need to get some things," I protested.

"Don't worry about it. We'll improvise. It's better that way, anyway."

Chapter Thirteen

GEORGINA

"Are you sure you're ready for this?" Blake asked when we reached his house again.

"If I say yes for the fiftieth time, will you believe me?" I replied. I was shaking, and tried to keep the rattle out of my voice. I hoped he couldn't see it.

"And you remember the safe word?"

I was a bit worried why he thought we'd need one, but he assured me it was simply best practice for anything like this. I'd chosen the word. "*Dissuade.*"

We were off the bike, and he opened the front door. It

squeaked as it swung and he looked down at me, serious for a second. "I just want you to feel safe in my hands. Figuratively and literally."

On that last word, he switched gears so fast it threw me, rocketing my heart into full speed. He scooped me up, flinging me roughly over one shoulder like some kind of caveman, or the Viking god he would play the part of so well.

I saw him grab something from the small table beside the front door but couldn't tell what because I was too busy squealing. Then I was bounced about as he jogged up the stairs to his bedroom.

I hit the mattress with a thud that matched how my heart was hammering. He was on me in an instant, grabbing my arms and hauling them up above my head. Something wrapped around my wrists, hard and rubbery, and I heard the click of a lock closing.

I twisted my neck to turn and look. He'd cuffed me to the metal top bar of the bedhead with a bike lock.

My hands were trapped, not an inch of give. Panic started to rise in me but then Blake's lips pressed on mine, perfectly gentle, and my eyes fluttered closed in pleasure. His tongue forced its way into my mouth, hungry and deep. Then it was gone. When I opened my eyes, I was flushed and breathing hard, and so was he.

"Stay there," he said.

"No problem," I replied.

He opened the door to the adjoining bathroom and casually began undressing. From my position on the bed, I could stretch my neck and pretty easily see what he was doing. He spun the shower taps, and stepped under the spray.

My pulse raced. I felt like I should look away, but I knew he was doing this so I *would* watch. And oh, dear god, if it wasn't the hottest thing I'd ever seen. Water trailed down the muscles of his back, forming shimmering rivulets. If I wasn't shackled down I would have been in there with him, clothes and all. I strained against my bindings almost instinctually, each restrained movement of muscle seeming to ignite the lust in me even more.

Blake returned. He stood at the foot of the bed, stark naked and hard. His hair and skin glistened with droplets of water.

He didn't say a word to me. He stared down, then walked away.

I cried out in pure anguish.

I hadn't really known what to expect when I'd decided I wanted to mess with bondage, but I'd had no idea it would feel like this. I had never wanted someone to touch me so much, and every moment he refused, that yearning grew.

Seconds ticked by, and I couldn't hear anything to tell me what he was doing.

I was stuck there, breathless in anticipation of what would come next, where he had gone, and whether he would even come back.

But he did, and he brought what looked like the sash tie from his curtains, and wrapped it straight over my eyes before I could see more of his amazing, naked body.

The darkness made me gasp.

I could feel the mattress shift and the warmth of Blake's thighs as he straddled me.

He pushed my loose dress and bra up to my neck in one swift movement. Goose bumps spread across my breasts and to my nipples. Somehow, still having my clothes around me, but exposed like this, made me so much more vulnerable. I could feel his hands again, lifting my hips and practically tearing my leggings and panties down and away.

He took a knee in each palm and pushed my legs apart. I squirmed, trying to close them. He held me firm, my soft legs no match for his strength.

Then he stopped. Blake wasn't doing anything. I had no idea what was going on. Shame made my face flush with heat.

My voice was rough. "What are you doing?"

"Looking at you. You are so fucking beautiful."

One of his fingers ran up my thigh. I whimpered as that finger pressed inside of me. I was so wet it slid into me easily.

And then it was gone again. I thrashed against my bonds.

"What are you doing to me?" I pleaded.

"Anything I want," Blake replied. His voice came from just below my chin, and then his teeth closed on one of my nipples. I cried out as they pressed firmly, his tongue grazing against me, then he was gone again.

"Do you know how hard it is not to just stick my dick inside you and ram you into the headboard right now?" he whispered near my ear.

Three fingers thrust into me then. My back arched near a foot off the mattress.

"Do it," I whimpered, desperate for release.

"Do it … what?" he drawled. He dragged his fingertips down from my collarbones, skimming the outer edges of my breasts, over my belly, down between my legs and inner thighs to my knees, pressing them apart wider.

"Do it!" I cried.

"That's not a very nice way to ask." He sounded angry, and a thrill ran through me.

He shifted position, and I could feel him holding his

weight up, straddled across my chest. The hot, smooth flesh of his hardness brushed against my cheek.

"Open your mouth. I want to see those amazing lips around me."

I opened, more as a gasp than in obedience, and the round head of his length prodded against my tongue. I closed my lips around it and Blake let out a rumbling groan, his body shuddering. I heard him slam a fist against the bedhead above us, grunt again, and then back away.

I could still feel and taste him in my mouth. I wanted more, like that taste had awakened a desperate thirst in me. I wanted him in me, in me everywhere, full and deep and hard. My body strained toward him.

"More," I pleaded, drunk on lust.

In return, all I got was the lightest tickle of his tongue against my clitoris.

I begged, weakly, "Do it, please."

"Good girl," he whispered against my flesh.

He pressed his whole mouth against me, lapping fast.

I bucked, out of control. "*Please!*"

He sucked in, tugging hard on that sensitive spot.

"PLEASE!" I screamed as the orgasm broke through me. Blake kept the pressure of his mouth on me for one more moment before shifting and plunging his hard length into me.

My thighs shook as I pumped forward and back, the pleasure blinding me more than the blindfold, burning through my brain in a rolling wave. Blake yanked my legs up and apart, slamming into me, with none of the consideration or gentleness he'd shown last night. Over, and over, and over again, he rammed into me in a way that shook my whole body and left me screaming. Then he tensed, staying pressed into me as far as possible as his breath dragged raggedly out his mouth.

He sagged down to the bed, half on top of me, his weight crushing and his arms wrapped around me. I wanted to bring my arms around him too, but instead pressed my face into his shoulder. Both of us were panting, covered in sweat, our bodies still vibrating with subsiding pleasure. His breath was warm against my face as he whispered soft little words.

"What did you just say?" I whispered, breathless.

"I think I've forgotten the combination to this bike lock."

I startled, jerking under him.

"Just kidding," he mumbled, nuzzling into my neck.

The blindfold was still on, and I enjoyed the warmth of him around me, so calm and protective after that intense experience. In the darkness of the blindfold, I could forget everything except his touch.

"Did you use, you know?"

"Of course." Blake reached down, and I felt him grab the base of the condom as he withdrew. He was gone again for a moment, and I took that time to try and get my breath, and mind, back to normal.

With infinite gentleness, I felt Blake remove my blindfold, and then unclick the bike chain from my hands.

I pulled my bra and dress down to cover myself, and little pinpoints of pain began in my fingers and forearms as the circulation returned. I sat up and tried to shake the feeling back into them.

"Shit, I left you tied up too long. I'm so sorry." He'd changed completely again. Caring, concerned … sweet.

"I'm fine." My voice broke.

Blake stared at me for a long moment. "Really?"

The lazy aftermath of pleasure dropped from me like a bag of bricks. I gritted my teeth together in an attempt to hold back the sudden threat of tears, but it was easy to see that my little act hadn't fooled him at all. "Yes, really. Stop acting like you care."

"I was just asking."

"I just answered." I was off the bed in seconds. "I have to go."

Blake pulled a pair of track pants on and sat on the edge of his bed, shaking his head at me. "Right. Fine. Call me

whenever, or whatever."

"Whatever," I said.

I grabbed my purse and headed for the door. I slammed it on the way out and stood on his steps, staring up at the faded stars above, my legs still shaking.

~~Make out with a stranger~~
~~Get to second base~~
~~Lose virginity~~ ✓ + bonus orgasm, wow
Sex on a beach
~~Bondage sex~~
Make love with a woman
Sex in a public place
Sex with two men
Sex with a ~~B~~

There was an invoice tucked under the wipers of my car windscreen from road service. I'd left my keys in Blake's letterbox and called earlier so they could get the battery sorted for me by the time we got back. I wasn't sure if I was glad or not, right then, that I was able to drive away.

I got in my car, started it, and pulled out of Blake's driveway, my hands shaking so much I could hardly hold the wheel. I was at the end of the street when he passed me, his body hugging his bike, which was slung low and dangerously close to the ground. He went around the curve far too fast, the roar of the engine echoing through my heart as he vanished from my line of sight but not out of my mind.

Chapter Fourteen

BLAKE

There's something wrong with her.

That thought kept running around my head, like a mantra of doom, as I gunned my bike down the highway. She seemed so intent on that list, too dead set on doing all those things. Not just for fun. Not just for kicks. Like they were life or death.

She was lying, too. A lot. It was obvious because she was not a good liar—another thing she wasn't experienced at. At first, I'd thought she was just trying to impress me, or keep things anonymous. But now I was sure there was more.

There had to be a reason for her wanting to do that list, and standing there in her dad's house, looking at that picture of her at fifteen, it had hit me—she was hiding something.

Then I had heard her dad say the wig was gone, and things started to click together in my mind. There was the long, thin surgery scar down the side of her left breast. While I had her tied up, looking at her, I saw small dots on her skin, spaced around her pale torso. Dots that were too tiny to be moles and too blue for freckles—tattoo marks, used to guide radiotherapy treatments for cancer. I'd seen enough medical dramas to know that, and it all added up to one thing.

Something was very wrong with her.

Maybe she's finished with treatment and is making up for lost time.

I tried to be hopeful, but the urgency with which she came at the list implied something more.

I couldn't just come out and ask. I didn't know her that well, and she'd made it clear she didn't want me to know her that well. I'd come into this—this what? Relationship? Agreement?—for the sex and for the ride. I didn't want to know her either. I didn't want complications, or feelings, or a relationship. Certainly not with someone there was something wrong with. Not again. I didn't want that.

I couldn't do that again.

So why did I care that she didn't want anything from me but sex? Fucking ironic mess. She wasn't the first girl to treat me like a piece of meat. I didn't know why it made me so angry. Hadn't I been after the same thing from her? Wasn't I just in this to see her with another woman?

Streetlights flashed overhead as I sped beneath them, pushing my bike too fast and letting that thrill of danger and the rush of cold night air cool my emotions.

The truth was, I didn't know what I wanted anymore.

Actually, I did know. I knew I wanted to drink. A lot.

So I did.

"Is she ugly, or mentally ill in some way?" the guy next to me at the bar asked.

I shook my head, rolling it against the cold bottle I had pressed against it. "No. She's fucking to-die-for gorgeous. She's the kind of girl that other girls would turn for."

"Let me see if I got this right. She took you to a great dinner, and then to a sex shop, gave you some pussy, then went home no-questions-asked, and now you're out having a brew. And you're complaining?" He sipped his beer. "Man, it's the perfect night. Don't tell me you're upset because *she* didn't want to cuddle afterwards."

I could hear the incredulity in Buddy's voice. I had no idea who the hell Buddy was. I thought he was called Buddy, or Mac, or Billy, or something, but he seemed to be calling me Buddy too, so I wasn't sure. Bloody Americans. He'd sat down next to me some time around my third beer, and we'd ended up talking. He'd just gotten divorced and I had my own problems, which made for us being great bar friends, especially after a few double tequilas. I supposed I was just drunk enough to expect some bloody sympathy—which, in light of the way he was looking at me, didn't seem like it was going to be forthcoming any time soon. It wound me up.

"Buddy, if you're done with her, give me her number. I could use some pussy right now."

That really sent me spare. My fist stopped a hair's breadth from his long and too-narrow nose. His eyes went round, and then bloodshot. I dropped my hand, hoping he wouldn't be a jackass and retaliate. That he would laugh it off, but the tequila was working, because he slammed his beer down on the bar hard enough to bust the bottle and shouted, "You wanna fight? Huh? You wanna have a go?"

The guy was maybe five-foot five but built like a brick shithouse. His wife had cheated on him with his own brother, which must have made for some uncomfortable holiday dinners. Worse, he'd lost his job over the situation. Buddy's brother had also been his boss, and clearly, keeping him employed wasn't worth the awkwardness in the work environment. The saddest part was he wasn't much older than me, and he was acting like his life was over.

Buddy had enough shit on his plate. He didn't need mine too.

I sat my own beer down and said, "Nah. Bloody hell, you'd kill me. Let's have another shot, and some of those hot wings. I am fucking starving. I'm buying. What do you say?"

The anger on his face dissolved, replaced by a grin that said Christmas had just come. "My man!" he said, throwing his arms around me in a bear hug.

I ordered wings and boilermakers. My head was already spinning. I was about to spend half my night puking and the other half with one foot on the floor, trying to keep the world from spinning me right off its axis. I couldn't seem to care. I wanted to escape all the thoughts whirling in my head, trying to work out just what was wrong with Georgina and what that meant to me. And the alcohol had settled in enough to make me think it was a good idea to keep drinking.

I had reached the stage of drunk where it felt like I was caught in one of those old foreign films, the ones where the people talking moved their mouths way before their words started to make sense. The edges of my vision blurred, and everything moved too fast, yet not as fast as it should.

I had been lurching toward the bathroom when I saw

her, her long dark hair tumbling down her back.

How'd she find me?

Didn't matter.

I didn't care. What mattered was she was here, and we'd work things out. I'd make sure she was okay.

"Hey, gorgeous," I said, and grabbed her and kissed her, right there in the hollow of her neck, next to the sloping curve of her shoulders.

As soon as my lips hit her skin, I knew I had messed up. Her perfume was wrong, and her skin shimmered with some kind of glitter dust.

The woman turned around. Her eyebrows had been plucked to narrow curves and she wore a bright pink lipstick and tight minidress to match.

She didn't look happy. "Gee, thanks, asshole. Next time, maybe you could give me some warning before assaulting me."

I backpedaled. "I am so sorry. I honestly thought you were someone else."

The girl put a hand on one hip, looking me up and down. Her pouty indignation started to crack as her lips curled upwards.

She half closed her eyes, smiling like a hunter setting a snare. "Are you saying you wouldn't kiss me if you didn't think I was someone else?"

The words made my tipsy head spin with tricky double

negatives. I didn't want to offend her any further. "Yes. No. Yes. No, wait. I mean, yes, you are a gorgeous woman, and I would have kissed you anyway."

"Really?" she said. In one smooth step, she had her hips up against me.

Her overly strong perfume assailed my nose as she leaned closer and pressed her lips onto mine.

Chapter Fifteen

GEORGINA

Last night with Blake was … it was almost more than I could bear.

My head was in the worst state. The things he'd done to me, the way he'd behaved while he had me tied up, and how considerate he'd been either side of that, left me utterly confused about the kind of man he really was. He seemed so ready to play the part, to use me however he wanted. Was that the real him, and he was just pretending to care? I had to remind myself that that was actually what I wanted from him—a man who was just after sex.

But despite reminding myself over and over that it didn't matter what kind of man he was, everything felt like it was getting way too complicated.

I drove to Blake's that day, fifty-fifty torn between doing the next list item and ending this arrangement.

I got out of my car and went to the door but just as I raised my hand to knock, the door opened and a girl with a face covered with smeared makeup and a neck covered in hickeys peered out at me.

"Holy shit, that sun is going to kill me," she said in this perfectly calm voice. The smell of alcohol baked off her, mingled with sweat. She raised a shaking hand, shielded her eyes, and added, "Wow. You must be her."

I blinked. "Her, who?"

"The girl Buddy thought I was when he kissed me the first time." She looked me up and down as I did the same to her. I was too busy wondering if she meant Blake was Buddy and what she meant about *the first time* to assess how similar we appeared.

"Dude, that guy drinks like a fish swims. I am lucky to be alive." Glancing down the driveway, she let out a long groan. "I think I threw up in my car. This is going to be one fucking rough ride home."

I followed her with my gaze as she wobbled across the

lawn and peeked in the windows of a blue sedan parked half on and half off the curb. "Yeah, I definitely threw up in there."

"Maybe you should roll the windows down," I said, because I couldn't think of anything else to say.

"Yeah, smart one. What time is it, anyway?"

"Two."

"In the morning?" She gazed up at the bright sky. "Duh, of course it's two in the afternoon. I am so fucking fried—fri—fired … both," she said. Blinking a few times at the sky above, the color dropped from her face and she dashed back from the curb to hurl in the neighbor's hydrangeas. Then she fell over and got tangled in the bushes, and yelled a bunch of words that might have been Spanish before making it back to her feet and getting into her car.

The windows went down, more yelling ensued, and then a pair of panties flew out the window and landed on the sidewalk. Her car lurched from side to side, and I winced, hoping she made it back wherever she had come from without killing someone.

Blake's front door was still open and I closed it, softly.

Tears sat in my eyes. I had no idea why. I shouldn't care who that girl was or what she'd done with Blake. He wasn't mine. That was the agreement. I couldn't get angry because he had screwed another girl. *Right after me.* He had every right to do whatever he wanted to just like I had every right to do what I wanted to do, and what I wanted right then was to get the heck out of there and go somewhere quiet to cry.

I was halfway down the path when the door banged back open and Blake's head popped out. He looked awful. His skin was a greenish-gray. There were dark circles under his eyes, and he gasped harshly when the sun hit his face.

I honestly expected him to burst into flames for a second. He must have too, because he wrapped his arms over his head and scuttled down the grass to where I stood. The old man from next door was out getting his mail again and watched the whole scene. Blake waved to him. The neighbor made eye contact with me for a moment and shook his head with disapproval.

"Where are you going?" Blake asked me.

"Sorry, you might have me confused with the woman that already left." I knew it was snarky but I was still stinging with jealousy and I didn't know how to handle that at all.

His red-rimmed eyes looked slowly to the street, now empty, then back to me.

Blake put his hands to his chest like he was making a vow. "Oh, no. No, no, no. Veronica? I didn't do anything with her, I swear."

"I couldn't care less what you did with her," I lied. "Just

don't lie to me like I'm an idiot."

Could I be any worse of a human being right now? My hypocrisy left a bad taste in my mouth, and I tried to walk away again.

Blake stepped in front of me, and wobbled like he might fall over. "I'm not lying. Why would I lie? I know you don't care. Look, just … this fucking sunlight. Come inside, and meet Buddy, and I'll explain."

"Buddy? She called you Buddy. She said you thought she was me, and you kissed her. More than once." I was letting him lead me up the path, letting myself hope he was telling the truth.

Blake winced. "I was completely bottled at the time, and I really did think I was kissing you. Things got a bit crazy, and all my new friends ended up back at my place."

We got to the front door and Blake pointed through at the couch. A man with pale ginger hair, wearing nothing but an old sheet covering his middle, was sprawled there, snoring loudly.

"That's … I'm not sure what his name is. I've been calling him Buddy. He hooked up with the girl that just left. I let them crash here."

"You let two complete strangers sleep at your place … possibly sleep with each other at your place?" I wasn't sure whether to think it was kind or crazy of him. Blake was picking up strays all over the place.

"Buddy needed a break. He's been having a rough time." Blake looked down the street. "I didn't really get to know Vicki at all."

"You called her Veronica a second ago."

"She might be Verity."

I shrugged, trying to hide the immense relief I felt. "She tossed her drawers," I said.

"Is that Yankee slang for threw up?"

"What?"

"You know, like tossing your cookies?" Blake asked.

"No, I mean she threw a pair of panties out of her car. But also yes."

"Ah." He stared at them on the sidewalk.

"You're just going to leave them lying out there, aren't you?" I asked. My mouth was twitching upward.

"Yep. I don't think I can face any cleaning up right now."

"You do look like you've been hit by the hangover bus. And then it reversed back over you a few times," I observed.

"I feel worse. You look great."

"It's the pure joy of not being hungover, radiating out of me."

Blake smiled, but it faded fast. He seemed worried by something more than his hangover. "Do you want to come in?"

"Better not wake Buddy. I was thinking maybe we could go do that next thing." I gestured to my sundress, the swimsuit underneath, the cues that a trip to the beach could happen. I was excited for this list item more than just for the sex. I'd never actually been to the beach before. It was a long drive from here, and since the lake was so close we always just went there instead. But I'd always wanted to go. My heart came alive at the thought of swimming in the ocean.

Blake blinked bloodshot eyes at me. "Seaside? Today? You trying to kill me? Maybe we can skip to the 'sex with a woman' part of your list."

Too soon. I bristled again. "Maybe you could call your new girlfriend back, see if we can't knock that out real quick so I can go do what I really want to do today."

Blake looked way too eager for a split second before my tone caught up with him. "Wow, can you hold the sarcasm a little? I'm about to drown in it. I thought you didn't care who I slept with."

"I don't," I lied, again. I could feel my invisible armor thickening, ratcheting tighter with each *click,* constricting my breath with each lie.

"Really?" His voice was soft, his forehead wrinkled with concern.

I swiped away the hand he reached out for me and my voice grew shrill. "I care that you *didn't* sleep with her. That you think that's what I want. You're not mine. I'm not yours."

Click, click, click.

Blake threw up his hands. "I didn't ask for this shit."

"I think I remember you did, when you were so eager to jump onboard the sex-list train. And I should have said no." I turned and walked back to my car.

"Don't run away again!" He wobbled down the path after me, and put a hand on my shoulder, but I wasn't sure whether it was to stop me or stabilize himself. "Just tell me what the fuck is wrong?"

I froze in place, ever muscle strained. My breath held like burning gas in my lungs.

"I'm sorry," Blake calmed his voice again. He spoke in low, soothing tones that shot into me like arrows. "I know there's *something*. Something hurting you, something making you act like this. It's okay, just tell me. Please."

My armor wasn't thick enough. Tears came. Too fast to stop.

Blake saw them and his face looked ashen.

He saw. He saw through my armor. Saw how weak and broken and sick I was.

Mortified, I turned and ran, slamming the car door and driving off, vowing never to come back.

How could I? How could I see someone so perfect look at me with such worry, pity, and pain? Someone I had grown to feel for, more than I'd ever planned.

I couldn't. I could never see Blake again.

No matter how much my heart wanted to.

Chapter Sixteen

GEORGINA

Without Blake, I had lost all interest in my list.

Without him to help, I wasn't sure how to get started on it again. I wasn't sure whether I still wanted to do the things written there without him, apart from the need to have it *finished*. Time slowed to a sludgy pace and all I could seem to think about was him, and how soon I might die. I went back to class just to fill in time and give my brain something to occupy it and stop it from going crazy.

I told everyone I'd had a bout of the flu, and after I told the counselor about my past chemo and resulting lower immune system they gave me a medical pass, so my scholarship was no longer in danger.

Julie thought I had seen the light, and even offered to help me catch up. I asked her how her physics knowledge was going to help with my graphic design assignments, and she just shrugged and moped away. I was being a bitch to everyone, it seemed.

I called her back and suggested we watch a movie. It took even more time away from getting assignments done, but it was exactly what I needed. We curled up on the couch together and watched *The Way You Do*. One of the actors in it was so intense, I started to wonder what was going on in her life. Whether she was going through something traumatic. Whether her life was any easier or worse than mine. I made up whole stories in my head about her. It helped put things into perspective.

Julie actually smiled when the movie finished, and I said I'd pull an all-nighter to get some work done afterwards. But when I closed my door on her and looked at the pile of work on my desk, I lost my motivation again. I'd been given extensions, but that just meant I had all of last week's assignments *and* all of this week's assignments to do. I couldn't even find it in me to panic.

I was numb to all of it. I just drifted through the days, trying to make sense out of things that no sense could be made of. I sat in class and stared at complex concepts and even more complicated people, wondering if anyone had noticed my absence, and if they would notice the larger absence that was to come.

Blake called me about a hundred times. I couldn't answer.

He stopped by looking for me twice. I hid. I couldn't face him.

And I couldn't stop thinking about him. I hated it.

It meant I cared about him, and I didn't want to. He was a hot, sweet, intelligent guy with a great future ahead of him. It was unfair of me to expect him to be there for a girl who was dying. What kind of life could we have together? A loved one dying from a terminal illness was only romantic in books and movies; in real life, it was messy and unbearable.

In stories, the heroine stayed strong, she was always beautiful, became more beautiful despite whatever disease was ravaging her body. I knew better than that. I had witnessed death all around me during my treatment. I'd witnessed my mother's death. Cancer took life and beauty away and gave back nothing. Blake deserved better. If he cared at all for me too, then ending it here was for the best.

Dad had called, inviting me to dinner on Friday, saying we'd be doing that instead of our normal Sunday thing. That was strange enough, but then I pulled up at Dad's house only to see Blake's bike in the driveway, plus another car I didn't recognize.

Oh god, do they know? Is this some kind of intervention?

I walked slowly into the house, ready to bolt if needed. Dad was sitting at the bar in the living room, drinking and laughing with Blake.

Dad put his tumbler of whiskey down on the counter. "There she is!"

He came across the room—a suspiciously immaculately clean room—looking joyful and slightly red in the cheeks. How long have the two of them been drinking?

Dad wrapped his arms around me. He seemed way too happy. What was going on?

"It's so nice you invited Blake to dinner again," he said.

I gave Blake a '*What the hell?*' look over Dad's shoulder.

With one more squeeze, Dad let go. "I've got someone I want you to meet as well."

I was given no time to assault Blake with questions before a blond woman walked in from the dining room, and Dad stood beside her.

She was a bit younger than my dad, maybe late thirties. Her bleached hair hung in a clean sheet down her back, and her overly-whitened teeth flashed as she smiled and extended one very tanned hand and said, "It is so nice to finally meet you. Your dad has told me all about you. Aren't you just so adorable?" She actually pinched my cheeks.

I stared at her. "Umm, hi?"

"I'm Louisa." She said it like I was supposed to know exactly what that meant. "I'm dating your father."

I gave Dad a steely look. I knew he'd been dating on and off since Mom died. Mostly off. But he always tried to keep it secret from me. I had no idea he was seeing anyone right now, let alone someone he now felt ready to introduce to his daughter. I felt utterly ambushed.

I'd probably brought this on myself. Maybe Dad had just been waiting for me to be the first person to bring someone home. Now it was an acceptable thing.

"Louisa. Of course. Dad has talked about you. A lot." I could see from my Dad's wince that he knew we would be talking a lot about her, very soon.

Louisa smiled even wider and put her hand on my shoulder, directing me into the dining room. An unnaturally clean dining room. Everything was unfamiliar.

"This is so lovely," Louisa said. "It's like a double date!"

"Blake and I aren't dating," I said.

"Oh, just friends. Gotcha." Louisa winked a very obvious wink at me, like we were girlfriends already. "Blake?" Louisa let her eyes linger on him. "I didn't catch your last name."

He hesitated. "Rowell. Blake Rowell."

Louisa's eyes narrowed very slightly, then she laughed. "When you say it fast it sounds like Blake Growl!" She leaned back and whispered to me, not quietly enough, "And *grrrrr* indeed."

Dad followed us, and when I glanced back at him I could see him alternating between giving anxious looks at me and making googly eyes at Louisa. This relationship was important to him, or she wouldn't be here. This was the first partner he'd ever introduced me too, and Louisa was obviously trying hard to win me over, in her own way. I knew I had to try as well. For Dad. He'd need someone, after I was gone.

The table was already laid out with Dad's finest plates and cutlery. Each setting was perfect, with folded napkins, multiple sets of knives and forks for each course, and a center-piece of yellow roses and calla lilies. Louisa stood next to it and flourished her hands. She'd obviously been working hard. I wondered if she'd done the cleaning too, or just inspired it.

I tried to seem enthusiastic, but it wasn't right. It wasn't the way we did family dinner. Sunday dinner was casual, just me and Dad and good food. It was Friday, anyway, but still. It was like she was already trying to create a new tradition. To take over.

Relax. She can't replace Mom. She's not trying to. You're just worked up.

I sighed and put on a smile. "It looks beautiful, Louisa.

Just perfect."

She beamed and Dad beamed, and my smile grew more honest.

The oven timer beeped in the kitchen and Dad headed that way. Louisa hurried after him, insisting on helping.

I immediately turned on Blake, who had been cowering behind the others. Now we were alone in the room, he backed against a wall, holding up his hands defensively. "Please don't kill me."

I hissed, "This is stalker behavior. You realize that, right?"

"I was just worried about you, that's all. And I wanted to apologize for being a massive prick. You didn't reply to my calls, or answer your door, so I just stopped by to ask your dad if you were okay. He kind of assumed I was here for dinner, and I wasn't going to turn down one of your dad's meals."

I half smiled. No one could turn down one of Dad's meals. "I don't want you to worry about me."

"Yeah. You've made that clear. But it turns out I do anyway."

The bottom fell out of my heart.

Blake stroked a finger down my cheek, looking far too concerned. "What is it you do want?"

You. All of you, up and down, inside and out. For every day I have left.

But that was selfish, too selfish. "I just want to finish my list."

Blake's hand dropped away. His voice sounded flat. "Made any more progress, since I haven't heard from you?"

"No. I just needed … some time. What about you? Do you still want to help me with it? It's meant to be fun. I want it to be fun for you too. *Just* fun. Nothing more. And I know which one you're looking forward to. It sounds like fun, right?"

Blake hesitated a moment, but then his lips pulled to the side. "I'd be lying if I said it hadn't been on my mind."

"Do you want to try tonight?" I asked. "You can help me pick up a girl, and then … I don't know. I guess we see what happens?"

Blake put his hand on his chest and said earnestly, "If you let me be part of what happens, even if I'm just sitting in the corner, I will be immensely appreciative. I'll try my best not to giggle like an excited schoolboy and ruin it."

I raised my eyebrows, not sure if he was joking. I dropped my voice to a whisper, worried about Dad overhearing. "You really want to watch me and another woman … make love?"

"Bloody hell, Georgie." Blake bent toward me as if I'd punched him in the belly. "Dinner with your dad and his new girlfriend, and I'm not going to be able to stand up all night."

I blushed as Blake hobbled over into a chair and

crossed his legs.

Dad and Louisa came back in, bringing plate after plate of food. They had cooked without me, but I didn't mind. An early dinner meant Blake and I could get away earlier too, and I was starting to get interested in my list again. Just seeing how Blake reacted to the idea of me and another woman turned me on. Made life spark up inside me again.

Dinner was a bit of a circus. Dad kept staring at Louisa, and trying to tell me every one of her many wonderful attributes. Blake stuffed about ten pieces of salmon covered in butter and dill sauce into his gut, and somehow still managed to have room for triple-cooked potatoes, half a dozen homemade sourdough bread rolls, and a huge helping of the creamy chocolate mousse my dad used to make just for me.

Louisa was nice enough but she kept asking Blake weird questions. Blake was too busy eating to notice that they were weird, or the way she would narrow her eyes a little right before she asked. It made me uncomfortable.

Dad had questions, too. Luckily, it was easier to answer questions about my classes now that I was actually going to them again. He backed off me in a hurry after he figured that out and he pretty much left Blake alone too, except for the occasional admiring glance when Blake managed to snarf down yet another serving of food.

As Dad started clearing the table, I excused myself to

the bathroom to clean up. I'd come dressed for a meal with Dad, not ready to pick up another woman. I wore a black, loose-fitting blouse with lace edges, belted around my waist with leggings beneath. I pulled the belt in as tight as possible over my just-fed belly to make my curves pop, and let my hair out, ruffling it with my fingers. I had some makeup in the car I could put on before we hit the bar, and overall, I didn't feel too frumpy. With Blake by my side, I felt confident.

I was about to leave the bathroom when the door I'd left ajar swung open.

"Hello there." Louisa leaned against the doorframe. "I was hoping we would get a chance to talk privately. A little bit of girl time."

"Sure, I guess. What did you want to talk about?"

She clapped her hands happily and the heavy gold rings across her fingers clacked against each other. She shuffled closer, propping herself up on the vanity basin beside me. "Just a bit of girly gossip! Won't it be fun to talk about boys together?"

"Except by boys, you mean my father." I grinned wryly.

She chuckled. "I suppose that could be awkward, couldn't it? I'll try not to tell you how dreamy I find him then."

I chuckled back, warming to her. But then those narrowed, fox-like eyes came back. "Blake seems like a nice guy."

"He is. But we are just friends," I said.

"Do you know much about him?"

"Not really," I admitted. I hadn't even known his last name until today. "But I've only just met him, and we're really *just friends.*"

Louisa waved her hand at me like the words "just friends" did not exist to her. "What I mean is, do you know who he *is*?"

I frowned, unsure where this was going. "He's just … Blake."

"Oh, honey! You really don't know?" Louisa shuffled along the vanity, even closer, clearly excited by something. "I suppose he was never really that famous. Just famous, you know, by association. But even I followed his Instasnap account for a while before it all ended."

Famous? "What all ended? Associated with who?"

"That's *Seyvia's* husband. I mean, they were young, but they had that high school sweetheart angle the press loved, and he was one of Sey-Sey's back-up dancers, so he was always right by her side in the news."

Husband? I leaned into the vanity basin, feeling faint.

Let us live forever,

Or let us die together,

Without you, what is life for?

The song lyrics floated through my head. That teen

pop-star that died young of an overdose not long after the song hit the charts ... Seyvia.

"Blake doesn't dance," was all I could say.

"Oh, it's him all right. You don't forget a face like his. I don't know what he's been doing since the tragedy, or how he ended up here with you." Louisa popped her hands over her mouth. "Oh, dear, I didn't mean it like that."

I just shook my head, trying to absorb the information. I couldn't even hate her for the slip-up. Of course, that was what any sane person would think. Why would someone like him be with someone like me? No wonder he was worried. No wonder he was trying to work out what my deal was. He'd already lost someone. He was probably trying to work out what risk I was to him.

If Louisa was right at all. Maybe she wasn't. It had to be at least three years since Seyvia had died. What was Louisa, anyway? Some kind of partners-of-dead-pop-stars expert? She probably had the wrong person.

But if she wasn't wrong?

Tears jumped into my eyes.

Louisa made a small whining noise. "Oh, darlin', I'm so sorry. I really didn't mean it that way. I was just trying ..."

I walked out of the bathroom. I had to find Blake. *To what? Confront him?* I couldn't be that much of a hypocrite.

If we both had our secrets, so be it.

But I still had to find him. To look him in the eye and see if I could identify the loss in there, the empty, unhealing wound a loved one carved there when they left us. To see his pain and decide if I could cause something similar in him again.

I found him out in the backyard, staring up at the tree in the middle of the lawn. Mom's tree.

Each step toward him felt as if I was held back by the weight of a ship's anchor.

The sky hung over our heads in softened shades of blue streaked through with pink and coral, ever darkening. Somehow, it made the purple flowers blanketing Mom's tree glow brighter.

"It's beautiful," Blake said when I reached his side. "I'm not sure I've seen a tree like this before."

"It's a lasiandra," I said. I looked at the tree too. "Dad and I planted it just after Mom passed away. In her memory."

I could sense Blake turn and look at me. I couldn't look him in the eye. I was such a coward.

His voice came quietly. "Isn't that painful? Having such a big reminder of her, right here in the middle of the yard?"

I took in a shaking breath. "Yes. And no. It's almost as though I put a lot of my memories of Mom into this tree. It was so small when we planted it. I could ignore it if I needed to—just turn away and not see it when it was too hard. But each year it gets bigger, more visible, as each year I'm more willing to remember, more able to remember without as much pain. And now, her presence will never fade away for us. She's here, growing stronger in this tree and our hearts forever."

Blake turned away to study the tree again. I took the opportunity to dab at the tears that threatened to spill.

The sky had shifted again, darkening into royal purples that matched the lasiandra, slashed through with neon orange as though set alight.

It was so beautiful it nearly broke my heart. I had been so sure before of my list, so sure it was what I needed and all I needed to feel alive for the time I had left. That sky, though? That never-ending stretch of color-washed space was enough to make me think that maybe there was something else, something that I might be missing out on.

The twinkle of the evening star appeared on the horizon.

"Starlight, star bright ..." I said, unsure what I would wish for that night. I couldn't bring myself to believe miracles happened. I'd seen too much death and suffering for that.

I would wish for something simple. That Blake would forgive me, and find happiness and healing after my list was done and I was gone.

"It's okay if you don't want to head out to a club right now," Blake said. His comment caught me off guard, and I looked right at him. His bright blue eyes seemed to peer right into my soul.

"I thought you were looking forward to this?" I teased.

"Boy, am I. But I couldn't stop eating for the sex life of me. Testament to your dad's cooking I suppose." He rubbed his stomach as he looked up at the fading sunset. "I am so full I'm sloshing."

I smiled, happy to be let off the hook. After tonight's revelations, I wasn't in the mood either. I needed time to find out if those revelations were true. Time to decide what they meant. "I guess this is good night then."

"Doesn't have to be. We could just hang out." Blake wrapped his hand in mine, dragging me toward the side gate. "Come on, let's go for a ride."

Chapter Seventeen

GEORGINA

Blake's body heat warmed my chest and arms. The air was cool and smelled of fresh-cut grass as we passed under tall oak trees, cruising slowly through the streets of my childhood.

That park was where Bobby Vaughn had kissed me when I was twelve, and when he kissed me again under the trees in the vacant lot behind it, I decided he was the boy I would marry. My best friend, Christy Roberts, used to live in the blue and white cottage on the left. She'd had a sleepover when we were fifteen and we had played spin the bottle with her older brother and his friends. One time the bottle pointed to her when I spun it, and after we kissed, half the boys in the room asked to go to the upcoming school dance with me. I was already going with Bobby, but I'd never felt so happy, so wanted.

Then, three days after that, my whole world changed. Then I wasn't the cute girl who kissed her friend at a sleepover. I was the girl with cancer.

Bobby went to the school dance with Christy. In his defense, he said that Christy was so upset about my diagnosis, and he was just helping make her happy by taking her to the dance. And I couldn't make it, since I was in the hospital that night, after all. What a hero.

The melancholy that lay heavy on my heart drifted off as we wound our way down the streets and to the lake. I knew where we were going as soon as the tires hit the old gravel road. The sound that came up from the wheels running over the rough ground was like a song I knew by heart, one that lightened my depression and made me smile.

The lake was empty, the road leading into it dusty. A few weeks before it would have been packed but since school had started again there were few people willing to come all the way out there. In this moment, it belonged to us alone.

Blake pulled into a space and parked. We headed down to the water. It gleamed black under the starry sky. Small insects sang in the grass, and the breeze ran over us in a long breath of air.

I drew it all in, as though I could pull all of existence inside me, become one with it all, enjoy everything micro and macro in that moment, from the soft lap of water tickling the lake shore to the twinkling universe above. Just being alive filled me with infinite happiness and sadness at the same time. Trying to find the joy and magic in every moment was painful, knowing how soon all this could end.

Blake stood at the lake's edge, staring into the water. "This is perfect sailing weather."

"Is it?"

"Have you ever been?"

"Sure. I've got my yacht around here somewhere." I checked all my pockets and peeked down the front of my shirt. "Damn, can't find it. Where's yours?"

I started prying into the pockets of Blake's jacket, and he just laughed. "I must have left mine at home too."

"Sailing is off the cards for the night then, old boy. Whatever else shall we do?"

We strolled along the shoreline a little farther, Blake holding my hand when the rocks got slippery.

"I was thinking about my first kiss on the way here," I said.

"I noticed it wasn't on your list."

"It was a long time ago. Nothing special." I side-eyed Blake. The things Louisa had said were still on my mind. Part of me had to know, and part of me didn't want to. I pried anyway. "How about you? What was your first kiss like?"

"Pretty standard too. Most of my firsts were by the book, very high-school-sweetheart stuff."

"Were you with that girl for a while?"

"Years. Followed her everywhere she went. Put my whole life on hold for her." He stopped walking and stared out over the water. "I always did so much for her, with her, but in the end it wasn't enough … I still can't dance without thinking of her. But that's over now. I'm getting on with my own life, trying not to get tied down again."

I inhaled a short breath, trying not to get flustered remembering getting tied down by Blake. *Stay focused.* Nothing he'd said meant he was who Louisa said he was. It was all too general. Could be anyone, any relationship past, even the dancing. I pushed a bit more. "How did it end? I mean, amicably or—"

"Do you like the woman your dad is dating?" he asked in a very unsubtle subject change.

It wasn't an admission. But it was enough that I knew. I just knew in my bones that it was him. That he'd lost his first love. And he didn't want to talk about it.

My brain stumbled to catch up, to not have a complete panic attack, to continue a normal conversation. I tried to frame a polite lie about how Louisa was *sooo niiice*, but quickly gave up. I'd lied to Blake enough. "No, I don't like her. I'm trying to be supportive though. This is Dad's first serious relationship since my mom died."

"I'm sorry," Blake said. "How did she die?"

"Breast cancer."

Something changed on his face. I hated pity, which was the normal response to hearing those words. But that was not the emotion written on his features. It was something deeper, more intense.

I put my arms up around his neck, swayed my hips softly. "Dance with me. It's a nice night for dancing. Maybe you can make some new dancing memories."

"I don't dance." Blake's body remained still as a statue.

"I'm not asking for a choreographed routine here, just—"

"I don't dance," he said again. His expression was unbreakable.

I dropped my arms away, feeling awful for having pushed him. There was pain there. A lot of it. Before I could apologize, his expression shifted again, and he gave me a wicked sidelong look. His hands were gentle on my chin as he tilted my face up to his and whispered, "Close your eyes."

I obeyed, closing my eyes tight. Confusion settled in even as his lips settled onto mine and his arms wrapped around me. I felt my feet leave the ground, and I couldn't fathom how he could be so strong. We were moving, still kissing, our mouths fused together as the cool water of the lake came up around us, closing over our heads.

Inky blackness washed my fear and sadness away. I scrunched my eyes shut tighter, reveling in all the feelings washing over me: the weight of my clothes, the strength of Blake's arms, the freshness of the chilled water. I felt so ridiculous, so happy, so *free*. I came up out of the water giggling and gasping. Blake stood solid on the lakebed, but it was too deep for me to touch. He kept me supported in his arms. His face and body were outlined by the silvery light of the moon, and droplets of water shimmered in his hair and dripped from his face. We swirled through the dark water as one, the surface reflecting the stars above us as though we danced in the heavens.

Mom, are you up there, dancing in the heavens too?

"What do you think happens after we die?" I asked in a barely there breath.

Blake's body tensed. I wanted to backtrack. I'd asked the wrong thing, gone too far. He let me go and I treaded water, about to change the subject when he spoke. "I never believed in an afterlife. Religions just never made sense to me. I always had too many questions and belief alone wasn't enough of an answer. But it does suck when some things don't have answers, and are so much harder to handle if you don't believe."

The chill of the lake settled deep within me. Frogs croaked nearby, blissfully unaware of their mortality.

"I don't know either. I wish I did. But I suppose that's the one thing everyone wishes they knew, and nobody ever will." I swished my arms slowly through the water, tipping myself up to float on my back. My hair swam around me. "What if it's none of the things religion tells us? What if there is nothing? And we know nothing, become nothing, are nothing, after this? How are we supposed to deal with that?"

Blake didn't reply.

I stared into the stars above. "Or, what if when we die we become dreams?"

"Dreams?"

"Like, if our consciousness, no longer attached to our bodies, just enters a constant state of dreaming. Or not even that we are dreaming, but that we become dreams themselves, within people who are still living."

Blake swam beside me, and kissed my cheek. "You amaze me, Georgina."

"Why?"

"You are either very brave or utterly crazy. I keep trying to figure you out."

"Maybe I'm neither."

His lips were soft on my cheek. "Or both."

Something slimy brushed against my legs in the water

and I ran out of the lake, shrieking, "Not brave, not brave, not brave!"

I turned back to watch Blake follow me out, worried some cousin of Nessy was about to snatch him away into the depths of the lake. The water ran down off Blake's shoulders as he emerged slowly, chuckling at my cowardice. He looked so utterly gorgeous I was almost ready to join him in the water again. Almost. Not quite.

The breeze raced against my wet clothing, and my teeth chattered. Beside us, there was an old fire circle on the banks that someone had left behind. Blake picked up a stick and poked through the remains. The blackened wood and the white ash scraped away to reveal some hot orange embers and nearly whole ends of pine logs.

"Want to see a magic trick?" Blake asked.

I giggled in agreement and before I knew it, he had backed his bike up so that the exhaust was pointed straight into the fire. He started the motorbike and revved the engine hard. The rush of fumes from the exhaust set the fire ablaze in seconds, and the world was lit up by a bright spurt of sparks that heralded long yellow flames.

I cheered him on, and he joined me sitting by the fire, sitting behind me and pulling me into his arms as our clothes dried.

"I wish we had marshmallows," I said.

Blake nodded. "I once roasted the pumpkin-flavored ones they sell near Halloween."

"I can't decide if that is brilliant or terrible. How did they taste?"

"I thought I'd be vomiting long before I finished out the bag."

My jaw dropped, aghast. "You ate the entire bag?"

"I wasn't about to admit defeat."

I could believe that from him. And the thought unsettled me. "Well, your work here is done, Sir Knight, starter or fires, taker of virginity, and ruiner of marshmallows."

"A gallant prince such as me? I thought my job would be to save the princess." His tone was light, but his face was tight with concern.

There was so much I wanted to say—to tell him the truth, to explain why the list was all we could have, to apologize for everything, but I couldn't frame the words. Not with him there, looking at me like he was a white knight and I his damsel in distress.

The earth was cool below my legs, but his body was warm as he hugged me. I let my head stay on his chest, listening to his heart beating. There was something so reassuring about that steady thud. He would be around after I was gone and that was more than okay—that was good. I was glad. I wanted to be nothing but a happy memory for him.

And for that to happen, he could never know the truth. This would have to end before things got worse. Before I got sick. "We'll have to find you a princess to save then."

A long silence fell between us.

Finally, Blake asked, "Do you want more than just your list?"

The smoke from the fire had curled into my nose, crisp and aromatic. It clung to our skin, and I breathed it deeply before answering, "No."

"What if I want more than your list?"

"You mean from me?"

"No, from Hello Kitty. Of course, from you."

"Then I'd have to say no to you, and I'd have to find someone else to help finish my list, and I don't want to do either of those things."

Blake lifted his chin, as though indicating everything around us. "This is more. This has been nice. What's so wrong with this?"

I got up, out of his arms and brushed myself off. "I'm sorry. We shouldn't have come out tonight. I'm sending the wrong signals. I'm not trying to play hard to get or some other game. I truly don't want more than what we've agreed to."

I held my breath, hoping he would let it go, and he did. He got up as well and started putting the fire out. He looked somehow exhausted, and I felt awful for turning him down when I'd love so much to say yes to him in every way. But it was for the best, for him.

If he'd lost someone he loved in the past, I couldn't put him through that again. I had to call this off. We'd do just one more item off the list first. I owed him that. I knew he wanted it.

We climbed onto his bike, and were back in front of my dad's house in no time.

The way he held me for a long time when he said goodbye galvanized my decision. I wasn't a princess he could save.

Chapter Eighteen

GEORGINA

I woke up the next morning unable to breathe. I couldn't force air into my lungs, and I sat in my bed with my mouth gaped open and my eyes bulging as I fought for air. Blurry blackness invaded my vision. My chest ached like I was having a heart attack.

I recognized it as an anxiety attack easily enough. I'd had my share. But even knowing that, there was always that inner voice whispering, *this is it. This is how you die.*

I counted out the seconds as I forced long, slow breaths, going through the relaxation techniques a counselor had taught me once. When my lungs worked again, I rolled over and burrowed back below the covers, wanting nothing more than to sleep forever. But I knew I had to get up.

I dressed in my comfiest jumper and leggings, and headed to the kitchen to eat the most decadent thing that could be found. The window was open, and a bubble floated inside. I stared at it in confusion, watching its rainbow swirls shimmer on the fragile surface until it popped in front of my face. Leaning out the window I saw the source: a couple walking with their toddler, who waved an automatic bubble-blower in the air as they went. It was such a joyous scene under the sparkling morning sun, with golden dandelions spotting the footpath around them. The world was so full of future and hope, out there.

Inside me, everything felt so desolate.

I rattled through the pantry until I found a box of praline chocolates and decided they would make a good breakfast, particularly paired with a half-empty tub of double cream I found in the fridge.

I was halfway through the box when Julie walked past, saw me eating them, and looked like a baby deer whose mother had just been shot.

"Shit," I said out loud. "These aren't mine, are they?"

"It's all right," she said, her voice flat. "You look like you need them more than me."

I bristled at first, and then let it go. I could never get a reading on Julie because of how she talked. It was like she was being dismissive, or sarcastic, or just plain mean from her tone.

But what if she wasn't? What if she just sounded like that? I tried to play that out, taking her words at face value, without any ulterior motive.

"I kind of do. Not sure there was ever a day that chocolate was more needed."

Julie eyed me, her face half turned and suspicious. "I've got another stash. If you want it."

"Do you want … Can we share them? Wow, I'm such a jerk—offering to share your chocolates with you. I'm sorry."

Julie edged a step toward me. "I've never had chocolates for breakfast before. My parents are strict about when candy should be eaten."

I jiggled the box at her, tantalizingly. "College is the time to be breaking rules."

And just like that, Julie and I were sitting at either end of the couch, tucked under the same blanket with two mostly eaten boxes of chocolates between us.

It was amazing what chocolate could do. I'd always assumed Julie didn't like me, but it was so clear to me now that that'd been my own way of keeping her at a distance. And here I was, accidently making new friends when it was a time when I most shouldn't.

An image of Julie and her wide, brown eyes, crying for me at my funeral made me choke up.

"Are you okay?" she asked.

"Yeah, just chocolate going down the wrong way." I swallowed, and shook my head. "No. That was a lie. I have become way too used to lying lately. I'm sorry, I'm an awful person. I'm going through some stuff, and I don't want you to have to worry about me."

Julie shrugged. "You're my housemate."

As though that answered everything.

"I can't believe this is the most we've ever really talked. What a waste of time, and chances for eating chocolate for breakfast together," I said.

Julie's expression didn't change a bit. "I thought you didn't like me."

"No. You're great. You're the best flat mate I could have hoped for. I've just been all kinds of bitch lately."

I put the empty chocolate box over on the coffee table and stood up from the lounge, stretching. "This has been really nice, but I've got somewhere to be today."

"Do you want … someone to come with you?" Julie mumbled.

I smiled at her and her offer. Even if I couldn't read her, she clearly had a read on me. But what I was about to do next wasn't quite the kind of relationship I wanted with Julie.

"Thanks, but I think I'll be okay. Blake is helping me with this one."

She smiled at the mention of his name. "He's a nice guy. I'm glad he's there for you."

Julie stood up as well, standing still a few steps away from me. Then she wrapped awkward arms around me for barely a second and disappeared into her room again, and it was one of the best hugs I'd ever had.

Chapter Nineteen

GEORGINA

I sat propped up at the bar, staring at the contents of my glass and trying not to giggle. Blake and I were scoping out potential women for me, or for us really. I did want to take it seriously, but the whole thing gave me the giggles. It was like kissing Christy Roberts while playing spin the bottle. We could barely keep our lips pursed we were laughing so much.

Blake kept making the craziest suggestions, like the woman with the big 80s hair and six-inch heels who looked like she was in her sixties.

"She's taken really good care of her body," I observed.

"Her legs look hot in those jeggings."

"What the heck are jeggings?"

I pointed up and down at the woman's legs, which were flashing with rhinestones. "Leggings made to look like jeans."

"Is that what those are? I was wondering how she got jeans to fit so tightly without popping an organ. Then again, most of the things women manage to do in the name of beauty confound the hell out of me." He slugged back half a beer.

My phone pinged with a new message.

Julie: I can't believe we ate chocolate for breakfast. It's so naughty.

You think that's naughty? I'm glad I didn't tell you about the rest of what I have planned tonight.

Me: You loved it. There's $20 stashed under the pizza flyer on the fridge. I'll love you for the rest of my life if you stock us up again.

Julie: As long as we can eat it together.

Me: Deal.

Blake watched me texting. I wasn't normally the kind of person to text when I was around other people, not that I was often around other people, or had anyone to text. I kind of liked having someone I could text. Still, I put my phone away and scanned the crowd again.

"There. What about her?" I pointed to a girl so thin she resembled a carefully whittled stick. With warm dark skin and long black hair, she had the face of a Disney princess. Shorter than even me, she wore a tight shimmery dress, and I swore if she turned side-on she would just disappear. "She is the most adorable thing ever. I want to put her in my purse and take her home," I said through a mouthful of sour-cream coated wedges.

"I'd be too worried we'd break her," Blake said.

"We'd probably lose her in the sheets."

Blake leaned across and grabbed some wedges from my plate. "How about we head back to the sex shop? Lady Pink Hair was hot for you, I could tell."

"I'm sure she makes an effort to appear hot for everyone that goes in there." I wasn't very good at the whole flirting thing or knowing when it was happening to me. I still found it hard to accept that anyone would actually find me attractive. Even Blake. He was probably just interested in me to get to this list item.

But getting this list item done seemed harder by the minute. It was already late. We were having fun, drinking, eating, and hanging out, but the odds of finding a suitable candidate seemed low.

Then, she walked in.

The timing was perfect, as a gush of wind and the rays of a car's headlights followed her through the door, making her hair shine and blow about her like she was in a movie.

She was so beautiful it was like she was being photoshopped in real time. She was bold, all character and confidence, an Amazon goddess.

Every head turned as she walked by. The man on the other side of the bar muttered, "Dear God have mercy."

Her hair was a glorious tangle of honey-gold curls. Her face held eyes that were a little too wide under brows that were thick and straight, a cute button nose, and a pair of lips fuller than any I'd ever seen. Nothing should have worked together. Her face was too small to hold those enormous eyes and mouth, but somehow that only made her even prettier. Her body, clad in a simple blue tank top and jeans, was a marvel of curves and angles. I ogled her openly, not caring about being discreet since everyone else in the bar was staring too. She was the kind of woman that made instant girl-crush material. I was so busy wanting to be her that I had to remind myself to want to be *with* her.

Blake appeared equally stricken. I couldn't even be jealous. Who wouldn't want her? She was the kind of woman someone like Blake was meant to be with. She was tall and would look perfect linking arms with him as they strolled into the sunset like two glowing gods. I daydreamed that if we could hook up with her tonight, maybe after I was gone the two of them could find happiness together. The thought left a bittersweet ache in my throat but solidified my resolve to try and bring this incredible creature home with us.

I elbowed Blake and questioned him with my eyebrows and a tilt of the head.

He replied with a slack-jawed stare and slow nod.

It all seemed too easy, like it was meant to be, when she came over, pointed to the stool next to Blake, and asked if she could sit there. Her voice was a low clear alto that reminded me of the blues singers my dad liked.

"Uh, yeah, sure." Blake had to clear his throat three times to get the sentence out, and I stuffed another potato wedge into my mouth to hold back the giggles, but some escaped anyway. She gave me a look that said she understood as she slid gracefully onto the stool and beckoned for the bartender to come our way.

"Bloody Mary, extra hot sauce please." Her voice gave me the shivers, right down my spine.

When her drink arrived with a sorry, wilted piece of celery sticking out, she sighed, took it out and left it on the bar, and downed half the drink in one hit.

I leaned past Blake and said, "This doesn't seem like your kind of place."

She chuckled. "I'm in town for a conference, staying at the hotel a few doors down. Was meant to be watching some speaker now, but even this dive seemed more attractive, maybe the kind of place I could find some fun. So here I am."

"You ran away," I said. "That's badass. Welcome to the

circus." We clinked glasses and drank, smiling at each other over the rims while Blake, unable to even speak, simply stared at us.

"I'm Georgina."

"I'm … Mary." Her grin said she was clearly not Mary.

Damn, smarter than me too. I knew giving a fake name was what I should have done.

She eyed Blake where he sat between us. "You two a couple?"

"No," I said, while Blake said, "Yes."

Mary looked on, her eyes growing more amused as we went through a little word shuffle that finally ended with Blake saying, "What she said."

Mary reached for the bowl of peanuts on the bar, shuffled through them with her long fingers, and placed one carefully on her tongue. I mightn't have been great at flirting, but there was something going on with this woman. She was older than me, and Blake, probably thirty, and simply radiated sexiness in a way that made it easy to get to the point.

The List Georgina is brave Georgina. I blurted out, "I'm just going to ask you. Because otherwise I'll have to put an ad on Craigslist."

She tilted her eyebrows up at those words. "For what? You need a new car?"

"No." My breath caught. Blake looked down at me,

amused, and offering no help at all. I had to keep going on my own. The worst she could do was laugh in our faces, and I had been rejected before after all. "I want a woman."

She didn't look shocked or even particularly surprised. "What did you want her for?"

"Um, you know …"

Mary just stared at me, waiting.

"For sex," I said, then instantly felt my cheeks turn red-hot.

Mary's full lips spread in a long, slow smile. She glanced at Blake sitting between us, then back at me. "Is he up for this too?"

"It's kind of my thing, but I said he could be part of it, somehow. I'm not really sure how it all works. It's our first time doing something like this." I was rambling. It was clear she was willing, and we all knew it, which only made me more nervous. I was excited, too. My nerve endings felt like they had been lit up with a blowtorch.

Mary's hand came out and caressed mine. She winked at me and placed her other hand on Blake's muscled thigh. "So you'd be wanting someone who could show you the way?"

She leaned across Blake toward me. Her head tilted toward mine and her lush lips parted. I swayed toward her, helpless to resist, and our mouths met. Applause erupted from the patrons and I could hear Blake mutter "bloody hell" above our heads. I almost broke away, but her hand had moved up my arm and to my neck. Her fingers pressed into my skin there, held me in place. Her mouth tasted like spicy tomato juice and cigarettes. Her hair was silky and slid through my fingers when I tangled my hands into it.

When the kiss broke, the bartender stood there, holding a tray of drinks in his hand. "Compliments of … oh hell, everyone!"

Beer foam sloshed over the rims of the glasses and shot glasses clicked together as he slapped the tray onto the sticky surface of the bar and wandered back toward the group of guys clustered at the other end. One of those guys gave Blake a double thumbs up.

Mary's face became serious and she locked my gaze. "Here's the deal. I want to fuck, you two want to fuck, and there is no reason why we can't all get what we want. Condoms are mandatory, and it can't be at the hotel the people I work with are in. Do we understand each other?"

Blake finally found his tongue. "Absolutely."

Her hand crept up my thigh, sending shivers down my body. I closed my eyes in involuntary pleasure and she chuckled, a rich and warm little laugh that reminded me, oddly enough, of chocolate brownies. "I am going to have so much fun with the two of you."

We shot down a few of the drinks, but left most on the

tray. The guys in the bar all stared at us as we walked out, and a couple of them high fived Blake. I wondered if I'd be brave enough to show my face there again, but if I was brave enough to do this, maybe I could. A buzz had hit me, and not just from the tequila.

Chapter Twenty

GEORGINA

Blake drove my car back to his place. Mary and I sat in the backseat, and she kept kissing me, her lips soft little pillows under my own, her mouth warm and moist. She took total control, which made it easy. The intimacy and pleasure of her touch made me feel more confident of what was to come, even eager for it. Every few seconds I would catch a glimpse of Blake staring at us in the rearview mirror, which turned me on even more.

Mary's hand moved up from my thigh, over my belly, and to my chest. When her hand gripped my breast, her thumb slid across the flesh of it and for one moment, she pulled back.

She knew. Blake had never felt a thing, but the first touch from a woman, and she noticed straight away.

"It's nothing," I whispered into her ear, and she paused for just one more second before she kissed me again.

We got out at Blake's house and made it inside in a haze of stumbling strokes and kisses. Blake led us up the stairs to his bedroom, and Mary made Blake sit in a chair across the room as she undressed me, and then herself. I trembled as I stood there, naked in front of them both. I could see the bulge of his excitement filling Blake's pants. I had no idea what to do next, but Mary clearly had a plan.

Mary grinned and looked at him. "Strip off and sit back. I'll let you know if you can join in."

I watched Blake get undressed, his muscles rolling as he dragged his shirt up over his head. A long shiver ran down my spine and settled between my legs as Mary took a step forward and pressed her hips against mine. She cupped my breasts gently in her hands, and placed those full lips of hers over my nipple. My eyelids fluttered, and I heard Blake exhale roughly.

"Fuck," he exclaimed, running a hand over his face.

Mary put a hand between my breasts, pushing me toward the bed with a wicked grin. "Your man has given us an order."

I landed on the bed, sitting on the edge of it, and Mary

stood in front of me. She reached for my hands and placed them on her breasts. I touched her nipples, and they hardened under my fingers. Experimentally, I wrapped my lips around one and tugged at it. It hardened even more. I knew the way it felt when Blake did that to me, and by Mary's moan I guessed she felt the same. Excited and encouraged, I sucked harder. Her fingers tangled into my hair, and she pulled me close. "I'm going to touch you everywhere," she whispered into my ear in a hot breath. "I'm going to fuck you so hard your man will beg me to stop, and then he's going to fuck you even harder."

She pulled back from me, leering at me in a way that made me catch my breath and my body pound with antici-pation.

Mary lifted one leg, putting her foot on the bed beside me and spreading her legs before my face. She looked down at me, challenging, daring me.

I licked once, cautiously. I gained courage as Mary groaned, deep and warm. My fingers stroked along the slippery seam of her and gently held her open so that I could use my tongue on her again. It was like exploring my own body, seeking the places I knew felt good, doing the things Blake had done to make me feel good.

"Good girl," she said, panting. "You're a fast learner."

She broke away and pushed me back onto the bed then landed on top of me, our breasts pressing together as she wrapped her lips over mine. She rolled us over, around, and somehow moved us into a sixty-nine position, with her on top and her tongue already delving into my most sensitive spot. Her hands ran up and down my thighs, spreading them wide.

Her mouth moved in a calculated rhythm. Firm, rolling, building. Rough, then gentle. Too much and then not enough. Her fingers joined in until I couldn't tell how she touched me and where—it was just one single, intense, and overwhelming sensation of *touch*. A sensory assault of pleasure and pain, rioting through me.

I tried to match her movements, her speed, her actions. Her hips thrust and swayed to the touch of my mouth. Our bodies trembled together. I pressed my tongue firmly against her, feeling her hot and engorged, and then sucked that throbbing nerve inwards. Her body went rigid above me, bucking against my mouth. I sucked harder, unwilling to break that hold. As her fingernails dug into my ass cheeks, my own orgasm broke through me. My eyes rolled back in my head and I could see Blake sitting in the chair with his legs wide apart, one hand rubbing up and down his firm length.

Mary flopped down onto the bed next to me, giggling and panting. I rolled away from her, lust heating my whole body and clouding my vision. The image of Blake touching himself was like the hit of a drug, and suddenly, all I wanted was him. I was thirsty for him in a way that drove me mad. I wanted him inside me. I *needed* him inside me. I crawled across the room to Blake, stopping between his legs, and placed my mouth around his hardness. He cried a long, anguished moan.

"Hey. Did I say I was finished with you yet?" Mary whispered from behind me.

I ignored her. I kept sliding my mouth up and down Blake, feeling the forms and shapes of him, the way he throbbed in my mouth, too blinded by passion to stop. I was determined to make him feel as good as he'd made me feel.

Mary smacked my ass, then lifted my hips. Her hand cupped my crotch, holding me firmly there in the small bowl of her palm, massaging the pleasure-swollen flesh. Her fingertips tickled against my skin, then she had her fingers inside of me, first one, then more, pushing harder and deeper than I imagined possible. I could feel her filling me, pumping against my wet flesh, inside and out.

Her second hand gently stroked down my back, down farther, spreading my ass apart. I could feel her fingers exploring every slippery part of my tender skin. So lost in lust, I would have let her do anything to me, touch me anywhere. I felt fearless, powerful, and entirely enthralled.

Between Mary behind me and Blake inside my mouth, the sensation of being filled entirely, pressed to bursting, made my whole-body thrum with an unrelenting need for more. I arched my hips up, trying to fill myself with Mary's hands at the same time as swallowing down farther over Blake. I wanted to push them both as far as I could push them inside me, as though that would ease that madness of desire that pulsed through me.

Mary thrust into me with the force of her whole arm, shaking my entire body and making me cry out each time. Deep, sobbing moans hummed against Blake's hardness in my mouth, and I heard him cry out as well.

"Stop!" Blake let out a rough, growling grunt.

He put his hands under my shoulders and lifted me off him and away from Mary.

For a moment I froze, stunned, worried I'd done something wrong.

But fire burned in his eyes when he looked down at me.

In one smooth movement, he threw me onto my back on the bed, then drove into me so hard I screamed. There were no warm-up or gentle strokes, and none were needed. The immediate and satisfying deep penetration was exactly what I wanted and needed.

His body slammed against mine, the force pushing me up the bed in an uncontrolled frenzy of passion. He filled me all the way, filled me in a way Mary had been unable to do. He filled my every yearning and longing and need. I knew, *knew,* that this was just a passing moment but all I wanted then was Blake, was this feeling of wholeness and completion and blind pleasure.

His mouth slanted over mine, kissing me with fierce desperation, and the weight of his body pressed me deeper into the mattress. His hands held my wrists above my head and Mary slapped his ass, a gleeful look on her face every time he drove into me.

She fell over onto the mattress beside us, her fingers working against her own flesh. In the blurry haze of pleasure and sex, I could see Blake staring at me. Only at me. Even when Mary cried out, her legs jerking and writhing beside us.

Blake's teeth imbedded into his bottom lip, and his blue eyes stared right into my soul. A huge orgasm burst out of me, tore through me, and left me sobbing and shaking.

We three lay together, a tangle of limbs, mouths, and organs. A pile of need and desire, sweat and sex. It was what I had craved for so long—all consuming, decadent, and so right I couldn't bear to think any longer. All I could do was respond to each touch, every movement, and every whispered word.

It was the sexiest thing I had ever done. Right then, in that moment, I felt more alive than I ever had.

~~Make out with a stranger~~
~~Get to second base~~
~~Lose virginity~~ ✓ + bonus orgasm, wow
Sex on a beach
~~Bondage sex~~
~~Make love with a woman~~
Sex in a public place
Sex with two men
Sex with a ~~B~~

Chapter Twenty-One

BLAKE

Georgina was sound asleep. She lay on her back, her eyelashes falling perfectly across pink cheeks and her mouth so slightly open. She looked far too innocent to have just done the things she had.

Mary pulled her jeans up, shaking her hips a little from side-to-side as she did.

"Let her sleep," she said.

I tore my gaze away from Georgina's face. "I don't think I could wake her up anyway." I didn't want to either. Most days she had dark circles under her eyes that proved she wasn't sleeping well. She needed the kind of slumber she had found just now.

Mary looked at her watch. "I need a ride back."

It was after three. A taxi would come, but that might take an hour or more around here. I wanted her gone. I wanted to lie down beside Georgina and hold her close. "I'll take you. Let me put on some clothes."

Mary left to wait in the living room. Maybe she needed some space or knew I did, but either way I was glad she went out. I stared at Georgina for a moment longer, and then threw the used condoms in the trash and got some clothes on.

I was still trying to get my head around what had just happened. The item on Georgina's list that had turned me on the most, that had made me want to be involved with her in the first place, wasn't at all how I'd expected it to be. It should have been a dream come true, but the reality had fallen short of what I had imagined. In daydreams, I never wished one of the women wasn't there. I never thought I would feel like I was doing something wrong. Or feel so damn jealous and possessive seeing someone, even a scorching-hot woman, give pleasure to my Georgina.

My Georgina? She's made it clear she isn't mine. That should suit me perfectly, but I kept wanting more.

Mary refused to go by bike, so I grabbed Georgina's keys and we were on the road. Mary lit a cigarette without asking if I minded. Since it was Georgina's car, I just rolled the window down on my side to try and stop the smell from sticking.

We passed dark streets, a cool wind blowing in the window, the radio so low it was just a hum.

There was something about that late hour. Most of the cars on the roads carried drunks going home or the cops trying to catch them. The world looked bare and tired, and a gloomy pall of depression filled the air. Maybe I was tired or just coming off a slow buzz that never really got a start, but I felt run down, exhausted, and sore in my chest.

I didn't want to talk but when Mary rummaged around in her handbag, pulled out a wedding ring and put it on, I couldn't help reacting. "You're married?"

A grin crossed her lips. "I travel for work far more often than we would like, and he knows I need certain things. Like the occasional gorgeous woman." She grinned again, the yellow of a passing streetlight flashing across her teeth. "I do this a lot less than I could, and we keep it honest. He's allowed to do what he wants as well, but we never bring people into our own bed. It works for us."

I shook my head. Maybe it worked for some people, but after tonight I knew I was only after one woman, and I wanted her to only have me.

Mary took another long drag of her cigarette and let

the smoke run out slowly over her lips. "What made the two of you decide to do this?"

I wasn't sure exactly how to explain it. I didn't really know why myself. "Georgina has this list."

"Like a bucket list?" She wound her window down and tapped the ash off her cigarette. "I thought it might be something like that when I felt that lump in her breast."

She said something else but it was lost in the roar that had started in my skull.

"Sh-she has a lump," I stuttered out.

"Man, breast cancer sucks. I take it the prognosis is no good?"

My hands gripped the steering wheel so tight my knuckles turned white. I had known. I'd known there was *something* wrong. I just didn't know what. I hadn't wanted to know what, not when we were pretending whatever we had wasn't going anywhere. Then it did anyway, and I felt things I shouldn't be feeling, things that were going to fucking hurt the both of us.

Georgina. She'd made it through something before, but she had it again and … she had what? Given up?

"She already had it, when she was a kid. And her mom—she died of it." Admitting it made my throat ache. I knew I didn't know for sure, but everything added up. There was that scar, and the fact that she had once worn a wig, and she had those tiny, damnable blue spots. She had a bucket list she was dead set on finishing. She kept telling me she wouldn't be around forever. She didn't want me to be attached to her. It all added up to a final equation I didn't want to solve.

A pain bloomed in my chest like a thorn-bush, tipped in poison, constricting my heart. I'd been hoping that after The List was over, Georgina would relax, and we could get to know each other properly, and maybe something real could come of this. It wasn't something I'd wanted for a long time. Not since Seyvia. But Georgina was so … ineffable. She awoke a desire in me for something more. Something lasting. But this was going to end. Everything ended, and too often too fucking tragically.

Seyvia. I still couldn't even say her name out loud. Couldn't hear one of her songs. Not after how she died. Not with knowing it was my fault.

I still couldn't deal with that pain. How could I go through something like that again?

I knew with Seyvia, too, in a way. I knew the fate she'd been headed towards. I'd tried to stay blind to it, to deny it, and it had happened anyway. It happened because I tried to deny it. Because I didn't help.

To be with Georgina would be staring down the possibility of losing her every single moment. Knowing that loss was coming.

But saying goodbye to her now would be losing her,

too. Removing her from my life by choice would have the same effect as losing her to death—that she wouldn't be with me.

And fuck it all, when all I wanted was for her to be with me.

"Fuck. Life fucking sucks." Mary tossed her cigarette butt out the window and yawned.

We didn't speak again. She got out of the car and headed into her hotel. She was just as hot and sexy as she had been when she came into the bar, and I watched her go, wishing I could go back in time and say no to the whole thing, yank Georgina out of there before we ever met the woman who wrecked my entire world.

I drove back home in a haze of pain. There was only one possibility—something was pushing Georgina into the actions she was taking, something dire, because under all of her bravado she was inexperienced and terrified as hell. And that something was probably cancer.

I got out of the car and looked for the evening star in the gloomy sky.

"She's dying." I said the words out loud, and they echoed in the stillness. A dog barked down the street. Tears filled my eyes, and I made it inside in time to keep myself from breaking down on my own doorstep. I wasn't strong enough. After tonight, I couldn't be with her anymore. I had to end this. I would in the morning. But I needed one more night with her in my arms.

I crept silently into bed beside Georgina and held her tight until morning.

Chapter Twenty-Two

GEORGINA

The next time I saw Blake, I would say goodbye to him forever.

Maybe that was why I couldn't bring myself to see him. I needed to buy some time.

After our night with Mary, I woke up in Blake's arms. His hands clung to me, and his face nuzzled deep into my neck. A small frown furrowed his eyebrows, even in slumber.

I lay there for a moment, my heart pounding against my breastbone as though it was trying to leap out of me and into him, fleeing this sinking ship that didn't deserve to feel the way his embrace made me feel right then.

So I fled, too. Snuck out before he woke up.

I didn't call him, and he didn't call me the next day. Or the day after.

There was a tension in that silence between us, but also a relief. As long as we didn't speak, the need to end this would be delayed. And I was still being a coward.

I tried to bury myself in class assignment work, but I felt a different calling. I dug through my supplies, found a large sheet of hot press paper, and cracked open my watercolor palette. Pencils and markers soon joined the dance, and form, hue, value, and pattern spilled onto the paper before me. I worked in a frenzy, splashing paint and then scrawling bold lines over it to accentuate the fractal shapes it dried into. Soon, something of beauty emerged from that chaos. I worked obsessively, breathlessly until it was done.

Mom, do you like it?

I fell asleep staring at what I'd created, surrounded by a litter of brushes and pencils. A fiery sense of purpose consumed me, and I knew exactly what I was going to do the next day.

But when it came time to do it, I needed moral support.

I had no idea how I talked Julie into coming with me, but I did.

I dressed in an outfit I hoped made me look tougher

than I felt—black T-shirt, denim miniskirt over old, ripped, black stockings, and a butt-ton of eyeliner. I thought I looked like a rebel, and that costume gave me courage.

It made Julie eye me suspiciously. She didn't join in the dress-up, and wore her usual cargo pants and a T-shirt with kawaii designs translated into broken English.

And that was how we walked into the tattoo parlor together.

I had imagined a dingy smoke-filled den crammed to the rafters with rough bikers and heavily tattooed people hanging out on stained sofas, drinking liquor from bottles. Instead, I found a bright, sterile room with a hint of funky flair in the massive color-splashed canvases and fairy lights strung along the walls above framed licenses and awards.

Behind the counter, a friendly woman with an etched buzz cut smiled warmly at us. Her arms were covered in tattoos, but not done in the traditional heavily inked black style. They were delicate, highly detailed geometric designs of leaping deer, surrounded by organic swatches of color, like paint had been splashed and left to dry on her skin. I smiled, instantly more confident I was in the right place.

She glanced over at Julie, then let her gaze rest on me. "Hi, I'm Glory. What can I do you for?" She gave me an appraising look. "Belly button piercing? Nose ring?"

"I want a tattoo." I spoke too loudly, but I couldn't help

it. Nerves were messing with my vocal chords.

The woman leaned forward on the counter, her pink lace bra showing clearly over the top of her plain white tank top. "Awesome, darling! Do you have something in mind? Working on an existing piece?"

"No. It's my first time. I kind of have some ideas, but some advice would be good." I hoped I didn't sound like too much of an idiot.

Glory just smiled wider. "That's how we all start out. Have a flick through the flash. Let me know if you see something you like. Start here—that's a good place for beginners." She thumped a heavy folder onto the desk and opened it to a section with tiny butterfly and love-heart designs. I looked down at them, feeling like the kid being sent to play in the ball pit instead of on the big rides.

"Actually, I was thinking of something like this." I opened my purse and pulled out my folded piece of paper, handing it Glory.

Julie peered over my shoulder as the tattoo artist opened it up. "Where did you get that?"

"Just something I drew."

Julie's dark eyes widened. "Pretty," she said, in her emotionless way.

Glory appraised the artwork, eyebrows raised. "Nice work. But to get that much detail, it's going to be a big tattoo for a newb. Sure you don't want to look at the smaller ones? I got some cute fairies."

Julie squeezed my arm as well, giving me a look. "Are you sure?"

The List Georgina is brave Georgina. The List Georgina says yes. "Yep."

"It will be on your skin. Your whole life."

"I do get the concept."

"Do you realize how long that will be?"

Much shorter than I want.

"I want my design. Can you do it all today?" I pushed on. If I hesitated now, I'd run away. The coward inside me would win. Because I was not at all as cool as I was pretending I was about getting this done. I was terrified, in fact. The idea of marking my skin forever scared me—until I reminded myself that my forever was going to be pretty short in the grand scheme of things.

Glory studied the design again for a while. "I'd normally do it in two passes, but yeah, if we simplify it a little it can be done today. It'll take several hours. And I don't give out pain meds."

I'd been through worse. The cost worried me more than the pain. But I didn't have anything to save for anymore.

Julie watched with a blank face as I signed the documents and paid upfront. "You're really doing this?"

"You want something too?" I smirked.

Her eyes popped. "No." Then her lip twitched. "Maybe. One day. Tell me how it was afterwards."

One day. Of course, Julie was still someone who had the luxury of 'one day'. "You can leave, if you want, since this is going to take a while. I mean, I want you here, it's nice having someone here, but I don't want to waste your time."

Julie shrugged. "I can wait."

Glory asked about where I wanted the tattoo. I didn't really know. I just wanted a tattoo because I wanted something permanent, something that was made to last. I had lived with the little pinprick tattoos from radiotherapy for years now, those plain black spots, and I wanted something to cover them up. I wanted to hide them with something beautiful.

I asked about getting the tattoo on my under-bust area, but Glory suggested it would fit better on my back. She told me to go to room number one, take off my shirt, and lie down.

"Be there in a jiffy," she sang.

The room was cold, and I shuddered. The entire space reminded me of hospitals and smelled of alcohol wipes, the kind I had to wipe the soft flesh of my stomach with before giving myself the post-chemo treatment needles that made my bones ache for days. The smell of those wipes still made me queasy.

Julie turned around as I stripped off my top half and

lay down face-first on what looked a lot like a massage table. She took a seat next to me and started playing a game on her phone.

Glory came in, and I heard her snap on some gloves. "All set? This is going to look so hot!"

I just nodded, and the needle whirred to life.

The pain wasn't very intense—it was just *there*. It settled into my back and my face pressed deeper into the low table's headrest. I stared at the tiles of the floor below. It was faultlessly clean, and that was one more thing that disappointed me. I wanted grungy, dirty nastiness.

The pain grew sharper as it went nearer my spinal column. I gritted my teeth, waiting for it to subside. Instead, it worsened, and I yelped.

Glory spoke over the hum of the tattoo gun. "Yeah, it's a sensitive spot. Want me to give you a break?"

"No. Keep going."

My eyes closed involuntarily, and a tear leaked out from one eye. Something ripped loose, the pain pulling away some emotional wall. That invisible armor I had locked on tight unclipped, and more tears began to fall.

Julie's feet came into view. Her hand closed around mine. It made the tears fall faster, splashing onto the tiles beneath me.

I couldn't handle this anymore. I wanted to be alive, to

have more than just a stupid list of things I was in a hurry to do because I would probably never get a shot at them otherwise. I wanted to have real friends. I wanted to really be with Blake. I didn't want my dad to lose me.

What would Dad do without me? He had never gotten over my mom dying. Even at my young age, I saw how close he'd been to giving up himself when he lost her. It was only for me that he kept going and stayed strong. How would he cope with me leaving as well?

The pain opened me up, letting loose an ache that had nothing to do with the needle stabbing ink into my flesh. I felt like a little girl again, losing my mother for the first time. It wasn't fair. I needed Mom. I needed her to have held me as a teenager when I suffered the same disease she did. I needed her now to tell me things would be all right. Even if they wouldn't. Even if we both knew I was dying, I needed to hear words of comfort from my mother.

It's okay. I know it hurts.

I could almost hear her voice.

It's almost over. You'll be all right.

It wasn't Mom. It was the tattoo artist. Her voice intruded into my clouded head.

"Aaaaand we're all done," Glory announced.

My eyes popped open. I wasn't sure if I'd fainted or simply cried myself to sleep right there on the tattoo table.

Time had passed, but Julie remained by my side, her hand still in mine. The gun stopped its whirring and the stinging pain no longer seemed as intense there on my back.

Some liquid was daubed gently over the area, and I held my breath for a few seconds as it sent fresh threads of fiery pain through me.

"It looks amazing," Julie said, deadpan.

Glory held up a mirror, and I looked over my shoulder to see. It did look great, swirling across the curve of my middle back and up toward my shoulder blades— red, bold, and defiant.

It was an artwork born of anger and strength. Bold lines created the silhouette of a woman, clutching a red heart to her chest as she was engulfed in flames that flew around her like wings. It was the first time I had drawn something just for me, just from my own inspiration, for a long time. It spoke to me. It said, "Hang onto whatever life you have got left. Burn bright as you burn out." This artwork was part of me, had to become part of me. And now it was, forever.

The woman swaddled me in plastic wrap. After dressing and being handed a sheet of care instructions, it was all done.

Julie took my keys and helped me into the car. I didn't ask her to drive, and she didn't offer—she just did it. She didn't ask me any questions, or say a word about how I'd cried and cried on that table.

I stared out the window all the way home, blinking up at the darkening sky with my fresh tattoo and my head stuffed full of things I didn't want to think about.

Chapter Twenty-Three

GEORGINA

It was over a week without any contact from Blake. My back had been itching like crazy. The yearning to scratch it raw was almost as strong as the yearning to see Blake again, despite what had to be done when I did see him. The weather had become muggy and oppressive, heavy around my body and heart. Even as much as I hated the cold, I started to crave it. Cool showers got me by, but I longed to be immersed in cold water, to float away in it as it chilled me to the bone. Throwing all caution and my tattoo aftercare instructions to the wind, I'd put my swimmers on and headed out.

I caught the bus into town. My head felt too clogged up and messy to drive. The air in the bus hung thick with the haze of sweaty humans, but to me, it smelled of life. I pressed my head to the window and watched the world go by, trying to glimpse into every house we passed, every balcony of every apartment block, every tucked away playground. I was playing voyeur to life, snatching up moments of other people's lives with my greedy eyes, but unable to live my own.

I'd lost all my courage and fire again. As much as I told myself the care and longevity of my tattoo didn't matter in the scheme of things, I just walked around the surrounding shops all afternoon, unable to go into the swim center as I'd planned.

Open hours for public swimming came and went. I hovered, aimlessly, until the shops started closing around me, and had to head back out onto the street to make my way home.

Then I saw Blake.

He walked up the footpath as I walked down, and there was no avoiding him, not when he spotted me too.

Then this is it.

"Hi."

"Hi."

"Hey."

"How's things?"

"How are—oh, good. How are you?"

"Good. Yeah. Good."

"Um, so …"

"Yeah, uh."

"I thought—"

"I was—"

"Sorry, you first."

"No, you."

"Really."

"Oh, I just, I need …"

The bumbling mumble of our conversation halted, and we both seemed to be very concerned about our feet, what with how carefully we scrutinized them.

I can't do it.

I couldn't look at that gorgeous face, so full of determination and fear and conflict and cause any more pain. I didn't know what I was going to do. All I could do was ignore everything and go on like nothing was the matter.

I was the walking embodiment of denial.

The air had become soupy around us until I could barely breathe, and dark clouds drooped low, grumbling with the threat of thunder.

"You going for a swim?" Blake finally said.

I glanced at my shoulder, and could see the edges of my red bathing suit showing under the light gray dress. The towel poking out of my tote bag was another giveaway.

"I was. But the indoor pool by the mall is closed now. I really, really could have done with a good swim. I don't know why I didn't go."

"Yeah, I could go for a swim too." Blake pinched the front of his shirt and wafted it. His eyebrows dropped, and his eyes looked as stormy as the clouds above us. "I know another place. If you want to come with?"

No. NO. Say you can't see him again. NO.

"Yeah, that sounds great. Let's go."

Blake led me back to his bike, and this time I insisted he take the only helmet since he hadn't brought a second one. I thought he would fight me on it, but he was only silent for a second, then put it on.

It was a ten-minute ride back to his place, which we managed in five. The clouds above us rumbled, but held steady, refusing to spill cooling rain. I expected Blake to change, which he did. But not only did he emerge with swimming trunks on, but also with a hefty-sized pair of pliers in his hand. *Bolt cutters?* I wasn't sure. I didn't question it.

He also brought out his spare helmet. I put it on, and within two minutes we pulled up out the front of an old-fashioned outdoor pool. It was big and rectangular, all blocky concrete and chipped lane markers, wrapped around with a high chain-link fence and a faded building with locked turnstiles at the front.

"It's closed, too." I don't know why I pointed it out. I knew exactly what the bolt cutters were for now.

Blake took them in one hand and me in the other, and we dashed around the edge of the chain-link barrier to a small side gate. We crouched slightly, but weren't making a huge effort to be discreet. There was no one around, and the thick clouds made the early dusk as dark as night.

I jiggled nervously on the spot, acting as lookout while Blake flexed his muscles and clipped right through the basic padlock that chained the gate closed.

This has got to be breaking and entering, a helpful little voice in my head pointed out. *That was definitely breaking.*

I entered anyway.

I glanced around, but couldn't see any obvious cameras. I wasn't even sure the pool was still in use, but the faint smell of chlorine as I drew closer told me it was at least being maintained. A few dead leaves floated on the surface, but the water was otherwise clean, and when I dipped a toe in, the chill of the unheated water raced a shiver from my feet to the crown of my head. It was perfect.

I dumped my tote bag and pulled my dress off over my head, kicking my shoes onto the still warm concrete. I was about to dive in when I remembered Blake next to me.

The way he watched me then made me catch my breath.

I'd bought a new, retro-style bikini with big red polka-dots that seemed cute and daring—for me at least. I suddenly felt naked, and my hands automatically moved to adjust the bottoms and cover my stomach.

"You're the most gorgeous thing I've ever seen." His voice sounded so sad.

He turned away before I could react and removed his T-shirt. I wanted to echo his compliment, but my voice caught in my throat, and before I could speak, I turned away as well.

"You got a tattoo?"

I suddenly wished I could cover my back as well as my front. I fought off my self-consciousness and lifted my long hair away and twisted it into a bun so Blake could see the tattoo fully. "Do you like it?"

"It's perfect for you."

Before I could ask why he seemed so sad, he took my hand again and pulled me into the water with him.

It splashed around us as we fell in, inelegantly. It was cool enough to make me gasp, and then sigh happily. It was exactly what I needed.

I surfaced with a laugh, and even Blake's stunning face lit up with a smile that broke my heart. His body brushed against mine, slick and firm.

Soon, I forgot any thought that we may be caught out here, breaking the law. For a little while, we forgot we were grownups at all.

We circled each other, splashed, shrieked, and laughed. We played Marco Polo and Blake pretended to be Poseidon, chasing a wanton mermaid. Blake grabbed my foot after I kicked water at him, and dragged me deeper into the pool. We ducked under the tiny rope with its floating blue and white baubles and floated underwater together, pulling funny faces at each other.

Lightning struck nearby, illuminating the whole pool. A huge rumble of thunder shook the chain fence, and the temperature dropped at least ten degrees. A slight steam rolled off our shoulders and I huddled next to Blake shivering and giggling. The damp air grew more humid, more chlorinated, filling my nose.

Blake took my arms and placed them around his neck, then held me by the waist, floating me within his arms. I wrapped my legs around his hips and we bobbed along through the refreshing water. Goosebumps covered my skin, and I clung to Blake's warmth. I pressed my mouth to his neck in light, nibbling kisses.

Blake shivered against me. I tightened the grip of my legs and could feel him firm under his trunks. My body wanted to take over, and I let it. I wanted to exist in moments of only action and no thought. Only sensation and no consequence.

I tucked my fingers and then toes into the band of

Blake's shorts, and then pushed them right down off his legs. He leaned in and kissed me, overtaking my mouth with his. I could have drowned, right there and then, in that water, in his kiss.

I settled my legs around him again, feeling his hardness against me, only the bikini bottoms separating us. With an arm still around his neck, I reached the other down and held aside the fabric. Blake groaned, pulling back.

"It's okay. I'm on contraception," I lied. I didn't care. I didn't want to think about consequences or futures and the pain it would bring. I'd deal with it all later.

Blake's kiss deepened, and he pressed up. The sticky pool water created a friction between us, and I could feel every movement heightened as he worked his way slowly inside me.

Every motion was deliberate and soft. I wanted to feel each shift of our bodies, to be in that moment, joined together as the water embraced us both. Soon, the friction eased, and we glided against each other.

Blake bit down on my shoulder and cupped my ass with strong fingers. He controlled my rise and fall with his hands, my body floating feather-light in the water. I lay back, letting him slide me over him as I watched his chest muscles roll, glistening in the water and lightning.

Lust consumed me, and I reached down to touch myself. I hesitated at first, seeing how Blake watched me.

Testing, I rolled a finger against my sensitive flesh as he pumped into me, and Blake grunted loudly. "Fuck yes."

His speed built, and mine matched it, the water swirling and splashing as pleasure built in even larger waves. Then the sky opened up, fast, fat drops of icy rain colliding with us.

My whole being was caught, trapped in the sensations, in how good Blake felt, how firmly he fitted inside me, how intensely he looked at me.

I tipped over the edge of pleasure, falling into an ocean of release. I cried out, just as Blake's own orgasm hit.

My head rolled back, and I saw a pair of feet clad in ugly, official-looking black shoes stopped right beside us at the edge of the pool.

"You two are in a hell of a lot of trouble," the uniformed security guard said.

Chapter Twenty-Four

BLAKE

We sat dripping in the front office, waiting for the cops to come.

Georgina had put her dress back on over her wet swimmers. She rummaged around in her bag. I thought she was going to call her dad or someone, but instead she pulled out her purse, and from it, that little black book of hers.

I could only gape at her as she clicked her pen and crossed out another list item.

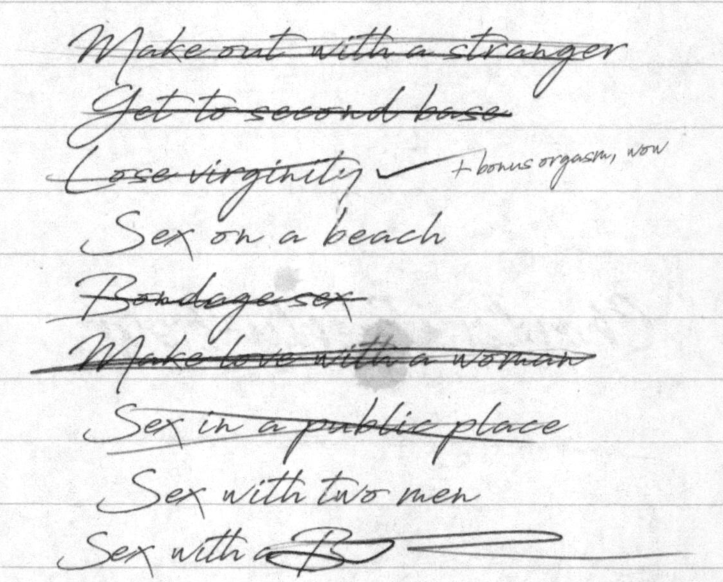

Anger made my hands shake.

Two police walked in, led by the security guard who pointed at us with the butt of his torch. The older cop looked like he wanted to laugh. The younger one looked new to the job, and kept blushing and checking a notebook.

We got put into the back of the cop car and sent on our way. Thankfully, the security guard had let me put my trunks back on before the cops showed up, but it was still awkward and uncomfortable. I couldn't even look at Georgina.

The cops talked to each other, laughing and making

jokes at our expense, all the way to the station where Georgina and I were left in a waiting room.

But Georgina didn't wait. She left me and went to talk to someone, then they went to talk to someone else. I didn't even get to make a phone call because they yanked me back out and put me in the wind so fast that I didn't have time to ask what the hell had happened.

I was free to go, and I knew Georgina was the reason.

I spent an hour pacing up and down in front of the station, getting soaked to the bone, before she finally came out, too.

Her eyes were raw and red, but her expression was bright. Calm. Even cheerful.

She walked up to me as if she had spent the better part of the evening having tea and crumpets with a bunch of old ladies instead of having her statement taken by cops.

She took all the blame. She swore up and down that she was the one who'd cut the lock. That it was all her idea. That she'd pay any damages. That she'd instigated everything. I wondered what else she told them about her specific situation that might have tipped the balance there. My breath became fast and shaky.

"They gave me a three-hundred-dollar fine and a black mark on my rap sheet. Not bad for a day's work."

It was the way she said it. She didn't give a flat flying

damn that she had just been arrested, or that there might be more consequences somewhere down the road. She didn't care about anything. She didn't even care to wear a helmet on my bike. She was fucking suicidal, and all that mattered for her was getting one more list item ticked off.

I pointed a finger at her as violently as a gun. "How long are you going to continue like this? Pretending nothing is wrong?"

She blinked, then her face went carefully blank. "What do you mean?"

"Stop. Fucking. Lying. To me!"

The rain fell harder, hiding what I was sure were tears on her cheeks. Her hands came up. She made a helpless gesture and then crossed over her chest, like she was trying to hold herself in. "Blake …"

"I know about the cancer."

She doubled over. It was like I had put my size-twelve foot right into her gut at full force. "How?"

"Mary."

"She felt the lump." Her words were hoarse and strained.

"And the scar on your breast?"

Her expression shattered. Her words were wracked with sobs. I'd never seen her cry, not like this. Like all the things she'd been holding in finally burst free.

I tried to reach for her, to say something, but she shrugged me off like I was an old coat.

Her sobs slowed and she spoke between them. "I've had breast cancer before. I found … I found a new lump. I'm pretty sure it's cancer."

"*Pretty sure*? You mean you don't know? Not for sure?"

Her voice shook, and she stared away, back up the station steps. "I know."

"Have you been to the doctor?"

"No. I can't. I just … I can't." She sighed, a long, low exhalation, then finally met my gaze again. Her eyes were red-veined, and wet strands of hair made patterns across her pale cheeks.

"You do know that the rest of us still have to live here after you're gone? That we have to live with how you've used us?"

Anger flashed over her features. "You chose this. You chose to do the things on my list with me. I have never forced you into anything. You don't get to decide what I do with what remains of my life."

I wanted to shake her. My voice raised, competing with the pelting rain. "You could be killing yourself. You could be doing all these things for no reason—acting like the end is near when there is nothing wrong. You have to get checked."

"I don't have to do anything. I won't. You don't understand."

"I don't *understand*?" Fury made my lips twitch. Lightning flashed. I blinked and saw Seyvia, lying in her own vomit on our bed, her skin blue. "You think you're special? That you have a monopoly on tragedy and loss? That I haven't lost someone I loved?"

Georgina's head shook. "I'm sorry."

"*Every* human life is a tragedy. We *all* die. That's the only way our stories can end, and the only way to ignore that is running away from anything *real*."

The rain thumped down harder. It was like the sky held an ocean and dumped it all out on top of us.

Georgina wiped her face and stared up at me with clear eyes. "Then this is it. This is over. We're over."

"You … You're choosing to run away?" I don't know why it shocked me. It's what I had planned to do. It's what I chose for so long. I've been running away ever since Seyvia. But this was real. What I felt for Georgina was real. I didn't want to run from life, or death, anymore.

"I won't see you again. This story ends here. Goodbye, Blake."

"Don't. Georgie, please—"

She turned and ran.

Chapter Twenty-Five

GEORGINA

I ran for two full blocks, blinded by rain and tears, breath
burning in my straining lungs.

He knew. He knew I had cancer.

My heart felt like a thousand butterflies were trapped
in the cage of my ribs beside it. I stopped under the shelter of
a closed mall entrance and leaned against the large window.
Inside, mannequins looked bright and happy in fluoro-colored
sundresses. My saturated gray dress sagged around me, clinging
and drooping against a body I hated in every way.

I collapsed onto the ground and dug through my bag.

My fingers closed around my phone, and thankfully, it was still dry and working.

I wanted to call my mom. Have her come and collect me and hold me. Be stern with me about my choices, but still love and forgive me and just be happy I was alive.

Mom, why aren't you here with me? I need you.

I couldn't call Dad. What would I say to him?

So I called Julie.

It rang out three times. I checked the time and realized she was probably on her way home from work. I kept ringing.

Finally, she answered. "Hi."

"Hey, Julie? Can I ask for a huge favor?"

Within twenty minutes, her tiny white smart car pulled up in front of me. The rain had eased a little, and I raced over and jumped in as quickly as I could. I landed on the passenger seat to find she'd laid down towels for me.

"You've got a strange idea of what a huge favor is," Julie said plainly. "I thought you were going to ask for a kidney, not a lift home."

"Thanks for coming to get me." My voice shook.

She looked me over properly. "Are you okay? You haven't been hurt by someone, have you?"

I shook my head, barely holding back my tears. "I'm okay. I just got caught out in the rain." *I'm the one who has been hurting people.*

"You sure? You can tell me. I can come with you to report it." Julie was as sincere as I'd ever seen her.

I shook my head, doing my best to look A-okay. "Really, I've done my time for the night. I just want to go home."

"No problem." Julie shrugged. She zipped back onto the road, her tiny car rocking with the sheets of rain, and her windscreen wipers pumping and squeaking their hearts out. "Oh hey, check it out." She thumb-pointed at the cotton tote bag beside my feet, which was full of chocolate.

I sniffled out a laugh. "Thank you. I need it more than you know."

"That's okay. Maybe we can do breakfast again. As long as you make the coffee to go with it."

I watched her as she drove, so calm and sure of herself, and in her support of the complete mess sitting in the seat next to her. Julie was a surprise in my life I'd never expected.

"You're such a good friend." I tried to say it lightly, but I choked up halfway through.

Julie stopped at a red light and looked at me, her brown eyes wide and worried. "You're my best friend," she replied. "You can tell me anything. I want to help."

Tears rushed from me harder and faster than the rain hitting the car. All the dams had broken inside me, and the truth flooded out. "I think, I think I have cancer. Again."

Julie put the car into park, right there at the lights. She reached over and hugged me without saying a word. I clung to her, gulping through my sobs. "I've been so awful to everyone. I'm lying all the time. I don't know what to do because I can't face it."

I kept trying to tell myself I was being brave by doing The List, challenging myself with the items on it as though they were dares. But I wasn't. All I was doing was hiding, running, lying. I couldn't face what was happening, and I was being a coward. The List wasn't enough. Nothing would be enough.

I wanted to *live*. I wanted more, more chocolate-eating time with Julie, more friends, more of a real relationship with Blake—more of my life.

Julie squeezed me tighter. The lights turned green, then red again as we stayed like that—me crying my heart out, her holding me. There were no cars behind us to honk us out of that embrace, and I clutched onto her like she was a life-buoy. Nothing could make this okay, but crying, being held, being honest, was a start.

"I'm not ready. I don't want to die." The words were wracked by sobs. "I don't want to!"

The universe didn't care what I wanted.

Neither did the car that smashed into us.

Chapter Twenty-Six

GEORGINA

I saw the pick-up truck coming over Julie's shoulder in the split second before it hit. It spun out over the wet road, coming too fast around the corner. I opened my mouth to scream, and then everything was wrenched apart. Glass sprayed through the air. Tires squealed. Metal crunched and groaned. Air-bags burst and slapped against us. I was thrown out of Julie's embrace as she jolted back and forth. The side of the car sheared away. My head hit the doorframe behind me.

Pain. Crushing sounds.
Darkness.

I woke up to the flash of lights. Red, blue, and the bright white of a paramedic flashing a torch in my face. She nodded at my blinking eyes, talking with other people surrounding us. People moved everywhere, but everything was jarred and blurry to me. Time skipped as memory and the present jumbled into each other. I was in the car seat as they cut the seatbelt off me, then I was on a stretcher. A man—the pick-up driver?—sat in the gutter, crying. I was in the car again, glass flying, suspended in slow motion, then I was being asked questions I could barely hear.

The only thing I could clearly see was Julie. Three paramedics surrounded her. There was blood. Her body looked wrong.

I was loaded into the ambulance, screaming out for Julie as they closed the doors.

I didn't know if I blacked out again, or if I was sedated. I woke in a hospital bed. I was stiff and sore, but alive.

My dad sat in the chair beside me. He stood and came straight to my side at the first sign of movement. The look on his face said everything.

My response was instant and primal. My face scrunched in on itself. Every part of the invisible armor I'd built had fractured in the crash, and now it shattered like the glass in the car.

"She didn't make it?" I sobbed.

"I'm so sorry, honey." He wrapped his arms gently around me, careful of my battered body. I wept into his shirt.

Every one of us dies. Was that what Blake had said? But not Julie. She wasn't meant to die. How could she be dead? She was the girl who had *one days*, with a carefully planned future and the drive and intelligence to get there. She was the one without cancer. The one without a ticking clock hanging over her. Who thought eating chocolate for breakfast was the naughtiest thing in the world. She was my friend.

And now, Julie was gone, just like that.

Her family—I couldn't imagine how they felt right now. Worse than I felt. How I imagined my dad would feel when he lost me.

Was that what life was? A series of painful losses? There was too much. I'd lost my mom. Blake lost his wife. Julie is gone. Dad lost Mom as well, and would lose me.

He almost just lost me.

I pulled away from his embrace so I could look at him. So I could look him in the eye and tell him the truth I had hidden for too long.

I could see how relieved he looked that I was still here with him. And now I was going to break his heart.

"Daddy, I found another lump." I barely got the words out. They rattled through my gasping breaths. I ached all over as I reached my arms to him. "I'm sorry. I'm sorry I didn't tell you sooner."

"A lump?" He froze in place, lifeless for a moment before he took my hands. Only the white circles around his eyes, put there by shock, gave away just what he was thinking and feeling. "I'm here for you. You are my little girl. We'll get through this together. I would do anything for you."

"That's why I didn't tell you. I don't think I can do it again. I don't think I'm strong enough to go through treatment a second time."

Dad swallowed hard. "Georgie, treatment is your best option."

"It wasn't for Mom."

"Things were very different then. There was nothing like the medicines they have now."

My lips trembled. "Daddy—you don't know what it's like."

"Is it better than the alternative?" Dad's bushy brows dropped over his eyes and he shook his head. "How long have you known?"

"I don't know anything for sure yet—"

"Since you started missing classes? Why did you wait so long to tell me?"

I flinched. Dad was rarely angry at me, but I could tell he was now by the strain in his forehead, pushing veins to the surface. I stuttered. I didn't want to keep lying to him, but

I didn't want him to know how I had ignored the problem so completely. So I lied again. "I'm still waiting for the results. I wanted to get them back first, in case it was nothing."

"Even nothing isn't nothing!" Dad growled, but then he snatched me so quickly into a bear hug I lost my breath. "You think waiting on results to see if you have cancer is *nothing*? I'm your father, Georgie. It's my job to be there for you when things are hard. I'm meant to protect you, not the other way around."

His beard scratched against my cheek, his arms squeezed me into his soft stomach, and I could feel my chest shaking with grief and guilt. I was like a five-year-old, sobbing into my daddy's chest because my mommy was never coming home again.

When I had stilled enough to accept some tissues to blow my nose, Dad stepped back. "Listen to me, Georgie. The only reason there are no photos of your mother during her last days up around the house was for you. I thought it would be better for you, for how you remembered her. But I think that was a mistake." Dad opened his wallet and pulled out a folded photo. It showed Mom in a hospital bed. Bald, and frail, with a tiny me cuddled up next to her. We were both smiling. "For me, she was always the woman I loved, right up to the end."

He carefully folded the photo and tenderly put it away, as though it were the most precious thing in the world. "That saying about making lemonade if life gives you lemons is bullshit. The lemons themselves are valuable, beautiful. Life is everything we have, and the bad is just as valuable as the good. It's harder. It's painful. But it's ours. It's proof we're still here, that we can *feel* things, which is a miracle in this infinite and unfeeling universe. We should do whatever we can to hold onto that for as long as possible. I will always love you, understand? Always."

I nodded.

"When will we know?" Dad asked.

"In a few days," I answered. "You will be the first person I call."

He nodded back. "I talked to the doctors about your injuries from the accident."

The accident. *Julie.* My face scrunched closed around burning tears. The smash seemed like it was a million miles away, separated from me by fear and disease. The pounding head and dull ache through my whole body could have been as much from emotional exhaustion as from the crash. I felt awful that that was all I'd suffered, when Julie had been irreparably broken. That wasn't fair. I should have been the one to die. I would have swapped our places in a heartbeat. I didn't want to die, I wasn't ready, but I knew what was fair, and this wasn't it.

Dad put his hand on my shoulder. "You're under observation for a concussion, and have some cuts and bruises. They think you'll be able to walk out of here in a day or two, which is a miracle as well. I'm so sorry about Julie, but I have to be happy I still have my girl. Do you need anything right now? Any painkillers? Do you want to see the counselor? Is there anyone you want me to call?"

"No." *Blake.* "I'm okay." *I am ripped open right down the middle.* "How about you? You want Louisa with you? She can be here for you if you want." *I want Julie with me again.*

Dad made a quick range of facial expressions that ended with a shrug and shake of the head. "I don't think I'll be seeing her again. I don't think she was right for us."

For us. Louisa may have been a bit pushy, but Dad had seemed genuinely happy around her. Then I'd reacted badly to her, and suddenly, she was no longer in the picture. I had blown Dad's chance at happiness yet again.

He was barely past forty. He had married my mom at twenty, and I had followed less than a year later. He was still young enough to start a whole new family, and that comforted me.

I was smart enough not to say that to him right then. Still, I hoped he might work things out with Louisa, or find someone else soon. He could continue living every moment, good and bad, for as long as he had. And maybe I should, too.

A doctor came in then to check me over, and Dad went to make some phone calls and talk to Julie's family. Once I was alone again, I lay back in the bed and made plans. Plans for the future. For whatever I had left.

Tomorrow, I had three things to do on an all new list.

Get a morning-after pill.

Apologize to Blake and end things finally.

And get tested for cancer.

Chapter Twenty-Seven

GEORGINA

Dad had almost closed his restaurant for the day to stay with me, but I'd sent him off to work. That suited all my plans, so I could cover my lies and mistakes.

I had the incredible luck that the pharmacist at the hospital was the same woman who had filled my scripts when I was getting treated five years ago. She was the sweetest woman who used to kneel down next to my lounge-chair while I was on my chemo drip and carefully talk me and Dad through the mountains of pills she was handing over.

I had walked down in my hospital gown, and explained

to her why I was in—both the accident, and the tests that were booked for later that afternoon. I knew she'd seen the tears welling in my eyes when I told her about both, and it was also incredible luck that I didn't break down again completely.

The loss of Julie still hit me harder than the impact of the pick-up truck had. I didn't have the capacity to deal, to understand it all. I kept thinking she was waiting for me back at home. That she was in class, or at work—just out of sight. I couldn't seem to comprehend that she was *gone*. And every time I tried to understand it, pain melted all rational thought into tears.

The pharmacist filled my request for the morning-after pill without a single question, and even offered me a prescription for the anti-anxiety tablets I used to get, which I accepted with gratitude. I had a feeling I was going to need them.

That was the first thing on my new list done. It was time for the next.

I knew I should just suck it up and deal with Blake in person, but I couldn't stop thinking about his face and the look on it when we fought outside the police station. And now I would have to be harsh with him—too harsh. I had to make sure it was over. How I felt right now, having lost Julie—I couldn't make Blake feel that way. I had to become just out of sight for him. I couldn't be *gone*.

I called him, and he answered right away.

He started to apologize for the fight, but I spoke over him.

"I wanted to let you know I went and got tested. I got my results, and I'm all clear," I told him. "I'm fine. The lump is benign."

I hated continuing to lie to Blake, but I needed to leave so he felt no further responsibility for me.

"Wait, what? When?" Blake said.

"I got in quick, and they pushed my results through fast because of my medical history."

"That's amazing news." The hope in his voice almost broke my will.

"There's something else we need to talk about …"

That was when I hit him hard. I had rehearsed my speech so many times, I ran through the whole thing in a minute, not giving him a second to interrupt. I told him I had used him, that he was nothing to me but a body. That I was messed up and not thinking straight. That all I cared about was finishing The List, not him. I apologized for all of that, and it was some of the truest words I'd spoken for a long time.

Then, I twisted the knife. "Now I know I'm okay, I have to move on. The List, and us, are over, and I never want to see you again. Seeing you is nothing but a reminder of the darkest time in my life."

"Georgie," His voice was pleading. "Wait, Georg—"

I hung up on him. Then deleted his number.

I knew I had hurt him, but it had hurt me as well. Saying those things sent pain so deep into my chest that it felt like I had eaten glass and the pieces were grinding together in there, cutting me and making me bleed.

I wanted to take it back, but I couldn't. I had lied. I didn't want Blake out of my life—I wanted me out of his. I was the cancer in his life in more ways than one.

I remembered how fun and happy he'd been when we'd first met. So full of life. I had leached that from him. I had brought him so much pain, and would only bring more. I had used him terribly, and the chances of me living that down were slim. Even if I did live, there would be other reasons I wasn't right for Blake. I might never have kids—I would run the risk of passing down my broken genes to them, and I couldn't stand that idea. I might have a double mastectomy and even if I had reconstructive surgery, I would never have the same body as I did before, never be able to breastfeed my babies, never be whole again.

I wanted to look at all these lemons with appreciation, see their value and beauty, but I wasn't quite there yet. Maybe I wasn't whole already, and hadn't been for a long time. I wondered if I ever would be whole, or if I'd die before I got there.

I changed into some leggings and a dress-length T-shirt Dad had brought in for me from home. Then I left my wing of the hospital and made the trek down to the breast cancer center to do the third thing on my list.

The waiting room was full of huge, fake sunflowers, but their happy yellow faces couldn't warm the chill that settled into my bones.

"Georgina Stone," I told the receptionist. *Stone.* That was what I could become. I might not be whole, my invisible armor might be shattered, but I could become stone. Hard and unbreakable.

The receptionist checked her computer and nodded. "Change rooms are just down the hall. Grab a gown and put it on with the opening to the front. Someone will call you in about five minutes."

I moved on. I knew the drill.

Once I'd changed, I sat in the more private interior waiting room, filled with women in their gowns, front openings out, readjusting the ties to make sure we were covered despite knowing those gowns would be right off again in no time. Sometimes, I didn't know why they even bothered making us put them on.

Most of the women were over fifty, at least. Some were hiding their bald heads under hats and wigs. They all turned to me as I walked in. I was used to the 'what are *you* doing here?'

looks by now though.

I wasn't used to finding someone else my age in the room, or two people.

The only seat left was to the side of two pretty, dark-skinned girls. One wore a robe, and the other didn't, but other than that, they were identical. They looked familiar, but I couldn't place it.

I didn't want to stare, but it was like looking back into my own past. I could see the nervous fear all over the one wearing the gown. This was clearly her first time. She was so incredibly scared it made me realize just how calm I was. I was becoming stone already.

They caught me in the act of gawking.

"We're identical twins," said the nervous one.

"Yeah, I think she noticed already," said the other. "Hey, you're in my print layout class, aren't you?"

So that's where I knew her from. I felt bad I didn't know her name. "I'm Georgina. I've missed a bunch of classes lately."

"Yeah, I noticed. I'm Priya," she said. "And this is Kaley."

Kaley just jittered her legs some more. "Have you missed class because ... because ..."

"What my terrified sister is trying to ask is if you've missed class because you have cancer," Priya said. "Which I think really isn't our business, but I felt like I had to help her out finishing her sentence, since I'm here to support her today."

I could feel the weight of both of their gazes taking in the empty space beside me. "I'm just getting tested."

Kaley's dark eyes lit up, glossy with tears. "You're not scared? I am so freaking out right now. I've been freaking out since I found the lump. Do you have a lump, too? My GP said it will probably be fine, but still, AAAALL the freaking out is happening. But we're too young for it to be cancer, right?"

"Sure," I said. *What a lie.*

Priya elbowed Kaley softly. "Chill out. You'd think we haven't faced scarier things than cancer before."

"Like what?" I asked, too fast. I knew lots of things could be scarier than cancer. Like knowing someone you loved could be taken from you any second.

Julie. I'm so sorry. You'd still be here if it wasn't for me.

Priya pouted. "Never mind."

The door to the waiting room swung open, and a pleasant-looking woman wearing scrubs covered with dancing bears holding balloons called my name.

Kaley reached out and snatched my hand, squeezing it for a split second. "Good luck."

Priya waved at me as I walked away. "See you in class."

Chapter Twenty-Eight

GEORGINA

I walked alone into the small room down the hall. I went past the nurse, holding my arms in to my sides. Nurses always try to be nice. Some even did the whole 'reassuring touch' thing, and I couldn't take that right now. The smallest act of kindness would have me sobbing on the floor. I'd barely held it together when Kaley had grabbed my hand.

The nurse asked me to lie down and undo my gown. I lay down on the bed, the sheet of protective paper crackling under me. I took slow breaths. Fear ate into me until acid spewed up from my stomach and filled my mouth, soured and bitter, stinging all the way up into my nasal passages.

The ultrasound technician felt around my breast with her cold gloved hand, feeling for the lump. She squirted blood-warm ultrasound gel onto me and rolled the probe all around my chest, tapping buttons on the screen as she did. She didn't say anything much, just a short gasp of sympathy about my age and previous run-in with cancer as she looked over my old scans.

"Too young. Just too young," she said, shaking her head.

With a frown, she called in a supervising doctor.

I knew that was never a good sign.

He reviewed the scans and announced he wanted to draw some tissue, and out came that scarily sized biopsy needle.

I didn't feel much. A local anesthetic took care of that. I just felt the pressure as the needle popped through my first layer of skin, forcing down into my breast. It was the same kind of biopsy I'd had that confirmed my cancer the first time, so I knew to brace myself.

Clack-BANG.

The biopsy needle sounded like a small gun going off as it extracted each sample. I tried to keep still and not flinch, and a single tear squeezed from my closed eye and down my cheek.

I squeezed the edge of the thin bed because I had no

hand to hold.

Clack-BANG.

Clack-BANG.

Pieces of me filled the syringe barrel and were taken away for testing.

The doctor left, and the nurse handed me a paper towel to wipe off the gel. She said they would be in touch soon. She told me I could change in there, that I could take all the time I needed, and walked out.

It all felt sort of anticlimactic, really.

I dabbed at the impossible-to-wipe-away gel. It was cold now, and sticky, and smeared off the towel onto my fingers. I gave up and just lay on the bed, exposed, raw, and wanting nothing other than to cry for days.

I stopped myself. I forced the tears back.

I had to be stronger than this. I couldn't take all the time I needed. I didn't have enough time. Every moment of my life now was limited and precious. I couldn't spend it lying in a medical examination room, crying, alone. The List was still unfinished. It didn't seem as important anymore, but part of me knew I had to complete it. I *had* to.

I would wait for the test results, and then I would know if I would only ever complete that list, or whether I'd have the chance to make new lists. Bigger lists. Life lists rather than bucket lists.

I would live what time I had as best as I could. Because I could, and Julie couldn't. I had to do that for her. I had to do that for my dad. I had to be brave, truly brave.

There was no point in staying there any longer. Everything that needed to be done had been done. I got changed, and walked out through the bright, flower-filled reception, feeling strong, like stone. I wouldn't cry again. I would be a riverbed during a bitter drought.

I would build myself up, build a wall of rock around myself. Until I was hard enough. Impenetrable enough. Strong enough to protect myself, and to protect my loved ones, for what was ahead.

I raised my chin, ready to walk out of this hospital and into my life.

The List Georgina pretended to be brave.

I wasn't pretending anymore.

Chapter Twenty-Nine

BLAKE

I didn't believe a word Georgina had said.

She'd gotten her test results back and she was okay, and her reaction was to end our relationship? *No.* It couldn't be true.

I heard the tremble in her voice when she told me she was only using me for her list, that she was done with that and wanted to move on. She'd never been a good liar. And I clung fiercely to the thought that she cared about me as much as I cared about her.

And yeah, maybe I should let her go. Regardless of those test results, I could still lose her to tragedy. Losing someone I loved once should have taught me some kind of lesson, but clearly, I was a slow learner. Or maybe I had learned. I'd learned that tragedy could strike anybody, at any time, and we should go after what we wanted anyway.

What I wanted was Georgina.

I had a plan.

A gusty wind blew through my hair, cooling the sweat on my neck and forehead as I hesitated on the doorstep. I probably looked as pale as the white stucco walls, nervous and unsure of how I was going to get what I had come for.

I knocked hard on the aged wood.

Georgina's dad opened the door, and stood before me, his eyes red raw under his bushy brows, and tears glossy on his cheeks.

I averted my eyes. "Sorry. I can, er, come back another time ..."

"Something wrong with the sight of a man crying?" Tom challenged. I looked up and he caught my gaze, unflinching and direct.

"No. I just don't want to bother you, if you're going through something right now."

Tom waved a hand and I smelled garlic and smoky whiskey waft from him. "When in life aren't we going through something?"

He pushed the door wider, an invitation to me. I took a

slow step forward, feeling like an intruder. "Are you okay?"

"I'm all right. It's just hard … It's always hard, this kind of pain and loss."

My heart clenched. I hadn't heard from Georgina for days—had something happened to her? Fear raced through me. "I thought the results weren't—"

"No, no. The accident, and Julie. Her poor family." Tom sniffed, shaking his head.

My blood chilled and ice trickled down my spine. "What happened to Julie?"

Before I knew it, I was sitting on the back step, staring at the purple flowering lasiandra tree, beer in hand. Tom sobbed into his beer beside me.

"Julie." I said her name again, unable to believe she was gone. I'd only met her for a brief moment, but she'd made an impression. Tears swelled and dropped from my eyes. *Fuck life, fuck this pain.* I felt like swearing and screaming at the sky, but wanted Georgina's dad to think I was a decent bloke. I said the only other thing I could say. "It's not fair."

And Georgina … she'd been in a car accident? Her roommate had been killed? And I couldn't be there for her. *God, she must have been in the hospital when she called.* She didn't even tell me. A sob tore hoarsely from my throat. I sniffed and wiped my eyes with the back of my forearm and took a long scull of beer. Tom patted my back, almost in time with his own short, hiccupping sobs.

It was refreshing, cathartic, to see him cry, to be able to cry like this with someone, with another man. My own father wasn't so forgiving about this sort of display of emotion. Just one more reason I'd been happy to leave him and my country far behind. Tom wasn't that kind of man though. There was nothing toxic about his relationship with emotions. I let everything out, my tears splashed on the mosaic tiled stairs and dripped into my mouth, mixing salt with the bitterness of the beer.

All the pent-up despair, guilt, and grief I'd locked away when Seyvia died rushed out of me. Tom must have thought I knew Julie really well, for how I cried. But I cried for Seyvia, and I cried for Georgina, and I cried for myself, and I cried for the pain and unfairness of life and how I still longed for this amazing, messy existence regardless.

"How do you do it?" I asked softly. "How do you deal? With everything you've lost?"

Tom put his beer down and picked up one of the purple petals that had fallen from the tree—the tree that had been planted in memorial for his wife. He held it delicately in his fingers as though it were a lock of his wife's hair. "When the heart is pierced by pain, it doesn't die. Those holes expand like a net and the heart grows even larger. It's more fragile, but able to carry more … more love, more grief, more life. Enough to carry those you've lost and the hurt their absence causes."

I stared at the yard, carpeted in those purple petals. My head bobbed, nodding as though it agreed before I could fully process the thought myself. My heart had grown larger. I had tried to deny it, pretending I had no grief to carry at all, but then Georgina had come into my life and filled me so fully with love that I found I did have room for it all. And I wanted it all. I wanted her.

"Georgina dumped me," I admitted.

"I know," Tom said.

I raised my eyebrows at him, wondering why he'd let his daughter's ex in for this weepy heart-to-heart. Maybe he'd needed it too.

"Georgie told me she wouldn't be seeing you anymore. She seemed upset about it. You better not have hurt her. I try to be the good feminist dad and not her relationship police, but she's my little girl and she's been through enough."

Fire and pain flared in his eyes, extinguished by a raw vulnerability. The desperate hope I hadn't hurt his daughter.

I wanted to tell him I hadn't. But we had hurt each other a fair bit just by being in each other's lives, when there was so much other pain to deal with. She'd hurt me as she dealt with the fear that her cancer had returned, and I'd hurt her as all my feelings of loss from Seyvia had resurfaced. The mess our relationship had become was more due to me finally dealing with that sadness than it was to do with Georgina.

"I didn't do anything to her. But it was a hard time, and I think everything became too hard, too confusing. And she called things off."

"Pity. I thought you kids were good for each other. Georgie's really come out of her shell for the first time since her cancer treatment."

Whoa.

Damn, it felt weird hearing him say it. *Cancer.* The word Georgina and I had done everything to avoid saying, or facing.

Tom must have read the surprise on my face. "I didn't just out my daughter, did I?"

"No. No, I knew. She didn't want to talk about any of it though. I can understand why." My beer had gone warm, just one last mouthful left in the bottom of the bottle which I swirled around. Talking about this was hard, and I wanted to just let it go, but I had a mission. "Did she make, you know, some kind of list back then? Like a bucket list?"

Tom wiped fresh tears from eyes which gazed far into the distance. "Yeah, I think so. Between finding the lump and getting the results. Not that she did anything with it. She went into treatment so fast, and it really hit her hard. She was one of the youngest cases the doctors had seen, just a kid."

I nodded, my heartrate increasing as my theory was

confirmed. I kept my voice as casual as I could. "Do you know what was on it?"

"Nah, she kept it private, in one of her journals." Tom shrugged. "Why do you think she made a list last time? Did she make one this time?"

I choked, and threw back the last mouthful of beer despite it being warm and flat. "Just curious. Thought it might be the kind of thing people did in that situation."

"You're still awfully interested in her."

I put my hand on my chest and looked at him with every bit of sincerity I could muster between the beers and the tears. "I think I'm in love with your daughter. I'm hoping to win her back. I want you to know that."

Tom laughed at me. It was full of ridicule and kindness and pity. He was a good person, and it showed. I only hoped I could be that kind of man, who could still be so positive after the life he'd lived. "Look, kid. If she doesn't want you then she doesn't want you. You just have to deal with that. I don't want to hear about you turning into a stalker. But I like you. Figure you deserve one more chance. Just the one, hear me?" He slapped me on the shoulder. "You know her past, and you know her future isn't certain. I need to know that my daughter won't get hurt if you decide this isn't the life for you after all. If you win her back, that is. I need to know you're sure this is what you want, for the long term."

I didn't even hesitate. "I am."

"So, did you just come around here to tell me that, or are you after a meal? I cooked a whole crockpot of beef stew and damned if I don't have anyone to eat it with me. You should know I put a full bottle of whiskey in it, so if you can't handle that you should probably stick to bread and butter."

I laughed. "It would take more than the threat of a hangover to stop me from eating one of your meals."

"I swear I don't normally drink this much." Tom became serious for a moment. "But it makes the waiting easier."

I wasn't sure what he meant by 'waiting,' but I nodded, tipsy from the beer and fog of emotions.

I excused myself to the bathroom, telling Tom I wanted a few minutes to compose myself so I could help him out in the kitchen. He nodded and said he'd work out something for us for dessert and went to do that.

And I snuck off to find Georgina's childhood bedroom.

Chapter Thirty

GEORGINA

I'd stormed out of hospital so brave, but it all fell apart when I got home, and walked into the space Julie used to share with me, used to live in. I stumbled into her bedroom, and crawled into her bed, under the sheets printed with flying chibi kittens. I stared at the posters of her favorite sci-fi show's spaceship schematics through eyes blurred with tears. I wished we'd watched those shows together. I wished we still could.

Emptiness hung in all corners of the house: on the lounge where we'd shared chocolate for breakfast, at the kitchen counter where we'd smiled at each other over the rims of our coffee mugs.

The loneliness of the space accentuated my separation from Blake. I already missed him with an intensity like a drill to the brain. I indulged in everything I shouldn't. I dug up the T-shirt he'd given me to wear that first night and put it on, clinging to the feel of it as though I were clinging to him.

I curled up with Julie's plushy collection, scrolling through Blake's long-abandoned Instasnap account.

It really was him, and he really was with Seyvia before she died. The photos were still there, confirming it, despite the account having no new photos added for years. Not a single post since the day Seyvia died.

Almost every photo in the account was of him with her, as though they'd been inseparable. Photos on glossy yachts, photos backstage under the glow of the spotlights, photos partying with other celebrities, photos from rehearsals. Always Blake and Seyvia together. Maybe it was just a PR thing, but the love I saw in his eyes as they posed for selfies, as she watched the camera and he watched her, was clear. There was nothing staged there.

As I scrolled through, I could also see a deep concern in Blake's eyes, wrinkling his brow ever so slightly as he looked at Seyvia, and as her own gaze lost focus more and more. She seemed downright out of it in some of the shots.

I didn't know the exact details of what had happened,

but I remembered the headlines: *Teen Popstar Dead from Overdose.*

Had he known she had a problem? Had he tried to do something to help her?

He must have. The Blake I knew would have.

To try, and to fail, with the result being such a tragedy … to lose the one he loved most …

My head spun. A black hole of pain opened up, sucking all lucid thought into it.

I slept through my despair.

Time blurred and passed. I stirred from my grieving slumber only when the phone rang. So many calls, but none were the one I wanted. It had only been a day since I'd been tested, and they'd told me there would be a two-to-three-day window for getting results. I still expected every call to be them, and my heart jumped into my throat every time the phone pinged.

I let all calls go through to voicemail, so I could listen without responding. Talking was too hard.

I listened to a message from Dad. "Hey honey. Just checking if the hospital got in touch yet? They seem to be taking a long time. Call me as soon as you hear from them, and I'll go in with you to get the results."

It was the third message he'd left with almost the same wording. I'd told him I'd been tested earlier than I really had, because I didn't want him to know I'd put it off for so long but doing that only succeeded in making him even more worried. *I do everything wrong.*

Next call came from an unknown number.

I listened to the voicemail. "Hi Georgina. Julie's mum here. Is it okay if we come by tomorrow? We want to … clear up … collect Julie's …" There was a long pause, a whispered sob. "You can text me, if it's okay. We have a key. Thanks."

The pain in her voice made tears stream from my eyes. I could barely see my screen when I texted her back, "It's okay."

It wasn't okay. Nothing was okay.

Blake called a lot. I'd deleted him from my contacts, but knew the number when it flashed on my phone screen. I didn't answer. He didn't leave messages.

Day bled into night and a new morning came.

Julie's family arrived. I answered the door, staring at them red-eyed and speechless. Her mother, father, and sister stared back at me, their arms filled with flattened moving boxes and plastic bags.

I let them in and left them to do what they needed to do, closing myself in my room to weep. I heard them through the walls, talking and crying as they packed. I hid from their grief like a coward. I felt like an imposter, my sadness an intrusion into their true loss.

I wanted to help them, but I wasn't strong enough. Julie

was *gone,* and knowing what her family must be going through made me feel like I could rot away entirely and leave nothing behind but a sad shade of blue.

The sounds of packing and loading out ended, and there was a timid knock at my door. I dragged myself out of bed, and Julie's mother stood there, her face red and puffy.

She held a narwhal plushy and pressed it into my chest without a word. I wrapped my arms around it, unable to blink fast enough to stop my tears. Julie's mom nodded silently, then left, and that soft, ridiculously cute sea animal was all I had left of my friend.

I cuddled it to me as I curled up on the lounge, and no call came from the hospital.

I didn't know if I wanted or didn't want that call. When the hospital rang and it was time to go in for my results, that would be the beginning of the end. I didn't even consider that the results could be good news. Good news seemed so implausible to me right now.

When it came to options I was wavering, torn between wanting to live and not wanting to go through the awful treatment again, feeling as though that suffering would be pointless anyway. The determination The List had given me to burn myself out in lustful life until it was over had vanished. I wanted more than just physical pleasure, and that was due to Blake. I wanted to be with him, and to love him forever—the exact reason why I had to let him go. Forever is supposed to be a long time—how could I promise him that? How could I give him a love that was doomed to end tragically after what he'd already been through?

Blake and Julie had been my anchors in the sea of all my confusion and fear. Without them my thoughts flung violently against the rocks of total despair. My world had been smashed to pieces and put back together all wrong.

My only option to stay sane was to keep busy. I decided that I'd just go on with normal day-to -day life until I no longer could.

On the third day, I started going back to classes.

The weather had turned, and a strong, chilled breeze blew straight through the light cardigan I wore. Heavy clouds hung low with the threat of rain, or impending doom. It was almost enough to send me home seeking warmth, but I moved on, determined not to give up.

I managed to make it through the whole day without breaking down. It amazed me how the whole world just went on being normal, as though nothing had changed. It almost made me feel normal too. Almost okay. Almost not completely broken and decaying.

As my last lecture ended, I checked the time. Julie's class would be over soon too and—

Julie wasn't in class. Julie wasn't going to be home soon.

Julie will never be home.

I knew if I went home alone tonight, all I'd have was the hard battle against crushing loneliness and mortality. I'd have to fight the temptation to call Blake, to go to him and beg him to take me back.

I considered going to the library, to find some quiet corner to study in, but on the way I saw a poster up for Student Happy Hour at the bar just around the corner.

I wasn't sure there'd be much happy about it, but a drink sounded good.

Inside, 'The Cornerstone' was decked out like an Irish pub and crowded with students.

I kept my eyes down, kept to myself, but as I moved through to the bar I couldn't help notice that I was turning heads. Maybe they'd heard the news about the girls in the car crash and were looking at me out of sympathy?

That was the voice of the old Georgina, always discounting any idea that she could be attractive. The looks I was receiving weren't looks of pity. I knew what those were too well. This was something else, something like the way Blake had eyed me when we flirted.

I bought the easiest and cheapest drink, a glass of house red, and settled into a threadbare vintage armchair in a warm corner.

I'd barely had a sip when a guy came and took the seat

next to mine. He had the build of a football player, and pretty brown eyes that reminded me of a Basset Hound's.

"Mind if I join you?" he asked, after already getting comfortable.

I shrugged a vague acceptance.

"I'm sure I know you. Are you in my environmental design class?"

"No."

"Architecture and Technology?"

I shook my head. "Sorry."

"My dreams every night when I imagine the perfect woman?"

I giggled and choked on my wine. "I'm doing a Visual Communications degree, but they haven't yet taught us how to astrally project into someone's sleeping mind."

He flashed a disarming smile. He was cute, and the way he looked at me warmed me as much as the wine I drank.

He's not Blake. The whisper came from deep inside me, unwanted.

"I'm Kevin," he said, as though in answer.

"Georgie," I replied.

"You like wine?"

"I like the warm, dulling effect of alcohol," I said, in my best deadpan voice. I must have been channeling Julie.

"I'll get you another."

All the well-established alarms about keeping an eye on my drink went off inside me, but Kevin returned with a full, unopened bottle and two clean glasses. He poured for both of us.

The wine was dark, almost purple. It tasted faintly of olives and cured meat, yet with a sweet and mellow aftertaste. It was potent and burned a trail right into my belly, a fire of life, burning memories of my pain away.

"Thanks. I needed this."

Kevin shuffled his armchair closer to mine.

I managed to keep up a steady stream of flirty conversation. Before my list, I had been awkward and insecure. The List had made me braver after all. And The List still haunted me. It still had two items on it that hadn't been crossed off. As much as I wanted to leave it behind, that incompletion gnawed at me. Maybe I could try again. Maybe Kevin could help me.

He could also be a nice distraction, to keep my mind off Blake and … other things. Maybe I could have casual relationships without hurting anyone, as long as that was clear at the outset. If things started to feel even remotely serious, I could stop them in their tracks. If I could cut a relationship off with Blake, I could do it with anyone.

Kevin ordered us food and we ate pulled pork burgers and spicy fries. My smile grew genuine, and the bottle of wine grew empty. We tumbled out into the cool evening air together and wandered slowly back toward the campus.

Kevin caught my hand in his. "My roommate's out late tonight."

He pulled me in close and when he kissed me, his mouth tasted of Shiraz and salt. His tongue was gentle and his lips were soft. He put his hands on my shoulders then dropped them right down to my breasts. It happened so fast that it almost felt accidental, but his firm grasp let me know he had planned it and liked his hands where they were.

I felt nothing at all—no tingles, no rising warmth in my chest, nothing.

I couldn't enjoy this. I couldn't enjoy anything. Not now.

I gently pushed him away.

He took the cue, stepping back and giving me space. I was immensely glad he wasn't the type to fight a refusal.

He said, "Sorry. Maybe I overdid it a little with the wine. Went straight to my head, and, ahh, other places that might be making me a bit frisky."

"It's okay. I'm just … It's not a good time."

"I swear I don't normally move this fast." He held up his hands innocently. "We can go slow if you want, get to know each other more. Maybe we could hang out tomorrow?"

I put my face in my hands, laughing into them and shaking my head at the absurdity of my life. "Slow isn't what I want. If anything, I want quick and casual. Before anything else happens, I have to make it clear that I don't want a relationship."

Kevin looked letdown, and then excited, all within the one breath. "So, friends with benefits?"

"Maybe just the benefits part. Sometimes. I don't know. I'm not ready to be with anyone right now. Not tonight."

He nodded. I fumbled in my bag for my car keys.

"You're not driving, are you?"

I'd thought about leaving my car there overnight but didn't want to walk home alone. "I live off campus. It's a decent walk."

"I'll walk you." He seemed to gauge my reaction. "Just walk you. Really."

"Really?"

"Hell yeah. You've offered me future benefits. I'm not going to blow that."

I let him escort me, grateful to have someone beside me through the darkness. We talked about everything and nothing. When we reached my front door, he moved to kiss me again. A single, soft kiss. "Just let me know when and how and what you want, and I'll be there."

I went inside, closed the door then leaned against it, sliding down to the floor. The dam burst. Tears poured from my eyes as though they'd been waiting to escape all night. I cried myself to sleep there at the front door.

I was woken by knocking. I squinted at the morning light, disoriented. Bedraggled, aching, and half asleep, I opened the door to a courier, delivering a dozen bright and fragrant roses. They were sunset toned, a cheerful yellow fading into the richest golds and scarlet reds. I took the blooms from the delivery woman, and buried my face in them, inhaling deeply. They were an old-fashioned variety with a sweet scent as dizzying as their color.

Nobody had ever sent me flowers before—when I wasn't in hospital.

There was no card. Could they have been from Kevin, or maybe Blake? I loved them regardless. They brightened my day and made me feel special and wanted.

If only I was certain I had a lifetime to spend with someone who wanted me, and that I wasn't going to wilt and die as quickly as these flowers.

Chapter Thirty-One

GEORGINA

I sat and ate my lunch on my own, surrounded by students coming and going in the huge cafeteria. I could hear discussions on plans for parties, games, dates, and everything except classes. The whole place smelled of tuna casserole and chai tea, and the noise levels were deafening. It was a beautiful mess, full of life. I let it all seep into me, churning with the guilt in my belly.

I shouldn't even be here. There was somewhere else I was supposed to be today. *I'm sorry Julie. I can't. It's too hard.*

I poked my fork into the creamy pasta on my plate, as

though that would help me hold myself together.

"I'm all clear! The results were negative." Kaley appeared beside me so suddenly it was as though by magic. She grabbed the empty seat next to mine, bouncing into it. "No cancer, just a fatty lump or something, but nothing to worry about, totally benign. It's all okay!" Priya followed not long after, taking the seat on the other side of me.

At nearby tables some other students sat alone, hiding behind their phones or laptop screens. How many were hoping someone would come along and sit beside them? I hadn't realized how much I had been hoping for that, how much I'd needed the company, and the distraction.

I smiled gratefully at the twins on either side of me then settled my gaze on Kaley. "That's awesome. I'm so happy for you."

"Right? I couldn't even imagine. I knew I was too young."

I blinked. I took a deep breath. "Just make sure you keep getting check-ups, just in case. Sometimes it does happen very young."

Kaley nodded, or maybe just kept bouncing. "We SO have to celebrate. You have to come! We could hit the Cornerstone after class, but I feel like we should do something more, you know? Go big or go home, baby!"

Priya put her hand on mine, speaking over her sister.

"How about you? Got your results yet?"

I froze. What should I say? I had too many lies and half-truths to deal with. Blake thought the results were in and I was fine. Dad thought I was still waiting but that I'd been tested much earlier. The twins knew when I'd been tested—they'd been there. The results should have been in by now, and the waiting stretched my anxiety inside me like heavy taffy. *Why don't I have my results yet? Is there a problem?*

I should tell them the truth. How likely were they to talk to Blake and mess up my lies?

I fumbled my words. The truth was hard.

Then the radio playing through the cafeteria speakers cut off and an eerie silence spread.

A male voice called from somewhere distant, "Georgie!"

"Huh?" My eyes went round. Why was someone yelling my name? Maybe it was meant for another Georgina, but the voice was familiar, and it made my face turn scarlet. I looked around and saw Kevin walking toward me. Was it him? No, he looked around as though searching for the source of the voice too.

Music started up again, louder than before.

Why can't I go back, take back the times I didn't say what I needed to?

Can you take me back, to the time my heart wasn't

broken by you?

Baby, take me. I want you, I want you back.

Six guys from a table across the hall stood up in unison.

Moving in time to the song, they kicked back their chairs, stepped onto the table, and ripped off their jackets to reveal matching tight white T-shirts underneath. Half the cafeteria started whooping and applauding.

Maybe I was dreaming, but the rest of the students were gawping and laughing at the sight as well. A random flash mob seemed weird enough, but even weirder was that they were looking directly at me, dancing toward me.

I shot Kevin an accusatory glare, but he looked just as confused as I felt. He stood there staring and cringed away as the dancers moved past him.

The group reached the widest walkway between the tables which ran down the hall toward where I sat. Students scurried away, clearing a path, and trying to grab the best seats to watch the show.

The music slowed to build for the first chorus.

The dancers parted.

Stepping up in the middle of those cut physiques was Blake.

He looked sinfully handsome in blue jeans and a white singlet that showed off his muscled arms. It clung across his wide chest, and teased the smallest strip of midriff.

He also looked embarrassed as hell, but smiled bashfully through it.

Seeing him caused tremors to shoot through my body. I didn't know whether to run to him or from him. I could only sit and watch, my jaw dropped, as he started to dance.

Blake doesn't dance, I thought, my brain dumbstruck.

But he was. He was dancing toward me. He was dancing *for* me.

And oh boy, how he could dance.

His body seemed built for it. The way it rolled and pumped to the beat was like a force of nature. It was a complicated routine, and the dancers around him clearly knew it better than he did. He stumbled over a couple of moves, twirling left when the others went right. It didn't matter. Blake was dancing. That was all that mattered.

The music picked up with the chorus, and he sang along. It was a song from five years ago, about wanting his baby back. His voice was as dreamy as his dance moves, his British accent making it even sexier.

And the song—I had loved it back in high school, complete teen-obsession loved it. I had fantasized about meeting the band, and being in their music clips, and which band member would ask me to marry him.

That was a teenage fantasy though, and this was very

real. Mortifyingly real. Like having dinner at a restaurant on your birthday and all of sudden, in the middle of your meal while you have a mouthful of food, there was a group of people standing around you singing, while everyone in the restaurant stared at you. Once, I heard someone say that there was only one thing more embarrassing than singing in public, and that was being sung to in public. It felt as true as my face was red.

Blake and the dancers started doing the side-to-side bop that was the signature move of the boy band that had sung the song originally, and half the girls in the cafeteria squealed in delight.

The refrain 'I want you back' began to sink in. I hunched low into my chair to hide from the stares and cheers of the cafeteria crowd, as Blake and his backup dancers descended upon me. I covered my face in an attempt to ease my uncontrollable, embarrassment-born laughter.

Blake ended the song down on one knee beside my chair. "I want you back. Give me another chance, Georgina?"

Kaley's jaw was practically on the table as she looked from Blake, to me, to Blake, mouthing, *"Oh. My. God."*

Priya had her phone out. She'd been filming the whole thing. "This is amazing."

Students across the cafeteria were calling out, "Say yes!" A few girls added, "If she says no, take me!"

On the other side of the room, Kevin stood stock-still.

His face wore an expression that said he had no idea what to do next. He shook his head as if to clear it, gave me shrug, and walked off. Blake was not an act he could follow. Poor guy.

The music had ended. The shouts to say yes were picked up by the rest of the crowd until the whole room was chanting. I had to say yes, and Blake knew it. How could I say anything else after that, in front of everyone? It was a giant setup, and that made me angry. I wanted to run. All those days I had missed Blake, fighting every desire to see him again, and there he was, in my college cafeteria, ambushing me with my own teenage fantasy.

"Yes," I squeaked.

Cheers erupted.

Blake got up off his knee and thanked his backup dancers with a quick round of fist bumps and high fives. Priya put her phone down, scribbled her number on a scrap of paper, and stuck it straight in the jeans pocket of one of the dancers, giving him a wink.

Blake turned back to me and took my hand. I could see the apology in his smile. "Let's get out of here."

The whole crowd applauded and wolf whistled as we ran out hand in hand.

Chapter Thirty-Two

GEORGINA

Outside the cafeteria, away from the crowd, I pulled my hand free of Blake's.

He turned back to look at me and winced. "I'm sorry if that was as embarrassing for you as it was for me."

"That was a total ambush. It's not fair to put someone on the spot like that. Me saying yes under pressure—it doesn't mean we're back together." My heart still raced from the public spectacle of it all, as much as from the feel of Blake's hand holding mine. It had been hard letting go, but it had to be done.

"I know." His voice was solemn. "I wouldn't have

chosen to do it that way, only it wasn't really my choice."

Of course he wouldn't have chosen that. He didn't dance. He used to; he used to be one of Seyvia's dancers. But her death must have also killed that part of him, the part that danced. So why dance now?

"Whose choice was it, then?"

Blake gave me a cheeky smirk. "Give me that one last chance. Go out with me tonight and I'll tell you."

I folded my arms. "Now you're adding curiosity blackmail onto public ambushing?"

"Bugger, okay. Not a good move." Blake rubbed his chin as though thinking it through. "But you are curious, aren't you?"

I snorted a tiny chuckle. *Damn it, don't let him know he's getting to you.*

He swayed his hips gently. "And that was kind of fun, back there, with the dancing?"

I failed to hide my smile.

"Just give me a go. A fresh start, without that list, free from what you were going through then. One night. One proper date. Please, Georgie?"

Looking into his blue eyes, how they gazed down into mine, my heart cracked open.

Say no. Say goodbye. You can't have this, no matter what you want. He doesn't deserve another tragedy.

My mouth opened but nothing came out. How could I say no to those eyes?

Maybe a compromise …

"Just one night. One last night. To say goodbye properly."

Blake frowned but nodded. He let me know when he'd be around to pick me up, then turned away.

Before he was out of earshot, I called out, "It was fun, back in the cafeteria. Like something out of a music video. It was nice seeing you dance."

Back home after class, I turned my wardrobe inside out trying to find something to wear. I had no idea where Blake planned to take me, which didn't help the decision process. I wanted to dress casual, but not too casual, just in case we went somewhere posh. I didn't want to look unattractive, but didn't want to dress too sexily. I didn't want to give Blake any false hopes. I didn't want to give myself any either.

I checked my reflection. I was fooling myself if I thought I wasn't trying to look appealing. I'd chosen my tightest jeans, a semi-sheer lace blouse, and ended up with more makeup on than I should have. Maybe the deep red lipstick was too much. I hesitated, knowing my full lips were one of my best features but not really wanting to draw his attention to them, because then he might want to kiss them. And I was supposed to be not wanting him to kiss me.

I really want him to kiss me.

A knock came from the front door, and I rubbed some of the color off my lips with the back of my hand.

I opened the door for Blake, and he came inside while I chased up my phone and purse.

Blake caught sight of Julie's emptied out room. "I heard about the accident. I'm sorry, about Julie."

I couldn't move for a full five seconds while I braced my emotions. I should have been grieving her, laying her to rest, not going on a date.

Blake moved a little closer to me. "You weren't hurt badly, were you?"

His blue eyes looked so worried for me. All I had was a light bruise from my seatbelt and a sore shoulder. I would have taken any injury if it meant Julie could have survived. Guilt made me shiver and I chased it away. "No, not badly."

I could barely talk to him. I could barely look at him. Having him so close was too much temptation when he was begging me for another chance. I should have been the one begging him, but I knew something he didn't know: that we had no future together. I should have been begging him for forgiveness.

Blake wandered over near the roses. Their color warmed the whole room from their vase on the coffee table.

"Pretty roses. Do you like them?" he asked.

"Did you send them to me?"

He smiled and made shifty eyes. "No card, huh? Completely anonymous? How will you *ever* know for sure?"

I frowned at him as I clipped my purse closed. "You could tell me. That's how I could know for sure."

He rubbed his chin. "Nope. I'm pretty sure there's no way you could ever know for sure."

I was almost certain now he had been the one who sent me the flowers. But if he was trying to win me back, why not send a card? Why not admit to sending them? He was being weirdly coy.

We took my car and Blake drove. The sun had just set, and stars poked through the darkening blue-green sky like tiny fairy lights. The spiced cake and aged wood scent of Blake's cologne drifted to my nose, and I closed my eyes, recalling the smell of it on his neck and the feel of his neck against my face as I buried it there. The feel of his chest under my fingers ...

The memory was so vivid it made my cheeks flush with heat.

I had to get my mind off his body, and I had questions to ask anyway.

"I used to love the song that you sang for me today. I would dream of being in their music videos, and one of the boy-band members falling in love with me."

"Is that right?"

"How did you know?"

"What makes you think I knew?"

The whole thing gave me a strange sense of déjà vu. Everything was so weird lately. Had he been conspiring with my dad? "Blake, it was … strangely specific. How did you know?"

Gravel rumbled under the wheels as we turned off the road into a parking lot. "Hey look, we're here."

"Perfect timing," I said, loading my tone with sarcasm like a big loud sarcasm gun.

'Here' turned out to be a carnival. We got out of the car and walked up to the entry gate.

Inside, multi-colored lights twinkled and flashed, and the smells of hot dogs and popcorn filled the air, along with the screams of people on rides and laughter from those trying their luck at the sideshow games. It was raucous and magical and full of joy.

Blake went to buy tickets. I froze in place, as though my insides had turned to solid ice.

Blake returned, and frowned. "Are you okay?"

I could only shake my head.

"You don't like carnivals?"

"No, I … I don't know. I've never really gone to one. It looks amazing. Too amazing. That's why I can't. I can't do this. Not tonight. How can I enjoy all of this, be here enjoying all of this? It's not right."

Blake put his hands on my shoulders. They moved me gently toward him, the solace of his embrace so close and tempting. I stayed frozen, refusing him. I didn't deserve comfort.

"It was Julie's funeral today." Admitting it aloud felt like a hammer to my chest. "It was her funeral today, and I didn't go. I was too scared, too much of a coward to be there with her family. I couldn't even be brave enough to say goodbye to her properly. I don't deserve to be here doing this now. Not when she's not here anymore."

My body tensed up, and my breathing quickened, guilt manifesting as a full-blown panic attack. Tears burned in my eyes, and I pushed them back with the palms of my hands. "Shit."

"It's okay. I mean, I know it's not okay, but it's okay not to be okay." Blake took me by the hand, and this time I let him lead me in through the entry, over to the side, out of the way of the passing crowds. "It's not fair, what happened. But it wasn't your fault, and you shouldn't punish yourself for it. It's okay to keep living. We can go in here, and have fun tonight, and we will take Julie, her memory, with us, okay?"

I put my hands over my chest, taking steadying, slow breaths. The Ferris wheel turned slowly in the distance, the seats swinging together as lights created rainbows of color around the circular frame. I could imagine Julie's big brown eyes staring up at it, her cute-yet-stoic expression showing the smallest smirk of joy. I could see her perfectly in my mind. Julie was still with me, just as my mom was still with me. That was where they existed now—in the love and memories of the people still here, still alive. And against all odds, I was still alive.

I already knew I needed to keep living as long as I could. It was harder, with the loss of Julie weighing on me, but Blake had just given me the reminder I needed. "Okay."

"Okay?"

"Yeah. Sorry. I'm not sure this is quite the angst-free evening you planned."

Blake shrugged. "Angst can come along too. You can't shut off your grief any more than you can shut yourself off from fun. Kind of sums up life, right?"

I nodded, a half-smile forming. Blake took my hand, and we ventured into the carnival.

Our tickets came with wristbands that gave us access to all the rides. We rode the tilt-a-whirl twice. The dizzy, spinning swirl of it seemed to throw the weight of emotions free from my mind, and I would have ridden it all night, but Blake dragged me off to other rides, trying one after another. While I queued for the bumper cars, he left me for a moment to go and talk to a family having birthday cake. Maybe he knew them. The line started moving again and he hurried back just in time. I actually laughed when Blake barely squeezed into one of the little cars but couldn't fit in enough to press the pedals and just spun in circles at the side of the track.

Contentment filled me as we climbed onto the Ferris wheel. It spun us high into the sky and stopped when we were at the highest point. As the cars swung softly over the scene below, Blake put something into my hand—a half-used birthday candle.

"Hold still," he said, and flicked on the lighter he held, lighting up the candle. The tiny flame swayed in the gentle breeze, but stayed alight. "For Julie."

A tear splashed from my eye onto my lap. I cradled the candle as though holding Julie's soul there in that precious little light. "For Julie."

I'm sorry I didn't come and say goodbye today. I'm sorry we didn't have time to become the great friends we could have been. I'm sorry you died.

The Ferris wheel started up again, and I held the candle close to me. "Goodbye, for now," I whispered, and blew the candle out.

Mom, take care of Julie for me.

We rode the wheel down, and I watched the ground rising up toward us. The operator was sending people away, saying there'd be no more rides tonight, and sadness crept over me. It was getting late, and soon all the lights would go out and this night would end. And one last night was all I'd allowed myself with Blake.

We meandered through the sideshow, and Blake pulled me over to a game where enormous teddy bears, and stuffed multi-hued unicorns, and purple dolphins hung around a wall of balloons. A range of smaller prizes, tiny, cheap plastic things, were piled in trays below. "I think you need one of those."

"A badly rigged game?"

"No, a unicorn."

I laughed. "No way you can win that. I'm pretty sure they're just for decoration. No one ever wins those."

"Challenge accepted." Blake went to the guy standing behind the booth and passed over cash. It looked like a lot more money than the prices on the sign, but before I could call him out on it, he grabbed the darts and started hurling them at the little balloons tacked by their mouths to a corkboard. He actually managed to pop a few.

"We have a winner," the guy intoned, grinning under the gaudy red and green lights. "Pick out whatever it is the lady wants, sir. Take your pick."

Blake took the unicorn. He handed it over, and I could barely get my arms around it. The sheer size of the toy made me laugh. It was so impractical, and so adorable, it filled me with joy.

"Oh god. It's so cute. But it's got some kind of … evil magic! I can feel myself regressing … It's turning me into a twelve-year-old. Oh no, I think I might squee!" I hugged it tight, mashing my face into its plush muzzle. Looking back at Blake again, I smiled and put all my heart into my words. "I love it. Thank you. For everything."

Blake took the unicorn for me, since it dragged along the ground when I tried to carry it. Happiness made me feel light and warm and full of beautiful heartache.

Our walk back to the parking lot was slow. Neither of us seemed to want the night to end. We squeezed the unicorn into the car and it filled the entire back seat.

We didn't get in the car ourselves right away. We just stood there, apart from each other. Blake seemed to be waiting for me. Waiting while I fought my ongoing battle of denial.

"I'll drive you home now," Blake said.

There it was—the end of the night. My body and mind went into a panic. It was too soon. This was our last night. I wanted it to go on as long as it could.

"Can you drive me back to your place?" I asked.

Blake took a step closer to me. "Yeah, of course. If that's what you want."

His face was so close to mine, dangerously close. I wanted to close my eyes, just lean into him and let him give me that long and lingering kiss that I had been thinking about ever since we'd split up.

"I loved tonight, today—all of it. It was the most amazing day I have ever had. Nothing between us is going to change. I still don't want a relationship. I only promised you one more night. But the night isn't over."

Chapter Thirty-Three

GEORGINA

I shivered, partly from nerves and partly from the cold of Blake's house as we walked inside, well past midnight. A chill had set in, making stepping into the unheated rooms feel like stepping into a freezer. It was like a sign, the cold, trying to drive me away, telling me what I was doing was wrong. Me being there, being with Blake at all, was sending him all the wrong messages and making it harder and harder for me to turn away.

It wasn't the cold that made goosebumps break out up my arms and down my back. It was being close to Blake—close enough to touch him. Everything about him tugged at my heartstrings, and at my body. It was infuriatingly ironic that I had this amazing guy, the guy I would have made up out of thin air if anyone had asked me to create my perfect man. And I couldn't keep him.

Blake asked me a question, but I didn't hear it. I was staring at the sofa and remembering the night I lost my virginity to him, and how tender and indescribably special it had been. I wished I could go back to that moment and change it all, say to him, 'I don't care about The List—all I want is you'.

Because it wasn't just the cancer holding me apart from him; it was all the things I had done. I wasn't ashamed of my list. I just regretted that those things, some of them, anyway, had hurt him, and badly. I had behaved horribly.

When I wrote out that list I'd had nothing to lose. Then that all changed. Blake cared about me. He kept trying to prove it to me and I just kept wondering what it was he saw in me.

My old enemy, insecurity, had come back to haunt me. It was funny, in a way, because Blake and my list had made me feel so confident. Right then, though, looking at his gorgeous face I felt like the same girl I had been back in high school— chubby, bald, sick, and lonely. I felt like the same girl who'd cried in the bathroom because a boy had pulled her wig off in the middle of class, the same girl who'd thought she'd always be alone.

What would I look like a year from now? Would Blake love me if I had chemo and lost all my hair? If I lost both of my breasts? *I mightn't even still be here for him to love. That's why it has to be only one more night.*

My mom had written something on a napkin before she died, a single line in flaming red Sharpie. She'd had a very bad day, or so my dad said, and she'd scrawled out the words, 'Pain is too beautiful to hate when it comes with the gift of one more day'.

I'd kept that napkin and held onto it through my own treatment, although I'd never fully understood it. Now, maybe I knew exactly what she meant.

I just wanted one more day. Just one more day with Blake. Or one last night.

I was truly, deeply, painfully in love for the first time in my life, and I couldn't bring myself to hate that.

I am in love …

I hadn't admitted it to myself before. But I could feel it was true.

Blake was staring at me, concern written in every angle of his beautiful face. He was probably wondering why I hadn't answered him, why I was just staring at him with an intensity that could bore through steel. In response to the question I never heard, I stepped forward and pressed my mouth on his.

Blake put his strong arms around me, and I felt a deep,

long sigh escape his lips. His body held mine up, his hands stroked my hair, and his lips brushed against my ears and my neck. He felt so good there, so right.

My heart gave an anxious flutter, like it had broken free from my body and fled like a frightened rabbit. *This will only hurt him more when you leave him again,* the dark voice inside me said. I closed it off. I'd been clear with Blake that this was our last night, and when it ended, we were over. Even if it hurt him. Even if it hurt me.

I ignored the churn of my belly that rose every time I thought of Blake being hurt, and lost myself in the taste of his mouth, the feel of his hands pressing against my back, and the spicy smell of his skin.

Nerves shook my hands as I led Blake to his bedroom then to the bed. It felt like my first time all over again, scary, intense, and full of wonder. Blake seemed hesitant, but I didn't let him stop to ask me if I was sure. With breathless confidence I took control, showing him this was exactly what I wanted.

I undressed before him as he watched, slowly dragging my shirt off, then peeling down my jeans. I pressed my chest to his as I undid my bra, then turned away to take it off and bent low as I slid my panties down. He placed his hands on the cheeks of my ass as I straightened up again and moved away from his hot touch.

It left him panting, desire clear in his eyes as he looked

my naked body up and down. Then I knelt before him, treating him like the Norse god he was. I lifted the hem of his shirt, dropping tender kisses across his abs as I unbuckled his belt, unzipped his fly. I could feel the hardness of him as I freed him from his clothes. My whole body felt heated through as though by an internal wildfire, the coldness of the room forgotten as lust rampaged through me.

I used my mouth on Blake as I had seen in the videos I'd once watched. I started slow, exploratory licks and strokes that elicited moans and gasps from Blake. My lips tingled as they slid across his skin and I plunged his shaft deeply into my mouth, suddenly desperate for him, trying to drink him in like he was my only source of water in a parched desert. He grasped at my head, his fingers tangling into my hair as he groaned through gritted teeth.

I writhed with longing as I sucked and massaged, enjoying the way he shuddered in my mouth, how he cried out my name.

"Fuck, Georgie, you're the sexiest thing I have ever seen," Blake rasped out from a hoarse throat. He withdrew from my mouth, kneeled with me on the floor. He whipped his shirt off over his head and kissed me hard as he pushed his jeans down a bit farther, grabbed a condom from the nearby bedside drawers, then pushed me back on the carpet. There was a growl in his voice and a sharp intensity in his gaze, but when he entered me, it was perfect—slow, sensual, and caring in a way that brought tears to my eyes.

I tempered myself, fighting against the urge to slam Blake into me, to fill myself with him in ramming, passionate desperation. I moved slowly to make every second count, make this night last as long as it could.

Blake seemed to have the same idea, and we washed against each other like a constant tide, each careful thrust matched by a soft and deep kiss. Each movement sent soft pleasure sparkling up from my tailbone to the base of my neck, gentle and warm and slow. I grew drunk on that contentment, letting it roll on and on, never wanting it to stop.

Caught in a haze of desire, we moved from the floor to the bed. I moved on top of him. He shifted behind me. Each change in position came fluidly, prolonging the cloud of passion we floated on.

It was so sweet, making love with Blake like that. There wasn't the urgency that came with ticking an item off a list, just the pleasure of our bodies becoming one, of both of us trying to make the experience last forever. Every part of it, from the first kiss to the last, to the slow-building climax that took my breath away, and the way Blake then curled around me with one hand wrapped around my hip and his body snuggled into my back, was incredibly touching and tender. It was the perfect night. The perfect final night.

The warmth of sunlight had begun to show through the edges of his closed curtains when we drifted off to sleep, his mouth pressed close to my ear.

"I have another present for you," he muttered just before he nodded off.

Nothing could have been a bigger gift in my life than he had been. When we said goodbye, I knew I would love this time we had together, forever.

Chapter Thirty-Four

GEORGINA

I cracked my eyes open, blinking at the sunlight and the casual chaos of Blake's bedroom. My heart dropped. Morning had come. The last night was over, and it was time to leave and never see Blake again.

He wasn't in the bed beside me, and when I squinted at the red LCD clock on the dresser it told me it was almost midday. The smell of bacon wafted into the room. *Is he making breakfast?* I smiled, then frowned, wanting to cry. Saying goodbye now was going to be so hard.

With a deep breath I got up and pulled back the

curtains, letting the golden sunlight stream in, warming my body. A quick glance down at the front yards below showed Blake's elderly neighbor collecting his newspaper, looking disapprovingly right back up at me standing naked in the window. I cringed and stepped back out of view.

I got my clothes on just as Blake walked in, holding a plate the same color as the sunlight. I could smell sweet dough and eggs along with the bacon.

"Brunch?" He looked incredibly proud of himself as he held the plate out and I stared down at the thing on it, unsure what it was. He must have read the expression on my face because he said, "It's a bacon and egg wafflewich. A sandwich on waffles."

I put my shoes on and shook my head as I tried to locate my purse. Maybe I'd left it downstairs. "Blake, our night is over. I have to go."

Blake looked defiant. "I know you promised only one night, and you gave me that, but there's so much more I want from you. I want to be with you, as long as I can. At the very least I want to share this magnificent breakfast creation with you and give you your present."

I was ready to walk away for the both of us, but something seemed more and more suspicious. He had never offered to make me breakfast before, and on top of the whole song and dance and carnival routine, the last twenty-four hours had been more than a little over the top. Why would he do all of this?

I raised my eyebrows, intrigued. "The breakfast isn't the present?"

"Nope. The present is out back."

"I really have to go." *This was Cinderella's last ball and it's way, way, way past midnight.*

He waved the plate under my nose provocatively.

My stomach growled like a bear, and the cramp of hunger that accompanied that growl was damn well painful. I took the plate and then took a bite of his wafflewich creation. He had put syrup on the bacon and eggs and it oozed out between my teeth. The waffle was puffy and delicious, the bacon crisp and salty against the sweet maple syrup, and the eggs were tasty and runny.

"So good," I got out through a mouth stuck together with dough. It was the perfect combination of sugar, salt, carbs, and fat that made happy food chemicals flood my brain. I took a second bite, then with great strength of will, put the rest back on the plate and started walking out.

"Present first," Blake said, and scooped me up around the waist.

"Blake, I'm saying no. This isn't funny anymore."

I could feel Blake tense. His voice lost the playfulness it had had before. "Just receive your gift, and then tell me no one last time, and I will never bother you again."

Out the back door, Blake set me down in the yard. An old concreted area looked out over an overgrown field of weeds and dying trees. A grumpy-looking garden gnome lay on the path half hidden in the tall grass. The drive-through garage was open at the back, showing a messy workshop filled with metal parts, two half-finished motorbikes, and grease stains. Parked just outside he had a gleaming new motorbike. It was cherry red, small, sleek, and simple, with chrome accents.

"What do you think?"

"Of the gnome?"

Blake laughed. "No, what do you think about your bike? I built it just for you."

Overwhelmed, the blood drained from my face. Again, that feeling of all this being somehow familiar came back. I couldn't figure it out though, nor could I understand why he was giving me a bike. A whole damned *motorbike*.

I shook my head, confused. "Blake, that had to be so expensive. You could sell it and make yourself some money."

"I don't care about the money. I want you to have this gift."

"I don't even know how to ride. I haven't wanted a bike since I was ... a kid."

The anonymous flowers ...

The music video scene ...

The carnival …

The unicorn …

The motorbike …

Oh.

My.

God.

My mouth opened and shut so fast I must have looked like a fish out of water gasping for air. It all made sense, a horrible and embarrassing sense.

"My list," I whispered. "I put all this stuff on a list when I … before I went into treatment at fifteen. But how did you know?"

Blake's eyes smiled at me. "I was wondering when you would work it out."

"You do have my list! How? Did my dad tell you? Oh god, do you have my diary?" I blushed so hard it felt like flames were going to leap out of my skin. "That was private! I wrote that a long time ago. I don't even remember exactly what I wrote on it. Wasn't there something about Niagara, or getting—"

Blake put a finger to my mouth. "Uh-uh. No spoilers."

I stood there, dazed for a few moments, blinking rapidly to fend off the threat of confused tears. "Why are you doing this?"

Blake took both of my hands, and sat down on the seat

of the motorbike so he was looking me straight in the eyes. "Your bucket list, as much fun as it was to do with you, came from a place of darkness and desperation. You told me once you had written another list when you were a kid. A list filled with hope and innocent dreams. I wanted to complete the items on that list for you. I wanted to do something for you that would bring back the person you were before you were ever touched by cancer."

My blinking stopped, and a tear dropped heavily from my cheek.

I wanted to say no because I knew that letting Blake work his way through my list of childhood dreams would keep me from being able to let him go when I needed to, and I needed to, whether I wanted to or not.

"I don't know. We're not in a relationship. We're not together. That's over now."

"We don't need to be in a relationship for this list. It's not like your last one."

I could see he was dead set on this. He'd sung and danced in front of a full cafeteria and built me a motorbike. I doubted he'd back away from this easily.

I bowed my head. "If you really want to do my childhood list for me anyway, maybe we can do some of it, but I get to see it first and approve the things on it."

Blake grinned, showing all his teeth. "Not a chance."

"But it's my list!"

"Yes, it is, but I have it and you don't, and that's just the way it is."

"That's not fair! I need to see the list again. I can't remember it all. How do I know you aren't getting me to do all kinds of wacky things that aren't even on it?"

"You'll just have to trust me."

"What if you take us out to rob a bank or have me hypnotized to howl like a Beagle every time someone sneezed? How would I know that wasn't on my list?"

Blake snorted a laugh. "Would you have ever put those on your list?"

"No," I admitted.

"Then don't worry about it."

I gnawed on my bottom lip. I trusted Blake, but I wasn't sure I trusted myself. I had cooked that list up when I was *fifteen*. At fifteen, my biggest ambition was to grow up to be a famous artist. Then, after the cancer diagnosis, I just wanted to *grow up*. What could I have I written on that list?

And *where* had I written it? Did I write it in my diary? Did that mean …?

"How did you get it? Did you read my diary? Did Dad give it to you?"

Blake gave a strong shake of his head. "Your dad didn't have any part of it. And I didn't read your diary."

I blew out a slow breath of relief. He must've had to poke around though. Who knows what he found or saw. I wanted to be mad that he'd gone through my private stuff, but only felt overwhelmed. I'd forgotten about my first bucket list like I'd forgotten most of my childhood dreams, and Blake had brought it back into existence. *For me.*

Maybe I did need some childhood dreams to come true.

Blake still had my hands held in his, and he squeezed them gently. "Come on. This bike here is an item on your list, and you should take a ride at least before you decide that you don't want her."

I pulled my hands free and wiped my cheek. "I don't know how to ride on my own."

"Then I'll give you a ride on it."

The bike gleamed and sparkled in the sunlight. All of a sudden I wanted nothing more than to be on it, my arms wrapped around Blake and the road flying past below our feet.

I nodded. "Take me for a ride."

We got on the bike and he revved the engine. The wind was cold but the leather jacket he gave me was warm, and the leaves blew down over us as we buzzed through the streets. Paused at a red light, I saw a tween girl in the car beside us looking at me with envy, and I could see myself reflected on the windows of the car she sat in.

My hair hung below the helmet, tousled and wild, my arms were wrapped around Blake's taut waist, and the sexy machine below us growled and thundered. I looked like someone else—someone who did exciting things just because she could. I looked brave, sexy, and free.

The bike shuddered as we peeled away from the intersection, heading into a long stretch of the city where the hills went straight down.

I screamed and laughed as we rode the hills. It was like the carnival all over again but a heck of a lot more exciting. Once the tires left the road completely and we hung in the air, suspended for a long heartbeat. Fear and adrenaline mixed with the sensation of Blake's body next to mine, his muscles flexing and tensing as he took us back down safely then roared to the top of another hill that spat us out close to the lake. We rode alongside it, the unsealed roads dipping into low valleys and rising up again on high peaks, showing glimpses of the sparkling water through the trees.

It was hours later when we pulled back into Blake's driveway, and I was exhausted and invigorated. He cut the bike off, and helped me to dismount. "What do you think?"

"I love it," I said sincerely.

I did, but I didn't want it for myself. I wanted to ride behind Blake, to embrace him for hours like that all over again. My inner thighs and arms, my chest, and even my palms all radiated warmth that had come from his body. His flesh had been imprinted onto my own, and I missed him even though he was standing a bare foot away from me.

"It's yours, Georgie, whenever you want it." His lips came close to my mine, and I wanted to kiss him. I could imagine that kiss happening, feel it in the tingle of my lips … but I drew back.

Nothing had changed. Blake was still the sweetest, most generous man alive, and I was still the tragedy waiting to happen. He could finish the new list, but he couldn't be mine.

Blake cleared his throat, breaking the awkward silence. "I'm glad you worked out we're doing your childhood list. It was fun, ticking things off without you even realizing, but the next item I couldn't really do without you knowing and agreeing. This makes things much easier."

"So I do get to know something on the list?"

"You agree to do it, then I'll tell you. If you can get it done this afternoon, I've got another surprise for you tonight."

I wasn't even sure why he felt he had to do this. Was it simply his attempt to win me back? Or was he doing this because he felt responsible for me? Did he love me, or was it some misbegotten sense of loyalty that he felt for me?

I wished I could just give in and be with him without any kind of bullshit emotion getting in the way, but it wasn't that easy. The way we had met made sure of that. I would never be able to be sure if he loved me or just felt obligated to be with me, thanks to my lists and my issues.

Still, I was going to let Blake work through this list for me. I couldn't say no to him, and half the truth was that I was dying from curiosity. I honestly couldn't remember what was on that damn list, but I wanted to know, and the only way to find out was to play the list out.

"I'm in."

Chapter Thirty-Five

BLAKE

Sneaking into Georgina's childhood bedroom was one of the hardest things I'd ever done. Harder than breaking and entering at the pool. Harder than any of the wild items on Georgina's bucket list.

The incredible guilt, the feeling of invading her privacy and her past overwhelmed me. Not to mention the fear of being busted sneaking around by Tom. I almost gave up and walked away. When she found out what I'd done, would she find it romantic? Or be angry that I'd intruded somewhere so personal without permission? Romantic gestures sucked like that. They were never as simple as they seemed in the movies.

But I was determined. A list brought Georgina into my life, and maybe a list could bring her back to me. Or if I couldn't win her back, maybe I could bring her some joy with what was on that older, more innocent list. Fill her with good memories of our time together to bury any pain she wanted to forget. That would be worth it.

I stared around at her room, filled with a huge collection of plastic ponies and stuffed animals, and shelves crammed with everything from coloring books to young adult vampire romances. The bedspread was printed with rainbows and fluffy pink clouds, and a teddy bear with a light-up heart still rested on the pillow.

Her dad hadn't changed a thing. I'd heard him mention once he kept meaning to turn the space into a walk-in pantry but didn't want the hassle of renovating. I think he kept it that way to remind himself of the girl Georgina used to be.

I sat on the small bed and opened the neon pink and rhinestone-decorated shoebox I'd found in back of the closet.

I wished I could tell Georgina how I had felt when I pulled the lid off and found her wig.

It was a lifeless, limp mess of brownish-red strands with a tiny bit of curl on the ends, nothing like her real hair which was dark and wild. I picked it up and held it. It smelled like dust and salt. Like tears and heartache.

I got lucky—under the wig was a journal, covered in sequins with one of those flimsy locks that had been broken open long ago. There was also a bottle of prescription-strength pain pills. A note had been stuffed inside, and through the orange plastic I read, 'You can get through this. Only take what you need.'

I stared at that for a long time, because the handwriting wasn't Georgina's, and the pills weren't hers either. They had belonged to her mother.

She had lost her mom, then had been fighting the same disease that had taken her mom away from her, when she was just a kid. How bad had it been for Georgina? I knew that it had put her through a lot physically. I could guess it had wrecked her self-esteem too.

And having to go through all of that while in high school … High school was easy for me. I was a big guy, good at sports, and was dating the hottest girl in school, who was already getting interest from record labels. What would it have been like if I had been sick, suffering from pain and exhaustion, and dealing with the loss of my mother?

I should give Ma a call tomorrow.

I'd been happy to leave Pa behind, and the rest of England, and all the hard memories of what happened there. I'd needed to start fresh and a new country was as fresh as I could get. But Ma was *Ma*. She was a good woman, and I missed her.

I should have told her that more often, and that I loved her. Life was too short and unpredictable.

Seyvia's was short, too short, but there was something almost inevitable about her death. I had felt her leaving me, slipping farther away every day. The more famous she got, the more distant from me she grew. For a while I'd just thought she was going to break up with me. She'd slipped far enough out of my grasp that I'd lost any influence over her, so when things got dire, when the partying and drugs got out of control, she wouldn't even accept my help.

I'd beat myself up over that for years. There must have been something else I could have done, something I could have said to wake her up to what she was doing to herself before it was too late. I'd never know. It had happened. And there was no coming back from death for a second chance.

That was why I needed this second chance now, with Georgina. I only had this life, and I was going to make it count.

Even if getting that second chance meant doing something terrible, like looking in her diary.

With a deep breath, I opened the journal. Inside was cute and incredibly girly, with little hearts drawn on most of the pages.

No reading. Just flick through. A list should be obvious.

It was hard not to read. Individual words would catch my eye as the pages flashed past under my thumb. Words like kiss, or stood-up, or hurt. Words stained with teardrops.

I almost gave up, then near the end I found a separate sheet of purple paper, folded neatly and tucked inside.

I closed the diary and carefully unfolded the loose page. *I found it.*

Her childhood list made me laugh and scratch my head. It was full of whimsy and childlike ideas of romance. Underneath all the list items she'd written, 'Make amazing memories that last forever'. This was her Forever List, and the pressure of making it perfect hit me.

How am I going to do these things?

It seemed impossible at worst, and at best, extremely embarrassing.

If past me knew that one day I would be dancing across a cafeteria to a song I never liked to get a date with a girl who'd already told me she wasn't interested, I would have thought I'd gone nuts. If it had been any other girl, I would have let her go, but Georgina wasn't just another girl. She was *the* girl, and I knew it.

Now that she'd finally worked out I had her list, it was obvious she was worried, but curious. She honestly couldn't remember what she'd written on it. That made things even more interesting. It was going to be a lot of fun playing it out.

After taking her for a ride on her new bike, I wanted to kiss Georgina and drag her back to bed with me, but she pushed me away. She'd said last night was our last time together, and she was sticking to that decision, for now. She was still refusing a romantic relationship, or being friends with benefits, or whatever it was that we said we were in the past.

But I planned to turn us into something more. We'd never really dated, and her childhood list was the perfect way to take her on perfect dates. To really get to know each other. To make happy, forever memories.

We would complete this list together, and maybe she would change her mind. Maybe she would let go of the insecurities or whatever was stopping her from letting me in.

If it turned out that after this we just became friends, I'd be okay with that too. I just needed her in my life, one way or another. She made me better.

Still, I wanted her. Badly. Real badly. She clung to me on the back of her bike, her thighs pressed around me as we flew along rolling roads, and I could have stopped the bike and thrown her over the seat and had my way with her then and there.

I had sent Georgina on her way for the next thing on the list. I offered to go with her, but after I explained what it was, she said she wanted help from some other friends. And I had my own work to do, preparing for tonight.

I was more nervous about this one than the dance in the cafeteria. Not only what I had to actually do, but with the nature of this item, it was going to be really hard keeping things platonic.

Chapter Thirty-Six

GEORGINA

When Blake told me the next item on my list, something I had to agree to do before he would reveal it, I almost took back my agreement and stormed off to never be part of this again.

I hadn't cut my hair since it started growing back after chemo. It was halfway down my back now, and not in the best condition, but I was fiercely protective of every strand.

Then I heard that voice whisper inside me, somehow younger than before. *The List Georgina is brave Georgina.*

This was something I had wanted when I was younger, and even now, part of me wondered *what if?* Could I be this daring?

Maybe I could. Maybe I did want this.

But I needed support.

I was browsing through images of different haircut styles online when I heard a rapping on the front window. Kaley's smiling face peered through, waving to me where I sat on the couch.

"Hey, girl." She gave me a quick hug when I opened the door for her. Priya followed her in, carrying a medium-sized make-up bag.

"Thanks for coming, and for doing this for me, with me, you know," I mumbled and winced, suddenly awkward having them in my home. They were so nice, and seemed to be happy to adopt me as a new friend, but I was still struggling to dive into that relationship as freely as they'd seemed to.

"No problem," Priya said. She flicked the ends of her black hair, which hung in a perfectly blunt-angled cut. "I've been wanting to change up my look too. Maybe you'll give me some ideas."

Both Priya and Kaley had hair that always looked like it had just been done by a hairdresser. They'd seemed like the perfect choice to help me with this mission. I'd sent Kaley a message asking if they wanted to come to the hairdressers with me to help me choose what I'd get done, and they'd revealed that they cut each other's hair, and were happy to do mine too.

"Pretty flowers." Priya brushed her fingers over the roses, inspecting them. "From your flash dance boy?"

"I don't really know. They came without a card."

"I bet it was him. Public serenades, anonymous flowers? You're living the dream," Kaley gushed.

I just shrugged, and blushed. Priya put her bag down on the coffee table near the roses and started pulling out scissors, combs, and a spray bottle.

"What are you thinking of getting done?" Priya asked.

I took a deep breath.

"Pixie cut." My heart had been pounding ever since Blake had said those same words. I almost laughed at how this made me more nervous than some of the things on my sexy bucket list.

"Wow. Big change." Priya squinted at me, assessing my face and hair.

Kaley gasped audibly. "Oh, oh, I can see it already. Look at her—she's going to be so fregging hot with a pixie cut. I mean, those lips."

Fregging. That was something Julie used to say, something from one of her sci-fi shows she fangirled over.

I tried not to think of her. Tried to fight the feeling that I was somehow replacing her.

I knew that wasn't really what was happening. I was allowed to make new friends. But it still hurt. I still felt like I was making a mistake letting anyone into the tragedy of my life.

I forced my derailing train of thought back to the task at hand. I reached for my laptop to show the twins some of the styles I liked the look of, but Kaley waved it away. She was drawing lines around my face with her fingers, talking about sweeping bangs, cheekbone composition, and making my lips *pop*. Priya nodded along, then shook her head, then nodded again when Kaley rebutted with, "But look at that chin line."

"I, um—" I tried to interject.

"Don't worry. We got this."

"I just …" I didn't know *just* what. I hadn't decided on the cut I wanted. When browsing online I saw half a dozen styles that looked nice on the models who wore them, but I had no idea if they would look good on me, and while they were all 'pixie cuts' they varied wildly in style. I couldn't choose. This was all feeling very sudden, and maybe having someone choose for me was the best option. The twins seemed to know what they were talking about, and based on their own hair, I trusted their tastes and skill. But I was still terrified.

"Okay. I'm putting my hair's life in your hands," I said.

Priya put a hand over her heart. "We're honored. Now, let's cut these locks."

A stool from the kitchen was brought into the room, and I sat there, taking deep breaths.

Snnnnnip.

I winced and squealed.

The first few chops cut a ragged line across the nape of my neck, and just like that, the bulk of my hair was gone.

I took in a lungful of air and slowly blew it out before reaching a hand back to feel. *It's gone. My hair is gone.* I looked down at the pool of black beneath me on the floorboards. *That's my hair on the ground.* There was so much of it. Adrenaline shook my fingers. There was no taking this back, no do-overs. We had to keep going now. *Mom, I hope this turns out okay.*

"Hold still now." Priya did most of the cutting, under Kaley's guidance. I had no idea what was happening or what I looked like. There were no mirrors in sight. Hair was combed down over my face this side and then that. Mist from the spray bottle cooled my neck and cheeks, and sharp little snippets of cut hair prickled through my shirt. The giant stuffed unicorn watched everything from its spot in the corner.

Kaley plugged in a hairdryer and took over. Dark strands gusted around my face, so light and short. My whole head felt wobbly, both from the nerves and the weight that had been removed from it.

"Almost done," Priya said.

Kaley put the hair-dryer down and stood in front of me with a huge smile, bouncing on the spot. "I can't wait for you to see this. Where's your bathroom?"

"Just down the hall past Julie's … past the empty room."

Kaley frowned, and nodded, and headed that way.

Priya came around to my front, tugging at the strands of hair around my face, checking their lengths and preening the shape. "We heard about Julie," she said, tilting her head toward the empty room. "I know someone who was in a class with her. I'm really sorry."

I looked down at the lifeless hair on the floor. "Me too."

Kaley bounced back into the room, carrying a large square mirror.

I laughed as she came around in front of me. "You took my bathroom mirror off the wa—WOW."

The first sight of my new look left me stunned. My hair was so short, shorter than I thought I'd ever dare cut it, but layered with long, sweeping locks that fell just right around my face. I looked sexy, and strong, like the kind of girl who could brave anything.

"It's … it looks ama—" I burst into tears.

"She doesn't like it," Priya and Kaley said to each other at the same time.

"No, I love it. It's awesome. I just … shit. I'm sorry." I sniffled back the ugly tears and came clean. "I haven't had my hair cut at all since I was fifteen, since I had cancer."

Kaley's grip on the mirror slipped, but Priya caught it and set it down on the floor.

"This is the kind of thing you might tell someone

before letting them do an already high-pressure style change on you," Priya said softly.

"Sorry. I really do love it. Thank you for doing this for me." I wiped at my eyes, but the tears wouldn't stop. I wasn't even sure anymore if they were sad tears or happy tears, or tears of pure relief, or tears of utter desolation. "I've just been going through a lot lately."

Kaley gave me a brief hug. "Losing a friend, getting a cancer test—sheezuz, girl, crying is totally the okay reaction."

Priya kneeled in front of me, and asked almost in a whisper, "Have you had your results yet?"

I shook my head.

"Shit," she said.

"Double shit," said Kaley. "Well, a change is probably a good thing, right? I get why you'd want a change right now. And you really do look so fregging hot. Like wow. Like whatchoo-doin'-tonight-can-I-have-your-babies hot." She winked and shimmied her bust at me.

I snorted a laugh, and the tears slowed.

Priya and Kaley helped clean up, and we all stood around the trashcan for a minute of silence together before letting my cut hair slide off the dustpan and into the rubbish. I made coffee, and they stayed, chatting in the kitchen while I had a shower—carefully keeping my blow-dry unsplashed. When I stepped out, clean and fresh, I felt like a new person.

With something else ticked off my unknown list, I felt braver, and better. I still wondered what else was on it, and what would be next. I wondered if Dad knew, and how much he'd been involved in Blake getting that list. The only reason I hadn't spoken to Dad about it was because I was avoiding seeing him at all. It was too hard after lying to him about my tests, and still having no results to share with him.

Kaley and Priya were leaned in close together over the counter, whispering almost conspiratorially when I returned to the kitchen.

Kaley nodded approvingly at my hair again. "We done good, sis."

Priya gave her a high five.

I had to agree. "Can I pay you for this? I would've been paying a hairdresser anyway."

"It's fine. Don't worry about it."

My phone buzzed with a message.

Blake: Ready for the next item on your list? Better be, cos thunderbirds are go tonight! Can't wait to see the new you, as much as I liked the old you.

I frowned in confusion at the rest of the message, offering the time, location, and the final instruction to dress 'in as little clothing as possible, in sympathy.'

Me: We're clubbing?

Blake: Not quite. Don't stress. It will be fun. For you at

least.

Me: Is this something I can bring friends to?

Blake: It's a public venue.

Me: *Should* I bring friends?

Blake: Only if you feel like punishing me.

My mouth slipped into a mischievous side grin. A little payback for him holding my list hostage sounded good. I turned back to the twins.

"Maybe I can pay you back by taking you out tonight. I can't tell you what's going to happen, but I'm sure it's going to be fun."

Chapter Thirty-Seven

GEORGINA

Priya and Kaley went home to get ready and said they'd meet me there.

I picked out the tiny tight minidress I'd worn the first night I met Blake. It was the smallest piece of clothing I owned, while still being considered outerwear.

When I put it on and checked myself out in the rehung bathroom mirror, I looked nothing like the girl who wore that dress the first time. She'd been so nervous, dressing up and playing a part. With my new haircut, and tattoo peeking out where my shoulders were bare, I didn't just look the part—I felt it. Maybe this new Georgina could move forward in life, and leave tragedy behind. Maybe her results would come in as benign and she would never have to face cancer the way the old Georgina had.

Maybe I couldn't leave tragedy behind. Maybe no one could. But maybe I could be strong enough to face it.

Do you think that could be me, Mom? Could I be that person?

The club Blake had sent me to was out in the funkiest section of town, near the sex store where we had been that one time. I walked hesitantly along the filthy pavement up to the entrance, triple-checking the address was right. I could hear doofy music playing within, and colored lights flashed out through the dark entryway guarded by a tired bouncer who gave me a too-old-for-this-shit look. Not many people were going in, but the women who did weren't in the age range to be carded anyway.

Kaley popped up beside me. She wore a hot pink dress that seemed to be more straps than coverage, her long hair in thick, perfect curls falling all around her. Priya arrived behind her looking as different as a twin could, with her hair straight and precise, and wearing designer ripped jeans, and an 80s-style mesh-and-neon-shirt combo.

Priya tilted her head at the venue. "This what we're doing? A strip club?"

"Is that what this is?" I studied the front of the building again and spotted a small chalkboard near the door that said, 'Ladies night.'

"You didn't know?"

"No. This is kind of a thing. I'm doing this thing where there's a list, and … look, I'll catch you up later."

Priya shrugged. "Looks like fun."

Kaley had the look of a toddler at Christmas and ran straight inside. Her squeals trailed behind her. "This will be epiiiiic!"

None of us were carded as we passed the bouncer. He barely glanced up from the e-reader in his hands.

Inside, the place smelled like old beer, and most of the surfaces felt like it too. The lights were dim but not dim enough to hide the fact that this bar had needed a renovation about three decades ago. It was two-thirds empty, so it wasn't hard for us to grab a table right up close to the stage. The stage was lit up by garish purple and pink lights, lined with feather boas, and featured a short catwalk and a few poles. I wasn't sure 'near the stage' was where I wanted to be.

Around the bar were middle-aged women who had perfected the cougar look. They were drinking and shouting boisterously, catcalling at the empty stage. While Priya and Kaley went to order drinks, I grabbed my phone.

Me: Where are you, and what am I doing here? Did I

have 'make a drug deal' on my list?

Blake: All will be revealed soon. Literally.

Okay, so he's sent me here to watch a strip show.

It made some sense. I'd been fourteen when the *Magic Mark* movie came out. My best friend at the time, Christy, and I had desperately wanted to see it because everyone had raved about the sexy stripping scenes. She snuck a copy from someone else at school against her parents' wishes. Because, as she'd said, life was short. We'd watched the movie together at a sleepover, hiding under a blanket, giggling and gushing through the whole thing. I'd had a huge crush on Magic Mark for a long time after that. I could easily have put something to do with that on my list.

That was right before I was diagnosed. When I went through treatment, Christy wasn't my best friend anymore. She just moved on. There were no fights or dramas; she just faded out of my life. Teenage years are hard enough without trying to stay friends with someone with cancer. Christy was just a kid. I didn't blame her. But sometimes I still did miss her.

The twins returned with beers, and I tried to explain to them why we were here, and the childhood bucket list Blake was intent on having me complete despite me not knowing what was on it. It was difficult to tell the whole story, or enough of it to make sense without completely humiliating myself or crying. I think they had the gist of it when we were thankfully interrupted.

A man stepped up on the stage. He looked like he could have been a movie star, twenty years earlier. His voice was almost lost as the women around the room whistled and hollered at his appearance.

"Hello ladies! Are we ready to paaaaaaaaarttaaayy?"

Excited screaming came from all around me, especially from Kaley who was up on her feet whooping with her arms in the air. The MC laughed, lifted his suit jacket at the back, and shook his sculpted ass at us. "I bet you want to see something a little sexier than me up here. This is way too much clothing, am I right?"

Assent at high decibels made my ears ring.

"Let's get this party started then with your favorite hunka-hunka burning love—Dirk Daring!"

I sat there, dumbstruck, as a man with a body that looked like he'd worked out six hours a day since the age of two spun out onto the stage, his muscles gleaming with oil. The leather chaps he wore framed his ass cheeks. They wriggled and flexed, and as he tore his shirt off, his pecs bounced up and down. He wore a brown fedora and carried a long bullwhip. When he let the whip loose with a loud crack, women up and down the stage screamed and tossed handfuls of dollar bills at him.

He pranced around the stage, sticking his ass up high

in the air, bending over, and then getting down on the stage to hump the floor. I tried not to stare, but I couldn't take my eyes off the man. As much as I wanted to pretend I was proper and sophisticated and not part of the caterwauling masses, I was getting turned on.

But where the heck was Blake? Was he too chicken to come along to this with me?

All around me, women were yelling.

"Take it off!"

"Yeah, work it, work it!"

Kaley joined in with, "Bring some of that beefcake my way!"

Dirk Daring jumped off the stage. He stripped down to just a bright red thong, and he started waving his crotch in women's faces. They stuffed money into his thong or held notes in their mouths for him to take with his own.

Then it was my turn for the 'up close and personal' show. I was giggling like a schoolgirl but managed to drag out a bill and slip it in the string around the man's hips. I didn't even see how much I gave him.

He spoke softly, just for the two of us to hear. "First time, darling?"

I bit my lip and giggled a little more.

"We'll make it extra special for you, just wait."

He winked and was off to the next woman, wads

of cash creating a frilly fringe around his waist. He made it back onto the stage, did a couple more one-handed push-ups, cracked his whip again, and ran off.

From somewhere out of sight, the MC spoke up again. "We've got someone new for you all tonight. Introducing, for the first time, Jungle Jim! Ladies, wouldn't you like to climb all over this Jungle Jim?"

The next guy swung in, Tarzan style, on a long rope painted green like a vine. Shouts almost tore the roof off the place.

I wasn't sure if I was ready for another show already. The first had been fun, if a bit confronting. I slunk lower in my seat to obscure the bright red shade I knew had colored my face, hiding behind my beer glass. *Have I completed the list item requirement yet? Can I go now?* Kaley and Priya seemed to still be having fun, so I hunkered down.

Kaley poked me in the shoulder over and over. "Omigod, omigod, omigod!"

The women went totally nuts, and I peered up over the rim of my drink to see what was going on.

The new stripper's body was familiar. He moved in a way that was—

It couldn't be.

It was!

Blake. The new stripper was Blake. He wore nothing

but a loincloth and a jaguar skin that was thrown over his shoulders where his caramel hair just reached, looking wild and tousled.

No. Way.

My mouth literally dropped open. I saw my expression mirrored in Kaley and Priya's faces as they recognized him too.

"I am so jealous right now," Priya yelled over the noise.

All the women around me were screaming and throwing money at Blake as he twirled down to the ground on the rope.

The last guy's moves were mostly just hip grinding and workout moves, but Blake put his dancing skills to perfect use.

When he ripped the jaguar skin off his shoulders and flexed his back muscles, I stood up from my chair and hollered with the rest of them.

Blake caught sight of me and did a double take. He mouthed, "*Wow,*" and fanned his face. I scrunched my nose and played with the ends of my now very short hair.

With a wink, Blake tossed the fake animal fur in my direction. Some other women tried to intercept it, but it landed safe in my hands, still warm and smelling of Blake. I looked up at him and realized just how nervous he seemed. I couldn't stop grinning and started egging him on with my calls like the other women.

He was as oiled up as the first man, and while he wasn't

as sculpted, Blake was way hotter in my eyes. He'd stepped up his dance moves since the cafeteria performance, and the money was flying. I could feel the flush of lust burning under my skin, shortening my breath.

Blake came off the stage and danced briefly for a half a dozen women. I tried to control my jealousy. He wasn't mine. I had no right to be jealous. Finally, he came over to me, and I sat back in my chair, suddenly nervous too.

He paused for a moment as he looked me up and down. Then he grabbed the back of my seat and dragged it and me away from the table and out into an open area. A spotlight followed us across the floor.

My eyes popped wide with panic. I was about to become part of the show.

Blake knelt in front of my chair, spinning and dancing on his knees as he worshipped me from below. Then the music changed, becoming more aggressive, and he grabbed my knees, forced them apart, and jumped up onto the space of chair between them. I gasped as he stood up, swaying his hips close to my face so all I could see was him and that spotty loincloth. My lips quivered in fear, and a longing built deep in my belly.

Blake jumped off the chair, and with a strong shove at the backrest I was falling backwards, then caught by strong arms before I reached the floor. Blake had me around the waist and off the chair, lifting my whole body with ease up onto him, wrapping my legs around his waist as he pumped against me, still dancing. The whooping of the crowd around me overwhelmed the music, and the drumming of my racing heart.

I was dropped down onto my knees, and Blake grabbed a fistful of my cut hair, rolling his hips toward my face. I groaned and gasped, each change in position and action happening too fast for me to keep up as Blake play-acted having his way with me in front of a screaming crowd.

With an impressive handstand and flip, Blake was then behind me where I kneeled, and he bent me over, grinding against me from behind. My face flushed, but not in shame. I could only feel the drunkenness of my lust for him.

When I couldn't take anymore, with a gentle lift and twirl, I was back in my seat.

My breath rattled hoarsely as I gazed up at Blake.

"What the fuck?" I mouthed, lust and laughter on my lips.

He bent toward me and I strained forward too, thinking he was going to kiss me, my whole body desperate for his. "Dressing room two," he said.

I looked over every part of him. I had come here tonight determined to remain cold and distant to him, to keep the message about our relationship, or lack of one, clear. The desire swimming in his eyes was almost more than I could take. Every fiber of my being was telling me to give in, to leap on top of Blake and take his remaining clothes off with my teeth. I wanted to feel the hard ripple of his stomach under my fingers and the swell of his manhood between my legs. I wanted him more than any logic or sense could fight.

I noticed the fur that had been dropped on the ground when I became a prop in Blake's show. I scooped it back up and held it close.

The song ended, and Blake jogged off stage to earsplitting applause.

I was halfway out of my seat already, then glanced back at Priya and Kaley. "Do you mind ... if I ...?" I was too breathless to talk.

They shared a look. Priya said, "Sure, but can we crash at yours tonight? It's just closer than our place."

I nodded without even thinking and mumbled where they could find the spare keys.

Kaley smacked my ass. "Go get that sexy man-flesh, girl. We're good."

A man in a cop uniform came on stage next, and as the rest of the women focused on him, I stood up, panting. My vision blurred with need, and I found my way backstage.

Was Blake a stripper? Had he always been one? Had he been lying about the roofing job to cover it up? Or had he done all this just for me? I was confused, but dressing room two would hopefully hold my answers.

I knocked on the door, my heart in my throat. I wasn't sure if I'd ever been so nervous to see Blake, and I didn't know why.

"Georgie?" Blake answered the door, still wearing just the flap of leather loincloth from his performance. I choked out a breath and stood staring at his body for all of a minute before my voice came back. *That body.* Yeah, that was probably why I was nervous. It made my knees turn to jelly and filled my chest with burning sparks of passion.

I still clung to the fake jaguar fur, so I handed it back to him. "What just happened out there? Was being part of a strip show on my list?"

A gorgeous expression of bashfulness came across Blake's face. "Your list had a line that said you wanted to date Magic Mark."

I stared at his lips as he spoke, the soft pink of them, the slight pout to his bottom lip, the light stubble beneath it. I barely registered his words. I was imagining those lips, all over my body.

"You're not Magic Mark," I mumbled.

"This was as close as I could get." He shrugged. The curve between his shoulder and bicep glimmered with sweat and oil, and I remembered how it felt to sink my teeth into his skin there.

"We're not dating," I breathed the words out. Flames

licked underneath my skin. We stood closer together. Had I stepped closer? Had he?

His face moved near mine. His voice was a low rumble. "I really did try my hardes—"

Our bodies pressed together. I wrapped my arms around him, feeling the heat radiating off his bare skin, the slick of oil and sweat as I dug my fingers into his back. Blake let out a ragged groan and mashed his lips down onto mine. He reached behind me and slammed the dressing room door closed, then slammed me against it. Our hands were frantic, clutching fistfuls of each other, wrenching at clothing. Blake's loincloth and G-string beneath tore away with ease, leaving him bare and hard between us. With a feral growl, he bent low, mashed his face into my cleavage, and popped the top buttons of my dress open with his teeth, letting my breasts fall free from their confinement. He kept his face there, wrapping his lips around mouthfuls of my soft flesh as though devouring me whole. My eyes rolled back, desire thrumming through me.

I could feel Blake's hardness rubbing against my leg and I tried to reach for him, wanting to have him in my mouth again, sick with passion and knowing his body was my medicine. As I tried to move down, Blake caught me under the shoulders and lifted me off my feet, pressing my back against the door. In one swift move, he dropped to his knees himself, threw my thighs around his shoulders and pressed his face between them. My panties were still on but the friction they caused between my skin and his mouth only drove me crazier. Somewhere in the distance, a tiny voice called out, telling me to stop, that I shouldn't be doing this. But it could have been calling from another planet for as much as I heard it over my frenzy of lust.

Blake's lips and tongue took me to the edge of insanity, working me fast then slow, hard then soft. He brought his hands up, pulling away the fabric of my underwear and pressing his fingers into me, opening me, plunging in and massaging me from inside. Each thrust pushed me farther up the door and Blake followed until soon he was standing, holding me up high, pinned there in pleasure. I bit my tongue, trying not to scream in ecstasy.

The orgasm hit me so hard my vision blanked out completely. I just hung there, pressed against the door, held up on Blake's shoulders, my mouth open wide, unable to make a move or sound as pleasure pulsed through me over and over.

As it ebbed and I started to slump, Blake lowered me down from his shoulders onto his lap, his cock sliding straight up into me as he did. I couldn't hold back a sharp, high-pitched moan, the fullness of him inside me making my whole body shudder. We made love there, pressed against the door. I rocked against Blake's lap for what felt like hours, and when he finally came I was right alongside him.

We collapsed onto the floor beside each other, and when we finally looked into each other's eyes again, there were too many questions, and too much desire. So we said nothing, and made love on the floor again.

Chapter Thirty-Eight

GEORGINA

I made it home in the early hours of the morning. Blake and I were only driven from each other's arms by him running out of condoms, and the club management kicking us out. I had dressed quickly and fled as Blake collected his takings.

Last night had complicated things to no end. I couldn't even be around Blake without giving in to desire. I wanted him too badly. I wanted to do the rest of my childhood list, to find out what else was on it. But I didn't want to hurt Blake by continuing to mess with both our feelings. I wasn't sure what to do next.

Blake was.

I had just tiptoed through the living room where Priya and Kaley were top-to-tailing on the couch. His message pinged into my phone before I stumbled into bed.

Blake: I love your new do. I'm taking you to the beach in the morning. Bright and early. Be ready.

My first thought was *Sex on the Beach*, one of the unfinished items on my sexy bucket list. But we weren't doing that anymore. I'd put it behind me.

For now. A small ball of anxiety ticked deep inside me, a countdown urging me on to completion.

This beach trip had to be something else. I didn't know what, since I'd been out to the lake a million times, and had even gone there with Blake.

I fell asleep while making excuses not to go—about how the beach at the lake was too rocky, the weather was declining, and summer was nearly over. The warmth had left the air and transferred into the leaves on the trees, changing their greens to sunset oranges and reds. They weren't falling yet but they would be soon. And I'd already fallen too hard.

It was way too soon to be awake again, but someone kept banging at the front door.

The banging merged with the sound of rain hammering the roof and walls. I put my slippers on then stumbled out of my room, throwing a fluffy robe over the old

T-shirt and cat-covered boxers I'd slept in. Priya shuffled out of the bathroom at the same time, looking like she'd been up all night too, but from uncomfortable sleeping arrangements rather than fucking a hot part-time stripper on a dressing room floor.

I got to the door and opened it.

I squinted out at the gray rain lashing down across my front porch and Blake.

He was dressed for the beach, in boardshorts, flip-flops, and a singlet top, and he even had a line of bright-yellow zinc across his nose. All of this, and he was already soaking wet. I eyed the motorbike on the lawn.

He rode over in this weather?

"You're not ready?" he asked as a greeting. "Or is your bikini hidden under those adorable PJs?"

"I just woke up. I didn't think we were still going. It's freezing. And raining. A lot." I frowned at the weather. I'd wanted to go to the beach with Blake more than I'd realized, despite my excuses.

"For one thing, I grew up in London. This isn't cold. Secondly, we're going no matter what. The water will still be warm enough to swim in, and the forecast looks promising. It will clear by the time we get there, trust me."

"By the time we get where? Not the lake?" This rain was set in; it wouldn't clear for hours at least. I'd been assuming we were going to the lake, but that was only a fifteen-minute drive away.

"I'm taking you to the ocean," Blake said. "I'm doing this for you. No excuses."

The ocean.

I'd never been. It was only a three-hour drive, but with the lake so close, and everything else complicating my life, I'd just never gone, despite always wanting to. I'd always wanted to swim in the sea. To watch real waves crash on the shore.

Screw the weather. I was going to the ocean.

"I'll go get ready. But we're taking Jiminy, not your bike. I'd prefer to drown at the beach, not on the way there."

I invited Blake inside, and he spotted the twins and the blanket fort of a lounge room. "Had a sleepover last night?"

Priya chuckled. "We could have if you didn't keep Georgie out so late."

My face flushed, remembering the banging of the dressing room door as we slammed against it.

I bit my lip and handed Blake a towel to dry off. His soaked and clinging singlet wasn't helping things at all. "Can we change up our plans a bit?"

I chatted with Blake about what we were doing, and we agreed to make it a group thing. I wasn't sure I could trust myself alone with Blake anymore. And with more people it would feel less like a date. Blake sent a message to some friends, and I asked Kaley and Priya if they wanted to come.

I got working in the kitchen, making hot coffee for everyone and trying to dig up some lunch and snacks for us. A container of leftovers from Dad's restaurant in the freezer had a mix of croquettes, meatballs, and truffle mini-quiches, which would defrost by lunchtime and be good cold. I scored when behind that I found a small batch of peanut butter balls I'd obviously forgotten about or they wouldn't still be there. I filled a couple of bottles with water and grabbed some napkins and cutlery. I didn't have a hamper so I put it all in an antique cooler I found under the sink that I'm pretty sure belonged to the old lady landlord.

Kaley floated into the kitchen like a cartoon character following her nose to the coffee pot. We let the caffeine wake us up, then got dressed and headed out into the pouring rain.

Blake and I loaded everything into my car, and waved off Kaley and Priya, who were going in their car. I took the wheel. *Mom, could you give us some help on the weather today?*

I was still a bit shaky on the road. Cars just didn't feel safe anymore, especially in the rain. But soon I barely noticed the drops splattering against the windscreen.

Blake seemed full of mischief today and sang along to the radio. Only he was singing different lyrics to each song, making them up as he went along, making them about me, or him, or lizards in top hats.

By the time he had finished perverting twenty minutes' worth of the latest pop hits I was weak with laughter. "You should do that for a living."

A ray of light had broken through the thick clouds, and hit the window beside Blake, making the edges of his golden hair glow. But his expression was dark.

His head dropped and his voice became low. "I did once. Not the silly stuff. But the songwriting."

I swallowed hard. Acted casual. "Yeah?"

"Me and my first girl, we used to write songs together." He looked out into the distance, then back to me. "You know Seyvia?"

I nodded. "I kind of already knew. That you had been with her. I wouldn't have picked it myself, but Dad's date at that dinner we had? She recognized you right away."

Blake chuckled ruefully. "Here I was trying to keep all that from you. Don't we suck at keeping secrets?"

I gulped again and focused on driving. "I know there are times when we're just not ready to share the truth. I didn't want to say anything until you were ready to tell me about it—about her." I reached across the gap between us and put my hand on his leg. "I'm sorry you lost her."

Blake grabbed my hand and squeezed it hard. "I didn't just lose her. It was my fault."

I tried to say no, it couldn't have been, but he shook his

head, words spilling out. "That night, I could see things getting out of control. I threatened Seyvia that if she didn't stop and come home with me then, that I would leave her." His voice cracked. "She didn't even care."

He paused for a long moment. "I wasn't going to leave her, not really, but that realization, that she didn't care if I stayed or left, it hurt me, and my pride made me walk away. I left her that night, and I never saw her again."

The night she overdosed. And the world woke up the next day to find their pop princess dead, and the saddest part was no one was really surprised. "It's not on you. Everyone knew what was going on; it wasn't your responsibility. She made her choices."

"If I'd just stayed with her, I could have been there for her, stopped things going too far. I could have saved her."

"You can't know that. And you can't save everyone. Sometimes, terrible things just happen."

Blake nodded, then reached up, and wiped his eye. "I didn't want to be that guy. A widower, at twenty? I shut it all away: the fame, the music, singing, songwriting, dancing, her … I ran so far from it all. For years. The only reminders have been the bloody royalty checks coming in like clockwork from the songs we wrote together. At least I've been able to get by on those while making a new life and haven't had to take too many roofing jobs."

He turned to look at me. "But it wasn't much of a life until you came along. Hiding from everything, I'd missed out on so much. I'd forgotten just how much I loved music, loved dancing and singing. You and your crazy lists—you've helped me rediscover that."

I breathed out slowly, the weight of emotions pressing the air from my lungs. I tried to be breezy. "What do you think you'll do next? Go for a career in economics, or get back to songwriting?"

"I'm not sure. I like both in different ways. Maybe I should just run away to join the circus. I once wanted to be a world-class juggler."

"You can juggle?"

"Not at all. Doesn't stop me from wanting it though. We don't always want things that make sense." Blake cleared his throat. "What did you want to be when you grew up?"

The rain had eased a little. I clicked the wipers down to a slower setting. "When I was young I wanted to be a chef like Dad, but I haven't got the attention span required. I always put things in the oven then forget they're there."

"I hope you have a quality smoke alarm," Blake said.

I laughed. "I should have wanted to be a ballerina or something, at least it doesn't come with the risk of burning the house down."

"I could have been a ballerina," he said with mock

sadness. "But I only have nine toes and these bad ankles."

I punched him in the shoulder. "You're goofy as hell."

"Anything to see that smile. But really, what do you want to do now?"

You wasn't the answer I should give, so I thought about it seriously. If I got the all-clear … if I had a life ahead of me …

"I wanted to be an artist for a very long time. After my treatment, I felt like I didn't have time for silly, frivolous dreams like becoming a professional painter. I struggled just to catch back up with normal schoolwork." I kept my eyes on the gray road laying straight out in front of me, watching it disappear beneath the car as we sped over it. "Now, I guess I would like to be an illustrator. I had this idea once: I wanted to write and illustrate a kids' book about a bald lion, to help kids deal with cancer."

"That sounds beautiful." He caught my fingers in one hand and kissed them. The touch of his lips sent a thrill racing down my spine.

I shivered, drew away, and tried to cover it by reaching for the bottle of water in the cupholder. "Or I could become a riverboat gambler."

"That's a good profession too. You just have to be a fast swimmer, if you're going to win a lot."

Would I ever know anyone else like him? Someone I could laugh with like this, talk about painful pasts with, and joke about our uncertain futures?

I grinned slyly back at him. "I'm already good with disguises. I have some experience with wigs, you know."

"I can see it now. You'd be the mysterious woman who shows up with cards in one hand, boobs busting out of a low-cut dress, and a cigar in your mouth. Take all the boys' money before vanishing into the crowd, suddenly a redhead with dark glasses."

"And I could become a spy if that didn't pan out."

"Do both. Make good use of your wig skills."

I'd never joked about the wigs like this before. It was a freedom I hadn't experienced and I felt myself opening up. "There was this guy in school—you know the kind—real jerk. He grabbed my wig one day and yanked it right off my head. He tossed it to his buddy and they started doing this whole 'keep away' thing right in the middle of the lunchroom."

I stopped. I'd thought I could share that like some funny anecdote, but my face and neck glowed with the shame that should have faded. I could feel it all over again, the baldness of my head, the shock, the pity, the laughter, and the whispers and the stares directed at me.

Blake said, "Some people are born assholes. Whatever happened to him?"

"He still lives with his mom. Unemployed, last I heard. He's bald now, too," I blurted out.

"Really?"

"As a cue ball."

"Karma works wonders sometimes."

Chapter Thirty-Nine

GEORGINA

As we rolled along the highway, the rain slowed then halted and the sun began to crawl out from behind the clouds, sending lemony-yellow light streaming into the car. *Thank you, Mom.* It suddenly felt just like beach weather.

We drove down through hills and I got my first view of the ocean, stretching off into forever. The air was instantly fresher, cleaner, and salty. We drove over a long bridge across a bay. The water stretched as far as I could see, high blue waves crested with foaming white caps. Seagulls pinwheeled overhead, and graceful cranes swooped toward the water, diving for fish.

Blake directed me from there until we reached an almost empty parking lot. Priya and Kaley's car was already there. The rain must have kept other people away, leaving the beach to us. I stepped out of the car, then ran for the water, kicking my sandals off along the way to feel the sand between my toes. The sand tickled. It had been warmed by the sun, and then it was cool and wet where it had been washed by gentle waves.

The shore was a sickle-shaped crescent, a small strip hugged by rocky cliffs either side and a long, thin wooden jetty reached out into the vast blue-green waters. Salty spray shot up in the air beside it. Dolphins danced across the waves in the distance.

Tears prickled my eyes at the beauty of it all. That all this magnificence could exist—that I was here to experience it … it was miraculous. And also so crushingly sad that I'd only be here so briefly, knowing such wonder. I smiled and laughed in the face of the terrifying splendor all around me.

My grin grew larger when I spotted Kaley and Priya, already in their swimsuits and sunbathing on a picnic rug not far away. I jogged over to join them.

Blake arrived with the cooler, and we stripped down to our bathers and soaked up the light. The sun warmed our shoulders and our faces as we laid out the picnic.

"Hey bitches, wha-what!" a woman yelled. A couple walked over the dune toward us, each person carrying two six-packs of beer.

The man hollered, "Buddy!"

Blake replied, "Buddy!"

I tried to pick where I'd seen them before. "Is that …?"

Blake nodded. "Veronica and Buddy."

"It's Vicki and James, jackass." Vicki dumped the beer on the picnic rug and stretched, bending her back like a model in her super-tiny bikini. "This guy—serious case of mistaken identity syndrome." Seeing her again, I could almost see how Blake had once confused us, at least from behind. She had hair like mine had been, and was a similar curvy shape. She held herself with a confidence I envied though.

James slapped Blake on the shoulder and sat beside him, cracking open a beer. "Dude, that night—can't blame him for not remembering our names. I barely remembered our names."

Blake laughed. "Glad you could make it."

"Glad I don't still have that never-ending hangover." Vicki sat down right on James's lap and draped an arm over his shoulder. Their hookup from that night at Blake's had clearly become an ongoing thing. James's face lit up as he looked at his girl, and I smiled. That was what love looked like.

My heart swelled. The sun shone down on us as we

shared food and drinks and laughs.

I could have stayed like that all day until Blake leaned over to me, and whispered, "This doesn't count as a trip to the ocean until you've actually been in the ocean. Let's go."

We walked out over the grayed and weathered planks of the jetty, the water making hushed splashes and gurgles beneath us as the color of the ocean darkened, the sandy floor disappearing out of sight under the swell of aquamarine. The sun had grown richer in color, turning orange as it lowered in the sky, and I looked back to see the others gathering driftwood. Vicki was chasing James around with a huge mess of seaweed, and I giggled. I was starting to like that girl.

Blake followed my gaze and laughed too. "I'm glad they came. I haven't made a lot of friends since moving from England. That night we met—after the mix-up and before the extreme intoxication—the three of us had a good time together."

"They're fun. I like them too."

I stopped and stared down at the water. It looked so deep, bottomless. I had planned to run all the way along the jetty and jump from the end, but had lost my nerve.

Blake waited patiently with me. He put his hands in his boardshorts pockets and said, "We talked a lot in the car, but we didn't talk about last night."

I folded my arms over my bare middle, feeling exposed.

"Do we need to?"

"I'm just feeling very uncertain right now about where we stand—what is okay or isn't okay with us."

I closed my eyes for a moment, turning to the sun and letting it shine bright red through my eyelids, and sighed. "These last couple of days have been so amazing, just a whirlwind of fun, and I can't even catch up on where I am or what I'm feeling other than happy. Can we just leave it there? Can I just be happy right now without worrying what we mean to each other, or what is going to happen next?"

Blake nodded slowly, then smirked. "You might have to worry a bit about what's next still, because I have your list and you don't."

I gasped in outrage, then laughed.

Before I could retaliate in any way, Blake jumped straight off the jetty, splashing down into the sea. His head came back up and he swam around, grinning at me like a lunatic. "Come on in. The water is awesome."

"You're going to get eaten by a shark!" I looked around, sure I would spot one of those dastardly fins lurking right nearby.

Blake laughed from deep in his chest.

"Or stung by a stingray. Or poisoned by a jellyfish. The ocean is full of terrifying, terrible terrors, you know that, right?"

"You're thinking about Australia." Blake chuckled, and then frowned, his eyes growing wide. "Bloody hell. I think something just bumped my leg."

He swam fast for the edge of the jetty and I ran to him, heart pounding. He reached up his hand for help and I took it, knowing only as his grin widened that I'd been a fool.

With a quick tug, he flipped me off my feet. The water closed over my head. Darkness descended, and salt filled my nose and mouth. I broke the surface to see him laughing at me.

"You … you …" I sputtered and he swam over, wrapped himself around me, and took us both under again.

I kept my eyes open. His were open too, and at first all I looked at was him, then I saw a school of fish swim past, and the waving strands of kelp. I kicked to the surface and the sun touched my face, and I inhaled sweet fresh air all over again.

"It's beautiful," I admitted.

"And warm," Blake added.

"And still terrifying."

"That's okay, because you're the bravest person I know."

We rocked on an endless tide, the water lifting us and setting us back down. I wasn't prepared for just how salty the water would be, how I floated and bobbed in the current. It was so different to swimming in the lake.

Up and down in the water we went. Once I swam down as far as I could and stayed there until my lungs were ready to burst, staring at the pretty pictures the sun made on the water over my head. The sparkles and colors made me feel alive, and inspired. I wanted to paint those shapes and hues, capture that beauty.

Blake swam around me, keeping his distance while always being nearby. He watched as I explored the water, floating on my back or diving under waves, laughing when I played in the shallows and helping me back up when I got dunked for the first time. The fading light sparkled in the droplets falling from his hair to his shoulders, in the water clinging to his eyelashes. I'd never seen anything more beautiful.

Soon it grew cold, and I joined Kaley and Priya at the fire they'd built. I wrapped a towel around me and stared into the glowing coals on the sand. Blake stayed back on the jetty with James, each trying to one-up the other with crazy jumps into the water. Vicki cheered and jeered, announcing the results with some made-up and probably biased scoring system. Dusk collected in the corners of the sky and bled into the center. Dark purple shadows clung to the surrounding cliffs, looming over our sheltered camp.

Kaley and Priya had been talking together most of the day, maybe even arguing, from what I saw once or twice. They seemed happy enough now, with Priya nursing a beer, and Kaley trying to cook a peanut-butter ball on a stick like a marshmallow.

"It will melt," I told her.

"If I just do it slowly though, maybe I can toast the outside—"

It slipped off the stick and sizzled in the fire.

"That was your third try; it's not going to work. Let it go." Priya laughed.

"I won't let it go. Some things you just have to do," Kaley said, very pointedly.

It started off a staring match that I didn't understand the cause of.

I shut my mouth and waited for the tension between the two of them to clear again.

Priya sighed. "Fine, I'll ask her."

I was at a loss. "Ask me?"

"You know how you've been going through some things lately?" Priya shot a glare at Kaley. "Well, we have too. And we kinda need somewhere to stay. Do you think we could lay low at your place for a bit longer?"

"Oh. I guess? I mean, yeah. Of course." What were they going through? Did they have nowhere else to stay? Why didn't they? There was so much about them I didn't know.

"We don't want to impose. We know you're not in the best place right now either," Kaley said.

"Oh fine," Priya snapped. "Make me ask her then you

be the one coming out with my reasons why we shouldn't."

"It's really okay." I put my hands up. "Maybe it's best for us *stuff-going-on* people to stick together, yeah?"

Kaley sniffled and glomped onto me. "Thank you."

"No problem. Do you need to talk about it?"

Kaley pouted. "It's going to sound crazy."

"That's because it is. *She* is." Priya peeled the label off her beer bottle, scrunched it up and tossed it into the fire.

"Who?" I asked.

"Our nanna, who we've lived with since our parents died."

"I'm so sorry, I had no idea."

Kaley shrugged, and mumbled. "Death is kind of a thing for our family. Nanna says we're cursed."

"We're not cursed." Priya's voice came out through gritted teeth. "Nanna is our curse. She's crazy and abusive. That's why we can't stay there."

"She's just traditional, that's all."

"She told you your cancer scare was your own fault!" Priya yelled.

A heavy silence followed.

How could someone in their family be so cruel as to even suggest that? I knew I still didn't have the full story, but I'd heard enough.

"You're definitely staying with me. As long as you

need."

Priya mouthed a thank you, then shuffled over beside her sister. "I'm sorry. But we can't keep making excuses for her."

"I know."

James and Vicki returned then, with her riding on his shoulders, and Blake following behind. The tone shifted back to beachside party, and the twins seemed more comfortable than before, laughing more freely.

Soon, we'd finished every last scrap of the food I'd brought, emptied the last beer, and Vicki and James coupled off and disappeared from whence they came.

Priya and Kaley excused themselves as well, saying they had some stuff to organize, and I nodded knowingly to them.

That left Blake and me alone. Just the thing I'd tried to avoid.

Chapter Forty

GEORGINA

We started packing up, covering the dying fire with sand. The sun was down, but there was still enough light left in the ocean-colored sky to see by.

Blake lifted and shook out the picnic blanket, and sand sprayed all over me.

"Watch it," I said, picking up a handful of sand and tossing it back at him.

"Don't start something you don't want to finish," he challenged.

I scooped a great ball of sand and flung it at his chest.

"That's it." He sprinted for me, and I squeaked, dashing away. On my short little legs, I had no chance. Blake barreled down on me, spreading the blanket like a net. He wrapped me up in it with him, and we both tumbled down into the gully between two dunes.

We were pressed together between the blanket, our bodies hot, sticky, and gritty. I spat sand from my mouth.

"This is very uncomfortable," I said.

Blake's voice was a grumble. "Well, if you're going to have sex on the beach you need all the stuff that goes with it—sand in your ass crack, sand burn on your knees, sunburn on your back, waves almost drowning you, seaweed in your hair, the potential of strangers stumbling over you. Sex on the beach should be a ridiculously uncomfortable experience, or you're not doing it right."

I looked up at his eyes, so blue, and so close to mine. "Are we going to have sex on the beach?"

Blake pressed the tip of his nose against mine, then ran it up the length until his lips were there instead. "That's up to you."

He was right.

At every turn, I blamed not being able to stop myself, blamed being out of emotional control, but the truth was it was always up to me. I'd always made my choices. I'd always wanted him. And I wanted him now, too. I was choosing him. I was choosing this.

I would choose him, and I would make this right. I would tell him the truth. I would make this work. How could I do anything else?

His breath blew across my cheek, then our mouths met and held in a long kiss. I tasted salt on his lips and tongue, tasted the ocean and sun and laughter in that kiss. His hands slid under my back, lifted me up and pressed me into him. The sand shifted below us. It trickled past my heels, tickling my ankles. The blanket fell down around us, spreading beneath us and blowing up at the corners with the small gusts of cool wind. The full moon came out, shining down a bright silver light over our sand-covered bodies.

His fingers caressed my hair, ran through it. More sand shifted and slithered, yielding below our bodies as our flesh yielded to each other's touch. When I sat up and took off my bikini top, he remained lying beside me and stroked his hand down my back, tracing the lines of my tattoo.

He hugged me, then pulled me back down onto the blanket beside him. My nipples tightened from the cold air blowing over them and then his mouth was on them, gentle but firm. Hot sensations crept along my spine. Excitement exploded within me, and I wrapped my arms around his upper body, pulling him closer.

He kissed me again, making me dizzy with lust. My

own mouth sought his. My tongue caressed his and asked for more.

His hands slid my bikini pants down to my knees and I shuffled them off the rest of the way. His finger pressed into me, slid all the way inside. I grasped at his shorts, finding them tacky with seawater, and I laughed as I struggled to pull them down.

Blake didn't help. He pushed me back onto the blanket. He bit his lip and rolled his fingers within me, making my eyelids flutter closed.

I heard hook-and-loop tearing, and felt Blake get something from his pocket, then push his shorts down. The crinkle of a condom packet opening made me moan in anticipation.

"Georgie," he whispered into my ear as he thrust into me.

He filled me completely, and made me feel whole. He moved slowly, his fingers circling and rubbing in time to his thrusts. I moaned, not caring if there was anyone nearby. Sweat appeared like dewdrops upon my body despite the breeze and the darkness, and I pressed my face up into Blake's chest, wrapping my arms and legs around him, trying to fuse myself to him.

He groaned and I could feel his stomach muscles tightening. He withdrew from me, moving down my body so swiftly

I didn't know what he was going to do until his tongue pressed into my pleasure-swollen flesh. The feel of his lips sent shockwaves and shivers across my hips and down to my toes.

Ecstasy shot through me. My mouth opened in a frenzied cry as his fingers went back into me, pumping and driving as I whimpered and writhed, riding his face and fingers until my whole body tremored and seized up, pleasure smashing through me harder than the waves crashing against the cliffs.

He came back up, kissing a path all the way up my body. I could only lie there, still shaking with uncontrollable vibrations, as though he'd set off an earthquake within me.

He parted my legs and slid in on a tide of hot desire, all the way inside me so that I could feel the pressure of him in the base of my back. He still didn't feel close enough.

The waves sang and sighed as they met the shore, and Blake and I matched that force of nature as our bodies met and sang together. As lustful sensation hummed through us with every movement. As love and need and sadness and beauty touched us with our every caress.

Blake clenched his teeth, clenched his whole body, as he growled and cried out with pleasure above me. I gasped for air. Tears ran down my cheeks, tears of joy and love, adding to the salt of the sea.

If I had to die, and I knew we all did, at least I could

do it having had this moment. The whole day had been perfect, even the rain at the beginning had made the sunlight seem that much stronger and sweeter.

Blake and I tangled into each other, a pile of pleasure-soaked limbs. There was nothing uncomfortable about it at all.

"That was amazing. I don't think we did it right," I said breathily.

Blake lay tiny kisses all over my neck. "Bugger. Should we try again?"

I wiped the tears from my cheeks but couldn't wipe the smile off my face.

"Thank you for today. I wouldn't have had any of this without you."

Blake squeezed me tighter in his embrace. "Can we call this a relationship now?"

"Yes."

After lying like that a while longer, we got our clothes back on and finished packing up. Before getting into the car, I checked my phone for the first time all day and saw a missed call.

The hospital had rung. I listened to the message even though I knew what it would say.

My results were in. They needed me to come in and hear them in person.

"What was that?" Blake asked, as I put the phone back

in my bag. I could feel the color gone from my face, the joy washed away, and I knew he could see it too.

"I'll tell you tomorrow."

I couldn't spoil today.

I asked Blake if he'd drive home, and then stared up at the stars the whole way.

Mom … please … please.

Chapter Forty-One

BLAKE

Georgina was silent the whole way home, and I was happy to sit in my own quiet contentment as I drove. It gave me time to think. And plan. Not just for the next item on her list, but for the future. My future. *Our* future.

I dropped her home and picked up my bike, and when I noticed a pawn shop still open late on the way back to my place, it seemed like a sign.

It took a while to find the things I was looking for back home. I'd put them in a safe place a long time ago, but safe really meant forgotten. Like I'd tried to forget that whole time.

But I finally found what I was looking for, buried in the garage under motorcycle parts, in a document box filled with record label contracts. I popped the ring box open, checking the contents, and saw part of my past that made my heart clench. One engagement ring. Two wedding rings. I snapped it closed again.

Then I was back at the pawn shop, waiting for the guy behind the counter to notice me.

I cleared my throat. The dark-skinned man with short-cut, pure white hair looked up at me from his crossword.

"No loans," he said in a tired voice.

"I was hoping you could give me a price on these." I showed him the ring box, and he waved for me to hand it over.

He reached through the steel grid that fenced the counter off and took the box, inspecting the contents, then raised a skeptical eyeball at me. He pushed the box back toward me and crossed his arms. "I'm not after fake shit or lifted property."

"They aren't. They're mine. They're real."

"Ha! Big young guy like you, coming in with merchandise like that? Come on." He went back to his crossword, grumbling something about kids these days stealing to pay for their gym juice.

I sighed, and reached for my phone. It took me a while to load up my unused Instasnap account, and then find the photo I was looking for. "See? They're mine."

"Hey! Is that Sey Sey?" The old man started singing. "*Without you, what is life for? Without you, what's a heart for? Without you-hooo-hooo, I am undone.*"

"Yeah." Everyone knew that song. The words I'd written. The words Seyvia had sung.

The man looked closer at the photo. It showed Seyvia and I in a cheek-to-cheek embrace, our hands out, flashing our brand-new wedding rings. "Oh, damn. That's you."

"Yeah."

"You're—?"

"Yeah."

"Right. Okay then." He shook his head, grumbling under his breath. He looked from the photo to the rings again. "I can't give you what these are worth. Not even close."

"Just give me what you can."

He laughed. "I like you, kid. I'm trying to be nice here, but you're the worst haggler I've ever met. Give me a minute."

He checked his cash drawer, then waved as he got up and hobbled around to a locked office behind him. He returned with a two-inch-thick wad of cash. "If you're happy to take this for these, you're a fool."

I chuckled. "Who's being bad at haggling now?"

The pawn shop owner shrugged. "I'm not that cutthroat. You've already lost enough. You sure you want to be parting with these?"

There was only a moment of hesitation as I went over the thoughts and feelings that had brought me here tonight. I was ready—ready to say goodbye. "Yeah."

He hesitated to hand over the cash. "You know, you'd do better auctioning them. I bet there are some fans out there that would die for these."

I was sure there were, but I had been hoping to part with these rings in a way that would see them just disappear into the system. I didn't want the media or anyone to know I was selling them. I didn't want some online auction going viral, digging up the past, and making ugly speculations about my life after Seyvia. It had been years; I was allowed to move on. I hoped this guy would just take the rings at any price, and then not turn around and auction them himself.

I'd said these rings weren't fake, but in some ways, they were. Getting married—it was never my idea, or Seyvia's. It was a plan from her PR people.

They had known that Seyvia was getting too wild. Dangerously wild. But they didn't care about *her*. They just cared about her brand. They wanted to take it in a new direction, something more wholesome. So it was decided Seyvia and I would get married. The childhood sweethearts, still so in love, making long-term commitments. It had worked for them and their plans.

I didn't object, not really. I'd loved Seyvia. I'd thought she loved me. I'd always planned to marry her, just maybe not that soon, that young. I'd thought we had all the time in the world, that we were going to be together forever.

I didn't even get to choose the rings. I didn't get to propose. It was all done by Seyvia's PR team, from the cut of the obscenely-large diamond to the celebrity-filled wedding extravaganza, to the careful photo shoot of the honeymoon.

My love for Seyvia had been real. But these rings were fake and meant nothing to me. I didn't need them anymore, but maybe the cash I got for them could be used for something that was real.

I didn't plan to rely on songwriting royalties my whole life, and they weren't enough anyway. Thanks to us being young and taking a bad deal, the amount I got from them only just got me by. The payment from the rings, and the cash from my night as a stripper, would help me finish Georgina's childhood list, and maybe help with the start of something new. That would be enough. After that, I had a whole life ahead of me to build my own career, to follow my own goals.

The guy looked at my expectantly. "We good?"

"Thanks, mate, we are. It's a deal."

We exchanged cash for rings, and I said a silent goodbye to that part of my life.

The man hid the rings away under the counter.

"Anything else I can help you with tonight? I need to clear out guitars. Maybe I can throw something in for you to help make up the difference."

"Yeah, actually. There is something I'm looking for."

Chapter Forty-Two

GEORGINA

It felt so good having told Blake the truth about not having my results yet. He took it well, as we sat for lunch over a huge fisherman's basket. It towered between us, salty and surreal. How was anyone, or how were any two people, supposed to eat all that?

"You have something on your chin," Blake said, and reached across the table.

The candles flickered as his wrist passed through the flames. It was dark, for lunchtime. The tiny points of light shimmered and danced, and then his thumb pressed against my chin.

Something slid down my face and I looked down, expecting to see a chunk of tartare sauce or lettuce lying on my blouse. Instead, a black slug-like shape lay there. As I watched, it began to crawl toward the buttons of my shirt. Panicked, I grabbed it. It was slimy and fat with blood, and it burst between my fingers. Another one poked its head from the collar of my shirt, its grotesque little body giving off a sickly shine in the dim light.

Crying out, I leaped up from the chair and ripped my top open. Black creatures, part slug, part snake, crawled all over my chest. I stared at them, at my bare flesh, terror freezing me in place. Then panic slammed into me like a freight train, and I flailed and screamed as I tried to scrape them away.

"Let me help you!" Blake shouted.

I turned to him, frantic and horrified. The repulsive things were everywhere. They had wriggled down into my pants. I could feel them sliding down my upper thighs, invading the backs of my knees, and worming their way under the thin skin near my ankles.

I sobbed. "Get them off! Get them off me!"

His hand touched my shoulder and my skin split open, tearing like tissue paper.

Instead of blood, more of the slugs poured out, a whole tide of them. They chittered and bit and dug nastily into my flesh, opening it farther and letting the ones still hidden beneath escape. I was torn apart in a flood of darkness.

I jerked up in bed, my mouth wide open and a scream trapped in my throat.

Breathe. *Breathe.*

I finally gasped air in, and that air was chased by wracking sobs.

There was a quiet knock on my door. "You okay?"

One of the twins. I didn't know which one. I could barely know anything over the racing of my heart. I forced my breathing back under control. "I'm fine."

She hovered there for a moment, her shadow visible under the crack of the door, then she left.

I wasn't fine.

I felt chilled right to the core of my soul. A pit of nausea consumed me from within.

I rolled over and cuddled Julie's narwhal plushie tight. My head ached at the base of my neck. *It's an aneurism. It's brain cancer. You've waited too long. You're riddled with cancer. You're dying.*

I grunted and rolled over onto my other side, pulling the covers over my head as though that could block out my anxiety. A bright point of pain burned in my left calf. *It's bone cancer. It's a blood clot. You'll be dead before morning.*

My heartrate sped and my mind blurred. I wondered if

this was what dying felt like. *Just STOP. You're imagining it. It's just a panic attack.*

A strange half-sob, half-sigh strained out through my teeth as I tried to breathe normally. If I could count to ten, and was still alive, I was probably okay.

Counting soothed me, and I started drifting off. Then the sensation of losing consciousness made my body sure I was dying, and jump started my heart again with all new terror.

There was no way I was getting back to sleep.

Even without the bad dreams.

I could still feel the black slugs squirming inside me.

I flicked on my bedside lamp and sat up. Beside me lay my little black journal, open to The List.

After getting home from the beach, I'd snuck in past the twins, sleeping on inflatable beds in Julie's old room, and went straight to get out that list.

I hadn't had sex on the beach with Blake to tick off an item. I did it because I wanted to; I wanted to be with him in that perfect moment. But I still came home and scrawled a line across the goal, like some kind of junkie getting a fix.

Now it sat there taunting me, unfinished. Just one item left.

Still shaking from the dream, I wrapped myself in my robe and went into the kitchen. I grabbed a tin of minestrone, emptied it into a bowl, and heated it in the microwave. The

~~Make out with a stranger~~

~~Get to second base~~

~~Lose virginity~~ ✓ *+ bonus orgasm, wow*

~~Sex on a beach~~

~~Bondage sex~~

~~Make love with a woman~~

~~Sex in a public place~~

Sex with two men

~~Sex with a B~~

soup was weak and thin. A limp noodle floated belly-up in the orange-red broth along with peas that had lost most of their color drifting past soggy carrot pieces. It looked as sick as I felt.

I wasn't even hungry—just too afraid to go back to sleep. Too afraid I'd never wake up again.

I didn't need a psychology degree to know what I'd been dreaming about. The nightmare disturbed me more than I would have liked. I wanted to be tougher than this.

Everything seemed so hopeless, and I wished I had never even gone for the test, that I didn't have to face getting the results. It was all so real now. It was just horribly, terribly, irrevocably real. This was happening, and I'd tried to hide all the things I felt about that by running full-tilt at the most base, primal lusts of life. Except things I had never planned on happening had happened, and things I had never imagined feeling were making me open up and feel them. I hadn't planned on falling in love.

When I had been sick the first time, I'd worked my way through the seven stages of loss. It was healthy, according to my doctors, to know what my odds were and to come to grips with the fact that death was unavoidable, even if I managed to cheat it that time around. I had simply accepted that I probably wouldn't live long enough to have the life I always wanted before cancer came knocking on my door.

Why did I just accept that? Why hadn't I fought harder, sooner? Why hadn't I gotten more done? I was pissed off. I was so damn mad I wanted to toss everything in the kitchen out the windows and onto the street. I wanted to kick holes in the walls, tear the bland framed art that had been there when I moved in off the walls, and break their thin glass with my fists.

I dumped the soup in the sink and went back to my room, back to the unfinished list. Staring at it, I could feel my lips twitching in anger. I was so close. So close to being finished. I couldn't leave it like that with this sickness that I knew was inside me, eating me up. If I just went to sleep again,

and never woke up tomorrow. If tonight was my last night …
I couldn't get so far and then give up. I couldn't wait a second
longer with my time ticking closer and closer to the end with
every breath.

I checked the clock. It was only ten p.m., two hours
after I'd gotten home from the beach. It was a Friday night. Not
too late.

I changed, grabbed my keys, and headed for Blake's
house without a second thought.

I pulled into his driveway. The lights were out and I
stood there, feeling like a jerk. Blake deserved better than this.
He deserved better than me.

As I turned away, his door opened. The lights inside
were down but the TV was still on, and Blake looked at me,
confused. He wore loose track pants, his chest was bare and
I ran into it, my tear-stained face pressed tightly against the
strong breadth of him.

His arms went around me and held fast. I knew I
should pull away. He hadn't asked for this, hadn't done anything
to deserve getting caught up with another woman who would
probably do nothing but die badly.

There was a time when he had just wanted to get laid
and had found my list interesting.

I hoped he found the last item on the list interesting
too.

Chapter Forty-Three

BLAKE

"You've got to be joking me." The words that had just come out of her mouth floored me, especially after the day we had spent at the beach. When I thought she'd finally accepted *us*. I'd never imagined she was still thinking about that damned list.

Only, she was.

She'd shown up on my doorstep, dressed for a night out just hours after we'd made love to the sound of crashing waves and she'd agreed to call what we had a relationship.

Her face was pale but determined. "I need to do this. It's the last thing on my list."

"It's fucking two dudes!"

She flinched but held her ground. "Why are you so horrified? You didn't have any problem with bringing Mary home."

"I just want a relationship with only you and me." That seemed reasonable. Not that I wanted to be reasonable at that exact second. She'd just announced she wanted sex with other men and suggested I was homophobic all in the same breath. I was stunned by fury.

I didn't want to share her. The thing with Mary had proved beyond a shadow of a doubt that I wasn't into that, that what I wanted, who I wanted, was Georgina and only Georgina.

"I'm going to do it. I have to. I can't leave things like this." Her eyes showed white all around the irises, and her lips shivered.

I knew girls who would do all the things on her list, and some who already had. Some of the girls who hung around backstage at concerts. They were the ones who always wanted people to know who they fucked, and exactly how they'd fucked them. They counted their conquests not in numbers but by deed. I didn't think that was the real Georgina—not really. I hoped the fear in her eyes proved me right.

It was clear she was scared, shaken to her bones. Lavender-colored circles ringed her dark eyes. Her new short hair made her neck look long and somehow frail. I could hear the tremble of her breath rush over her lips, and wanted to kiss her gorgeous mouth until she forgot about that last thing on her bucket list. That fucking list. I thought it was over, that we could bury it by checking off an older, more innocent list. I thought we could move on.

"Why, why now? After today?"

She just shook her head. "Come with me, then we just need to pick up one guy. We can do it together, like before." Every word was rushed, rambling.

I ran a hand over my face, unable to even comprehend. "No. Fuck no. How can you even ask me this? I won't. Georgie, please …"

"Then I'll do it without you."

She turned and left without another word. She dashed to her car and sped off into the night.

My fist hit the wall beside the door, going straight through the plasterboard. *Fuck.* Fuck her and her list. I was sick of playing a body part in her little soap opera. It was clear she would never think of me as anything more, and I wasn't going to break my heart again over some girl who didn't give a shit about me or even about herself.

Chapter Forty-Four

GEORGINA

Desperation and mortal terror took the wheel and I ended up in the parking lot of the club that had been my original hunting ground for The List. I almost went in there, but the twang of guitar and a mellow voice filled with sadness reached me from the other side of the road. It drew me in, singing to the pain in my heart.

I stormed across the street into the country and western joint, sat at the bar and downed three shots in a row. Fury blurred my thoughts as much as the alcohol, but even then, I knew I was about to do the dumbest thing I have ever done. And I barely cared.

I only cared about completion. As though if I finished my list, everything would be okay.

Completion was the only thing I had left to cling to. I had to scratch that last item off my list—I *had* to. It was as though crossing it out would cross out all the pain I'd ever known, would stop the ticking time bomb inside me in its tracks. *Black slugs, eating me from the inside out ...*

With dry, sore, determined eyes, I scanned the club. Men drank at the bar made of old fence palings, men played pool, men sat around watching a dog race on a big screen. I was one of very few women in here. *This should be easy.* From my seat, I spotted two guys sitting in a booth in the darkest corner of the timber-filled space. One was tall, thin, and wearing clothes that would have been better suited to someone twice his weight. They swamped his lanky body but didn't hide the prominent Adam's apple or the knobbly bones of his wrists. When he caught me looking he elbowed the guy next to him, gesturing toward me with his head.

His friend had painted-on skinny jeans and a shirt that gave the impression of someone trying to be a cowboy. He had long brown hair and a nice enough face, if it weren't for how he leered.

I knew those looks they were giving me. They were the same looks I got from the kind of guys who back at school would tease me about being fat while staring at my breasts. I could see even from here they were assholes.

I walked right up to them and sat down at their table.

"Hi. I'm Mary," I said.

"Rick," said the wannabe cowboy.

"Austin," said the other.

"You guys up for a threesome?"

A cynical part of me had learned something these past weeks. I was attractive, attractive enough that some men would at least be willing to have sex with me if offered bluntly. There would always be those who would be shocked, or gentlemanly, or taken, or gay, but otherwise, sex on a plate was as good as sold. Still, it was no mystery why I was as blunt as a knife made of cheddar that night. Deep down, I wanted them to say no to me like the crazy woman I was, to tell me to fuck off.

"You a cop or something?" Austin retorted.

"No, just looking for a good time." I tried to inject as much sultriness into my voice as possible but it still came out too fast, almost like a final gasp.

"Nah, she's a hooker." Rick tilted his beer up, swallowing it down in long gulps. "We don't pay for pussy. We don't need to get high either so move along."

I should have walked away. But the offense of being rejected stung. I wasn't that same scared, sick girl who got rejected anymore. I *couldn't* be her anymore. I had to do this.

I leaned across the table so they could see the deep valley between my breasts and smiled at them both. "I am not a cop or a hooker." I delivered each word slowly, eyelashes lowered, my lips caressing each sound. "I'm horny, and I want you two guys to fuck me."

They wore matching looks of shocked disbelief tinged with a lecherous hope. Austin sat his beer bottle, greasy with his fingerprints, down on the table, and gave me a long up and down look. Then gave his friend a long look up and down. Rick shrugged in a clear "what the hell" expression.

"You want two dudes to fuck you? We are two dudes with hard dicks. We can make this happen. Shit, we even have a room out back tonight." He clinked his drink with his friend's, laughed, then paused. "We can go one at a time, right?" he asked.

"Together. All at once, or no deal."

There was fear in their eyes as they looked at each other. Eagerness too, but fear to be the first to say yes. I arched my back and ran my fingers across the top of my cleavage.

"Fhhhuuuhhhuck," Austin breathed out. "All right. I'm game. You game?"

"Dude." Rick slammed back the rest of his beer. "Fine, I'm in. Need another drink first."

The guys bought a round of shots. I tossed mine back, needing the numbness the whiskey brought to push me along to my goal.

I didn't sit down, eager to move things along. Rick scooted closer to me and put his hand on my thigh, running it up and down the bare flesh. My first instinct was to push him away. It wasn't that there was anything particularly wrong with him, except that *he wasn't Blake.*

Screw Blake. I'd asked him to do this with me and he refused.

My jaw shook, and I clenched my teeth to hold it still. I could do this with someone else. I could. I would.

The List Georgina is brave Georgina. The List Georgina says yes.

Rick's fingers were cold. They pressed so far into my muscles that they ached, no gentleness at all—only hunger. It made my breath catch.

The shots had hit my system and my thoughts blurred. I walked away from the table. Rick caught me, pulled me back the other way. "Where ya going?" he slurred as his fingers twisted into the bottom hem of my dress, brushing against my panties.

Where was I going? My body had moved first, but then my mind caught up.

I was leaving. I'd changed my mind. I couldn't do this. I wanted to go back to Blake.

My insides were at war, each side violent and

panicking. Go back to Blake, or get The List finished?

I have to finish it. This is my last chance. Tomorrow might never come.

I let Rick and Austin lead me to the rear exit, each of them with an arm around me, supporting me between them. The more the alcohol ran through my blood, the more it made sense that if I just finished that list everything would somehow right itself.

Yet everything felt so *wrong*.

Out the back was a long expanse of weedy, derelict alleyway. Cars with flat tires rusted against the curbs, and stray dogs huddled below the scant orange glow of flickering street-lights. The apartments behind the bar were seedy, broken-down wrecks. Their red-brick walls were covered in graffiti. The thought of going into one of those dwellings made my stomach churn.

The thought of being with these two men made it worse.

But I wasn't backing down.

Chapter Forty-Five

GEORGINA

The lights went on. Dazzled, my sore eyes took a moment to adjust. We were in a living room. It stunk of moldy food. Fast food containers crowded the counters, and empty beer cans tumbled from the sink. The smell made me gag.

Austin sat on the couch and pulled me onto his lap. His bony knees struck my ass cheeks, and I could feel he was already hard, his firmness nudging against my flesh as he massaged my hips with his hands. He licked my neck.

I cringed away.

"Come on, this is what we're here for. Don't be a prick

tease," he whispered near my mouth, his beer breath filling my throat.

We just need to do what needs to be done.

I stayed on his lap.

"Have another drink, that'll get you going," Rick said, appearing with a can of beer in each hand. He pushed one open can into my hand and it sloshed out the top, all over my dress.

I gasped and they both laughed at me. Austin started patting me down, being completely conspicuous about groping my breasts at the same time, a huge grin dripping from his face. He took the opportunity to tweak my nipple.

"Bags the top end," Rick said. "Those lips are so fuckable."

"Fine by me. I'm ready for some of this big booty." Austin pushed me over so I flopped across the arm of the sofa, exposing my ass to him, which he then slapped hard.

Austin slid my dress up over my hips and Rick came around in front of me, his belt buckle rattling in my face as he worked it open.

I tried to relax into it. To get into the mood.

This isn't right. This isn't me. This isn't Blake. I don't want this.

I felt tears welling up. Big, messy, snotty, tears.

The List Georgina is brave … The List … says yes …

NO.

I didn't care what fantasy I'd imagined when I'd added this item to my list. I didn't want them. I didn't want this. Not anymore.

I pushed their grabbing hands off me. "Stop. I've changed my mind."

They didn't stop. They both pawed over me like dogs who'd found a lame possum.

I slapped them away and rolled off the couch. "I'm going."

Rick stopped, fly half unzipped. "Fucking, what? Are you kidding me?"

"No way, slut, you're not ringing the dinner bell then walking out on us." Austin grabbed the back of my dress, wrenching me toward him. I fell roughly, knocking my head on the floor.

"Ow, that hurt!"

They just laughed at me sprawled there, dress up around my waist. "I think she changed her mind again."

Rick and Austin fell upon me where I lay in the middle of the room. Hands were up my dress and down my dress. Too many hands. The wrong hands. I screamed.

Chapter Forty-Six

BLAKE

I paced over worn carpet, dumped myself on the crackly old couch, then paced, replaying the whole conversation over and over, torturing myself. Was I overreacting? Was I being too prudish or jealous or trying to own her? Why did it hurt so damn much?

How dare she even ask that of me?

I'd known it was on her list right from the beginning. Shouldn't I have expected it? Or was I always too fixated on the 'sex with a woman' part to think of it reaching this point? What did that make me?

My eyes ached and I grabbed my hair with both hands, making fists against my scalp.

I should have given up trying to make this anything more than just about her sex list. I should have given up on her long ago.

But I just couldn't let go.

And deep under all my anger, fear sloshed around, slimy and rotten. Fear for Georgina.

My pride stung, still feeling the slap of Georgina's rejection. I wasn't going to go after her. I refused.

"No!" I yelled it at the front door, as though it was trying to convince me to go.

Georgina would have to look after herself. She'd made it clear she didn't want or need me. Just like Seyvia did.

I had given up on Seyvia, and that decision had haunted me every day since.

Shit.

I threw on a jacket and boots, grabbed my keys and helmet, and headed out into the night.

Speeding along the quiet night-time roads, cold air reached its fingers through the gaps in my jacket, chilling the bare skin beneath. My teeth chattered—anxiety shook my core. I headed first for the bar where we'd picked up Mary, but I couldn't spot Jiminy in any of the streets nearby. I tried another local club, then headed for the one where we'd first met. That was where I saw her little green hatchback, bright against the other black-and-white cars in the lot. I jumped off my bike and headed in. The bouncer looked disapprovingly at my track pants and motorcycle jacket combo, but my dark expression was all I had to wear for him to let me in.

Pushing through the crowd, I got more than one filthy look as I checked through the strobe-lit corners and smoke-filled dance floor. She wasn't there.

She's already gone home with someone.

I didn't want to believe that. I had to keep looking.

Back outside, the flashing red sign over the old saloon-style building across the road caught my eye. Maybe she'd gone there instead.

She's with someone else right now. Two someone elses.

Denial sent me into the country and western bar. I kept telling myself I still had a chance to find her. I'd keep looking all night.

I didn't have to. As soon as I stepped in far enough to hear the line dancers stomping the floor, I saw her. I saw her disappearing out a back door with two men.

My charge toward her was caught by the bouncer. He had followed me in through the entrance where I'd walked right by him. He put a hand on my shoulder. "Dude, dress code."

"I'm just here to get my girl. I won't be long."

"Mate, that's what every bloke is here for, and it can

take a lot longer than you'd hope. Especially dressed like that. Out."

I threw his hand off my shoulder, and he reached for something at his hip. It could have been pepper spray or a taser or a gun for all I knew. *Fucking Americans.*

I put my hands up in a peace gesture. "I'm leaving."

She wasn't here anymore anyway. I had to be able to get around the back some other way. I jogged out the entrance and around the building, a trashy side alley leading up to a strip of equally trashy rental rooms. I couldn't see Georgina or the men anywhere.

But I could hear her.

She screamed.

I raced to where the sound came from and put my boot through the door. The decayed wood burst open.

The scene before me made white-hot rage fill my head, burning from my eyes like molten steel.

Georgina lay on the ground as those two men, those beasts, clutched and tore at her as violently as walking dead hungered for flesh.

My charge into the room drew their attention, but I only saw Georgina's eyes look up and meet mine. They were red with confusion and fear, slick with tears.

One man came at me. My fist flew into his nose with vicious glee. He fell back.

I knelt down beside Georgina. "I've got you." I scooped her up, holding her close to me and wanting to take her from this place and erase the knowledge that this had ever happened, to go back in time to the beach and the sun and the happiness that felt so long ago.

Georgina gasped, "Watch out!"

I turned just in time to see a full beer can being swung at my head like a club. I dodged back, but it clipped my eyebrow, breaking the skin.

Georgina pushed herself out of my arms and onto her feet. She put herself between me and the man attacking us just as he swung again.

The blow hit the side of her head.

She crumpled. I reached for her, catching her as she fell.

No, NO.

The man had frozen above us, can in hand, as though shocked by the result of his actions.

I tried to rouse Georgina. She was completely passed out. But she was alive.

At least she wouldn't have to see this.

I had barely any control of my body, or the sensations raging through me, but I could name the emotion I was feeling. *Murderous.*

I left Georgina on the floor, straightened myself back

to full height, and glared at the remaining man from under eyebrows dripping in blood.

He scrambled back. I stalked across the room after him. My hands clenched into fists and released, then clenched again, as though champing at the bit.

"Who even are you, man? We were just having fun."

I had no response but a feral growl.

"I … I'll call the cops." His eyes were wild.

Georgina groaned from behind me, drawing my attention, my heart, straight back to her.

It gave my target a chance to dash, and he ran for the other room.

I let him go.

On my way back to Georgina I spotted her purse on the floor near the couch and grabbed it, then lifted her too, cradling her into my arms, tucking her head under my chin.

I was glad the parking lot was empty as I carried her like that—apparently lifeless as blood dripped from my own forehead down my face—back to her car.

I rested her carefully down onto the passenger seat, checking over her scalp with my fingers. The blow hadn't broken the skin, but a lump had formed where she'd been hit. I took the driver's seat and squeezed the wheel like I was trying to wring blood from a stone.

Maybe calling the cops was the right idea. Those guys

shouldn't be allowed to get away with this.

But I knew how women in a position like Georgina's were treated. I couldn't put her in that situation. It would have to be her decision. And she still wasn't fully conscious. I had to get her to a hospital.

I started the car, and she startled awake.

"He hit you," was the first thing she said, staring at me with wide eyes.

I didn't know what to say. I couldn't say anything, my voice lost in confusion and anger and relief.

She reached gingerly for the wound on the side of my head. I took her hand before she could touch it. "I'm fine. Head wounds bleed a lot—that's all. It's not that bad."

Her face scrunched in on itself. "I'm sorry. I'm so sorry."

"Do you want me to call the police for you?"

She seemed confused for a moment, guilt in her features clearly confusing my meaning. Her words were tired and slurred. "No. It was my fault. I just want to go home."

"It wasn't ..." My hands squeezed the wheel tighter. The car sat idling, still and directionless. "I was taking you to the hospital."

"No, no hospital. I can't be in hospital again." She looked as scared as she had when she lay on the filthy floor beneath two men. "I'm fine. Really. Barely a headache."

She was lying. "I'm not leaving you alone tonight."

"I can't—"

"No, you're coming home with me. And if you start hurling, it's straight to the ER." My mates back home and I had had a rough enough childhood to know the symptoms of concussion.

Her mouth opened, but she didn't say anything. She lay against the car door, her head pressed to the cool glass of the window.

We said nothing else on the drive back home. But she was here, with me, and safe now.

I wondered though, with Georgina, if anything would ever be safe. Or if this was life—a constant series of challenges and hardships. How could I ever protect her from it, or protect myself, my heart, from whatever lay ahead?

I didn't have any answers. I couldn't see the future, except for one sure thing.

I wanted Georgina to be in that future, for as long as possible, no matter what.

Chapter Forty-Seven

GEORGINA

I dipped in and out of a tossing and turning slumber, tainted by sickening dreams. Rick stood over me, his dick hanging exposed. The head was swollen, the shaft engorged with blood, and a heavy vein ran along the side, pulsing with a kind of terrifying life.

"I bought you drinks," he said in a mosquito-like whine. "You owe me."

I tried to run but got caught in a giant web. A man in a white coat skittered to me along a sticky strand, telling me to relax, that everything would be fine. Austin stood below me, jacking off furiously while the doctor jabbed me with giant needles that turned into other dark and horrifically unknowable *things* under my skin.

Each time my eyes peeled open in fear, Blake was there, sitting on the side of the bed, watching me, brushing back my hair from where it clung to my sweaty forehead.

Finally, my stomach stopped roiling and my mind cleared.

Then the reality of the night before flooded in. Shame struck me. So did horror—how could I have done that? What if Blake hadn't showed up?

He saved me.

What the hell did he see in me? I was a wreck, and I was wrecking him.

I could have gotten him killed.

Just like Julie. It was my fault. I was death. I was poison. I could have killed the man I loved.

I hated myself for endangering him like that, for not even considering that he would come after me, that I was risking him with my behavior as well as myself. Those two guys could have killed Blake. They could have had guns. They could have called the cops on us both. I could imagine dozens of different endings to the night that were so much worse than where we were.

Why did he come after me?

Of course he came after me. He's Blake.

I lay there thinking all of this with my eyes closed, unwilling to open them and face the real world. But I knew every moment I stayed there, Blake was sitting guard over me, losing his sleep to keep me safe.

My eyelids burned with the effort of opening. Blake was the first thing that came into focus. He sat hunched over, elbows on knees, face in hands, hair hanging in golden strands like a curtain around them. He wore only track pants, and even in the dim light, the sight of his bare chest and shoulders was something so beautiful I wanted to cry.

He looked like he'd fallen asleep. I moved slowly, quietly, both for him and my aching body. I stood up, and my head throbbed. I reached tentatively for the place that hurt. An egg had formed there, but it was already smaller than it was last night. I pressed at it and hissed in pain.

Blake's eyes flew open and he looked up at me.

He didn't have to say anything. It was all over his face. I had hurt him. I had hurt him so badly.

My voice was a static hiss and pop. "I have to go."

"Your car is out the front."

My head gave off a few more sickly thumps as I tried to bend over to reach my shoes. "I'm sorry."

"I don't care." I risked a look at his face and wished I hadn't. He had grown hard, cold, and it was my fault. Before

I could think of anything to say, he spoke again. "That stupid stunt you pulled could have ended a lot more badly than it did, you know."

"I know." My face flamed. "I didn't mean for you to have to come and rescue me."

Blake just shook his head. His eyes were swollen from lack of sleep, his features still blurred, almost smudgy. "Did you even consider that they could rape you? Or kill you? Do you ever, even once, stop to think about yourself? Your safety, I mean. Your life, not your stupid selfish list. Those guys were scum, and what pisses me off the most is that you somehow think they are all you deserve, that you deserve to be treated like that. I am so done with this, Georgina. Do you hear me?"

I winced away from his anger. I'd finally pushed him too far. I had gotten what I wanted, what I thought I deserved— his hatred. Him no longer wanting me.

I was ready to dig my own grave, and cry in that hole until death took me.

I tried to walk away but he stood in front of me.

I had never seen him this angry before. I stood there, to hear him out and take each stinging blow. Because that was what I deserved.

I knew he was right about those two guys. They would have raped me. They wouldn't have even seen it as rape. I had offered them something, and they would have taken me up on that offer, even if I had changed my mind. I'd invited the worst to happen to me as though it was inevitable. Maybe it was never about completing the List. It was about making this life seem so terrible and cruel that the threat of cancer and death paled in comparison.

And it would have been terrible, being with those men.

To them I had been just a body. I had treated Blake the same way.

I was no better than those two assholes from last night.

That was a rude awakening. I prepared myself for the worst, waiting for Blake to lash me with words harsher than my own thoughts.

Blake's face softened. "Do you even know why I came after you?"

His question confused me, and I didn't have an answer. I shook my head.

"I came after you because you do deserve more. Because you should want more. Because I love you."

Tears raced down my face. Blake pulled me to him, to his chest, where I could feel his racing heart through his warm skin.

I wanted to tell him too. I wanted to tell him everything—how I felt, how I feared.

I wanted to believe him. I wanted to believe I could deserve someone like Blake, that I could deserve his love. But I could only cry, and cry, for everything that had happened last night, and every moment since I found that damned lump.

"I want to break something," I blubbered into his chest.

"Other than my heart?"

I thumped a fist softly against his chest.

"Come with me." He held me as we went downstairs. He passed me a box of tissues then disappeared into a spare room, rattling around until he came back out with a cricket bat. Then he led me silently into the backyard.

Outside, the sky shone with the shimmery pale blue of morning, too early for the sun to have brought warmth to the world yet. It was still hiding somewhere unseen.

Blake handed me the bat. I raised it like a weapon, my knuckles white around the handle. I looked for a target. I couldn't spot the gnome, probably cowering from me in the untidy lawn. One of the trees caught my eye though.

It looked almost dead, its trunk gray and riddled with rot. Its roots were mostly above ground, and a long black streak showed on one side where it had been burnt. Had lightning struck it, or something more mundane? The leaves were overly large, spotted, and turning—not the spectacular reds and golds of the leaves of the trees around it, but a sickly brownish-yellow. It looked as though it was suffering.

I took off at a dead run, the bat over my head, grass rushing against my ankles. I brought my weapon down on the tree so hard that a shudder ran all the way up into my arms. The pain just made me angrier. I screamed and yanked the bat back before striking again.

The tree crackled and crunched, and dried rotten bark shattered away to reveal a ghastly white underbelly. The morning birds had fallen silent but my voice only grew stronger. I hit the tree again, swearing a blue streak, making up words when I ran out of known ones to hurl at the tree, the sky, and any gods that existed. I smashed dry branches off, splintering them with screeching blows.

I fell to my knees in front of that dying tree. The dirt and grass was soft under my knees.

"I'm sorry. I'm so sorry." My words coughed out between sobs.

Blake knelt down next to me, put a hand on mine. "You don't need to apologize to the tree."

I wasn't. I couldn't speak any more. I wrapped my arms around Blake, wailing.

Crickets began their songs again nearby, and the lights went on in the neighbor's yard.

"Shut up over there, you damn degenerates!" The old man next door had apparently had enough of us. Blake scooped up the sobbing mess I'd become and carried me back into the living room.

He put me on my feet, holding my hands, keeping me

steady. I took deep, calming breaths. His hands felt so perfect holding mine. I still felt the urge to run from him, pull away. Instead I tried … just staying. It was one of the scariest things I'd ever done. Just holding his hand, lingering there, letting myself have that.

I cleared my throat. "I am sorry about your tree."

Blake shrugged. "Did it help?"

I breathed out slowly. A calmness had followed my violent outburst. "Yeah. It helped. Thank you."

He brought my hand to his mouth and gave it a light kiss.

I stuttered, averting my eyes. "Sorry for making your neighbor yell at us."

"Nah, he's already got it in for me. Probably because I nicked his garden gnome."

I surprised myself by smiling. "You stole that poor old man's garden gnome?"

"It brought itself home, so I don't think it really counts."

"What?"

"There's this garden gnome that moves all by itself. I swear it does, and it gives me shifty looks. I pinched the creepy-assed thing a few times and ditched it, but it just keeps coming back."

"No wonder he was calling us degenerates."

"Well, that, and the number of times he's managed to

catch me without clothes on. Honestly, I don't think he's ever seen me fully dressed. He came over one day when I was just out of the shower and since I had no clean towels, I answered the door with nothing but a pillowcase wrapped around my waist. Come to think of it, that's when the gnome began to give me shifty looks. He and the old bloke probably talk."

Laughter filled my mouth, stretched my chest open, and made my belly ache. It was the kind that makes everything fade for a moment.

"You need to learn how to take better care of your house and your relationship with your neighbors," I said.

He pulled me closer to him. "You need to learn how to take better care of yourself."

I put a hand on his shoulder, feeling his body heat, and I imagined what it would be like when I died, when the heat lifted away layer by layer until only an endless cold remained. Tears came back but I held them in.

I had never had to deal with so many emotions all at once: pain, fear, laughter, guilt, *love*. When I was fifteen and going through treatment, I'd been a child, really. Everyone else felt things for me. I had to keep my brave face on for my dad, for the kids at school, and even for the doctors sometimes. There had never been time to *feel* anything. At fifteen, death was such an abstract concept, it barely filtered in. I knew what it meant but not really. Now that I had lived a little, now that

I had met someone I loved enough to not only live for, but wanted to create a future and life with, there was nothing at all abstract about it.

I started crying again, and when Blake reached for me again, I crumpled into him.

"I'm sorry. I'm so sorry. I lied to you. I'm such a coward," I sobbed.

"What are you talking about?"

I could barely force words out, and they emerged as a husky whisper. "I lied to you about my results, saying I had the all clear. I don't."

Blake tensed, waiting, breathless.

"I didn't have the results yet. I still don't. The hospital called yesterday, but I'm not ready. How can I go in there and face that? Because if I do have cancer again, how do I face what that means? Knowing the treatment might not work?"

"You'd prefer to just ignore it and risk dying sooner?" There wasn't any anger in his voice, only honest, tired curiosity.

"People who jump from burning buildings don't believe they'll survive the fall. They just don't want to burn."

Blake held me by the shoulders, and placed his forehead down on mine.

It wasn't just the treatment I was scared of. It was as though I believed treatment meant death. It wasn't only the cancer that had halted my life at fifteen. The treatment and

everything that went along with it had saved me, removed the cancer from my body, but it had taken so much from me as well. I knew I should be grateful that I had been saved, but I was scared, and my fear had been driving my every thought, my every action. My body had gone into fight-or-flight mode, and I'd been flying away from life faster than a peregrine falcon all the while trying to convince myself I was running *to* life, that I was living and being brave with that stupid, sexy list.

I saw my purse on the coffee table. I separated myself from Blake, picked it up, and pulled the little black journal out of it.

That list. I glared at it, sighed, then tore the page free from the notebook.

I ripped it in half, then half again, smaller and smaller until it was nothing but confetti. I threw it in the air and watched it drift down like snow around us, settling onto the old couch and the stop-sign coffee table.

"All done with?" Blake asked, his tone guarded.

"Done. All done."

He walked up behind me, wrapping his arms around me, and kissing my neck. "Forget about that list. Forget about the results, for now. Let's just be, just live, for a while."

"We're not over? You're not done with me?"

"Are you serious? How many times do we have to go over this?"

"I lied to you. I've been horrible. I'm so sorry for everything I've done. I'm a mess and I'm trying to be stronger, but I can't promise you I won't hurt you again. How can you want that?"

He turned me around to face him. "Every life is just made of moments. Ups and downs. Pain and pleasure. No one can guarantee a happy ending. Yeah, you hurt me, but I can understand why. I know how fear can control you."

"I treated you like shit," I whispered.

"You did, and you almost lost me."

I let that sink into me like a punch to the gut. "I

screwed up so much."

He shrugged, and a small smile emerged on his lips. "Everyone makes mistakes."

I laughed out loud at his understatement of the year.

The birds outside were singing their morning chorus, and golden light spilled in through the front window, the sun finally showing its radiant face. I tangled my fingers up into Blake's hair, never wanting to let go.

He whispered, close to my ear, my partner in crime, "If you're not ready, let's run away. I'm okay with that, as long as we do it together. We'll run away, and finish your childhood list. And when you're ready to come back for your results, we will face that together too."

My heart echoed him. *Together. Together.*

Chapter Forty-Eight

GEORGINA

I dropped Blake off where he'd left his bike the night before, and was incredibly proud of myself for not breaking down in a teary mess just for being in proximity to the country and western bar and those memories.

After that I managed to drive myself safely the rest of the way home. Alone.

I didn't want to say goodbye to Blake even for a short while, not again. But he said he had some things to organize, and I had to go home and pack.

He said he'd be with me soon. That made me feel

strong.

The house was quiet, except for a soft snoring sound. For a heartbreaking moment I thought it was Julie, then I remembered Priya and Kaley were staying here now. It was early enough in the morning that they were both still asleep. They probably didn't even know I'd gone out. Everything that had happened the night before, my whole crazy night of danger, didn't even exist to them. I liked imagining it that way, as though, from the right perspective, you could just change your existence. Erase your mistakes.

To complete the illusion, I cleaned the run and smudged make-up away, then showered, and got into my pajamas. It almost made the hot lump of regret in my stomach less noticeable.

The rims of my eyelids were raw, dry, and stinging. From the moment I'd found out about Blake doing my childhood list, through getting my haircut and the night at the strip club, to going out to the ocean and then my stupid attempt to complete my sexy bucket list, the past days were a sleepless blur. I just wanted to put my head down on my pillow and stay there for a week.

My stomach grumbled, hungry and alive, in spite of everything I'd put it through. I grabbed eggs and a stupid amount of bacon from the fridge, and started cooking, as though this were any normal lazy morning. I worked quietly, but either the sizzle of the bacon or the smoky smell woke the girls, and they came to join me for breakfast. Sleepy-eyed and bed-haired, they looked completely at home. Priya popped some bread into the toaster, Kaley laid out plates, and I smiled at how natural it all felt. I wondered what things had been like at their home with their nanna. They seemed at ease here, able to be themselves in this space. I was thankful they were with me.

I checked how they liked their eggs, cracked a few more into the pan for them, and got the coffee brewing.

We sat at the breakfast counter, chasing runny yolk around our plates with toast and bacon dippers. "What's the plan for today?" Kaley asked, enthusiasm and awe in her voice. "Casino? Sky diving? Tiger wrassling?"

I crunched my toast. "You know, I don't do something amazing and adventurous every day of my life."

Priya tipped her head to the side, her look no-non-sense. "I bet you don't even know what you're doing. I bet Blake is organizing another big surprise."

I hung my head, laughing at myself. "Fine. I don't know. He's got a plan. I was told to pack."

Kaley and Priya both squealed.

They squealed again when a knock at the door revealed Blake, ready for our next adventure. He wore nice jeans and a buttoned dress shirt, making me feel frumpy for having gone straight to the pajama option when I got home.

He'd showered too, and although there wasn't a trace of blood from the cut above his eyebrow left, I still imagined it. I shook the image away. I couldn't pretend last night had never happened, not really, but we were here, we were safe, and we were moving on. *Together.*

Blake dumped a stuffed travel backpack next to the front door. "You're not packed?"

I thumbed back to where the girls were still eating. "We did breakfast."

Blake's eyes lit up. "Any left for me?"

Priya patted the bar stool next to her. "Georgie cooked a ridiculous amount of bacon. Come and join us in Bacon City."

Blake groaned loudly after his first crunchy bite. "You cook the best bacon. If I didn't already love you, this would be the tipping point."

My heart ku-thumped. Kaley and Priya looked at each other with openmouthed grins.

I tried to reach for another piece myself, but was swatted away by Blake. "You need to go and pack. You've got twenty minutes."

"What? But I don't know what I'm packing for."

"Okay, I'd wanted this to be a grander reveal. I was planning this next list item for a bit later on, with a bit more fanfare, but it will make a good getaway now so I've bumped up the schedule. So, ta-da, I guess." He took a wad of folded papers out of his back pocket and handed it to me.

Something home-printed, with confirmations, dates, times, names.

Tickets. Airline tickets. *NIAGARA*. The word jumped out at me, and my heart dropped into my belly. Niagara Falls had been on my list, I was sure of it. I used to dream about it being the most romantic place ever, back before it was considered cliché or kitsch.

Kaley leaned over my shoulder to see, and nodded. "Yeah, that's better than tiger wrassling."

I flicked through the pages. Business-class flights. One way. He'd booked accommodation too. He'd scribbled out all prices, but I could tell from the details it wasn't cheap. Why book business-class? Why the fancy accommodation? Were those on my list too, and he was spending so much on my behalf? What else was my list going to force him to do?

"Blake," I whispered. "I can't afford this, and I can't accept it from you. You can't afford this."

Blake waved away my words. "Don't worry about it. It's sorted."

"I already owe you so much."

"This isn't some kind of barter system. You don't owe me anything."

Priya watched us from the counter, popping crunchy

bacon bits into her mouth like they were popcorn.

Blake grinned then. "Besides, I paid for these tickets mostly with my stripping money, which was from your list, so it's like it's yours anyway."

I looked at the tickets. I thought about the lump, about going in and getting my results.

I looked at Blake. "Twenty minutes? Okay, I can do that."

I heard Kaley asking Blake if he was planning any more stripper shifts as I dashed to my room.

My first problem was that I didn't have a suitcase, or a travel backpack like Blake had. I'd never been anywhere.

I dumped out the large messenger bag I used for college and grabbed it and my biggest handbag. Between them there'd be enough space. Maybe. I didn't know because my second problem was I had no idea what to pack. I stuffed as many clothes as I could into the messenger bag, then topped up my handbag with some toiletries, my phone charger, and, on a whim, a sketchbook and some pencils. My heart was racing from adrenaline as I threw on some comfy but classy clothing for the flight—woolen tights and a collared shirt dress—with only a few minutes left.

I took a deep breath to calm my nerves, to think through what was happening. Was this madness? Running away with Blake with twenty minutes notice?

When Blake said he loved me, it was hard not to say the words in return, hard not to let the thrill that ran right down my body show on my face.

I was afraid. For him. For myself. For what was going to happen to our lives, or my lack of one. Denial and fear raised their voices at me again, their old refrain that I should say no to Blake and end this, once and for all.

Or I could pick up my bags, and walk out the door and into Blake's arms. I had to choose. I had to believe I deserved more, and I had to do it right now.

Maybe I already had. The bags were packed, the lights switched off, and my purse was in my hand. I looked up at the ceiling.

Am I doing the right thing? Help me out here, Mom.

The messenger bag fell off the bed, landing on my foot hard enough to make me gasp. I stifled a shriek, glared at the ceiling and a muttered, "Geesh, fine. I get it. You don't have to be so mean about it."

I stepped back out into the living room. Then dashed back into my bedroom for my coat, a scarf, and underwear. I couldn't believe I'd forgotten to pack underwear.

Finally all done, I hugged Kaley and Priya goodbye. "See you."

"When are you coming back?" Kaley asked.

I looked at Blake. He shrugged. "That's up to Georgie."

I shrugged too. I didn't know when I'd be ready. But I knew I couldn't leave it too long. "Soon."

Priya nodded. "Thanks again for letting us stay."

Blake took my larger bag for me. "All set?"

"Yeah. Just one more thing I have to do."

I dialed Dad's number and asked him to meet us at the airport. He was working at his restaurant, and I hated asking him to drop everything for me, but I needed to see him, and he didn't think twice.

He arrived not long after we did and greeted us with a smile.

"This is all very spontaneous." Dad wrapped me in a one-armed hug, then gave Blake an equally loving hug, all the while balancing a brown paper bag under his other arm.

"Yeah, thanks for coming down to say goodbye."

"You've cut your hair."

I twirled a finger into the barely twirlable length. "Yeah, everything is a bit spontaneous lately."

He raised a bushy eyebrow. "Like missing class again?"

"Sorry, I know. This week's been—"

"Hard. Of course it has. Waiting is always hard. Don't worry about it; I'll sort things out with college. And your new hairstyle is beautiful." Dad smiled under his thick moustache.

He helped us with our bags as we walked through the long building, seeking our check-in point. I breathed in the courage I needed to tell the truth. "I don't actually need to wait anymore. The hospital rang yesterday. My results are in, and I have to go and get them."

"And your doctor has moved to Niagara?" Dad deadpanned.

"No. I … Maybe waiting isn't the hardest part. The part that comes after waiting is, and I'm not ready for that yet."

We all stopped walking. Other travelers flowed around us, like we were pebbles in a stream.

Dad nodded slowly. "I understand. It's okay to run sometimes. Just not for too long. We all have to face the truth, to face life, eventually."

That was a truth I was becoming ever more acquainted with every day.

"I'll be home soon."

"And we'll go get those results together," he said. It wasn't a question.

Together.

I gave a single, strong nod, unable to open my mouth for the sobs that wanted to come out.

"Here." Dad opened the paper bag he'd brought, and revealed a few takeaway containers filled with food from his restaurant, still steaming. "For your flight. Airplane food is terrible."

Blake snatched the bag from him, sticking his face into

it and breathing deeply. "Thanks, Tom. You're the best."

I hugged Dad again and never wanted to let go. Then an announcement for final check-in was called, and we said our goodbyes and headed off.

A sudden fear that it would be the last time I'd ever see him stole into my heart. I was starting to see my fear clearly now, see how it wormed its dark thoughts into my every action and decision, trying to block me. I saw how it tried to control me, and I tried to fight back, but still found myself scared.

As we made our way through security, I whispered to Blake, "I've never been on a plane before."

"Don't worry. You just sit around until they get you where you're going. At least we'll be comfortable. I have to go business-class or I barely fit in the seat. But either way, flying is boring."

Boring? We would be up in the air, higher than I'd ever been. Or at least, that was the theory. What if the theory went wrong? We'd face a fiery and horrible death, that was what.

I knew the odds were small, but fear told me I could die. And I didn't want to.

More than anything, I didn't want to die. I knew then that if I had to, I would go back into treatment and fight the cancer. Even if it was the whole deal: surgery and chemo-therapy and radiation and hormone therapy. Even if it was the full mastectomy. Even if I had to lose parts of myself. I just wanted to live. Anything for the gift of one more day.

Flying for the first time scared me, but I decided to do what I had done when I was in treatment for the first time. I plastered a giant smile on my face and put one foot in front of the other.

I kept waiting for some bells and whistles to go off while the guy guarding my line scrutinized us and our stuff. I thought they'd decide that the long-haired girl on my ID wasn't the same as the short-haired girl in front of them. We went through a futuristic X-ray machine and I wondered if they could see my lump on there—if they would haul me out and demand I get my ass to the nearest hospital immediately.

We made it onto the plane and to our seats. Blake rested his head back and held my hand, smiling at me reassuringly as the plane started rolling down the runway.

My breath caught when it rose into the air, engines roaring, seats shaking and rattling. I forgot about trying to smile and act calm and buried my face in Blake's shoulder. The plane leveled out, and through the window I could see the swirl of green and brown and gray that was the earth far below. I snuggled in next to Blake, looking out and losing my heart to the sight of the tops of clouds. I'd never imagined seeing clouds from *above*, never imagined they would be so beautiful. Blake watched me, smiling as I took it all in.

"You have the most amazing face," he said. "It's like I

can see everything you feel on it, and you feel so much."

"What am I feeling right now?"

"You're terrified, and you're loving every moment."

As soon as we could put our tray tables down we shared the food Dad gave us before it got too cold. We talked about the craziest stuff—whether or not pizza on a stick would be a moneymaking venture, and what it would be like to live on the moon. Soon, I'd forgotten we were even in the air. We watched a movie together, sharing the earbuds, and I fell asleep with my head on his shoulder.

I woke up disoriented, positive that the plane was going down, and it was.

We were descending into Niagara.

Blake put the blind of the window up and I stared out, no longer frightened. Lights flared and shone, like little candles in the distance. The day had darkened, turning gray. Soon those tiny lights became long streets filled with cars and headlights, streams of glitter on a tiny world that we skimmed the surface of.

My heart pounded in excitement as the wheels hit the ground. I floated out of that airport, high on happiness.

Above all of that was the feeling I had gotten while doing my bucket list. That I was *alive*. I could feel the blood in my veins, the breath in my lungs, and the warmth of my body.

I was alive, and I was in love, and I was in Niagara.

Chapter Forty-Nine

GEORGINA

I wanted to drink in every moment, but my body rebelled. I was so exhausted and wrung out that I barely noticed the scenery as it went past the windows of the taxi. Blake took us to a large building on a quiet tree-lined street. I only saw pieces of it. Blake and I staggered into our room, fell across the bed, and went to sleep without even stopping to get undressed.

I woke up the next day to sunlight streaming in through the sheer curtains, and looked around with wide eyes. The ceilings were high and decorated with carved panels, the floors were polished hardwood, and the walls were painted a delicate blue-green, like the crashing water of the falls I could just hear in the distance. We were in the penthouse apartment of a posh B&B, set up in a heritage Tudor mansion. Blake must have made some decent money stripping.

The bed was huge, and as soft as I imagined the tops of clouds to be. The covers were silky and light but so warm. I could stay in there forever. I rolled over, seeking Blake. His eyelashes lay against his cheeks, golden-brown with stunning pale tips, just like his hair.

I knew the hair that lined his upper thighs was the same color. A birthmark on his right shoulder vaguely resembled a star, and a long thin scar from a bike accident marred his right forearm. I'd come to know his body so well. And his heart too.

He was kind, and intelligent, and funny. He was amazing in bed. He was perfect.

I lay there, looking at the shadows his eyelashes cast on his cheeks. I wanted to trace the curve of his jaw with my eyes. I wanted to remember the way his lips looked slightly parted, his breath a soft whisper over them. I wanted it all forever.

I imagined that he would stay handsome as he aged, and when he did finally leave the world he would be old and beautifully worn out from living and loving to the fullest. His face would look just like it looked right now while he slept— content and at peace.

How badly I wanted to watch him get older, see him get a little silver in his thick honey hair. The idea of forever, the impossibility of it and the yearning for it, formed tears that dripped onto the sheets.

Blake stirred beside me, and I wiped those tears away as fast as possible. I didn't want to be a cause of sadness or worry to him. Not now. Not today.

He blinked up at me and smiled, and my heart was even more his with every second.

"Morning." His fingers stroked my throat and jaw and I shivered, needing his touch all over my body.

We were interrupted by a knock at the door. Blake grumbled. "I thought I'd ordered breakfast for ten in the morning." He glanced at the clock. "Oh, right."

He got up to answer the door, looking the very definition of 'just rolled out of bed', and it was the single sexiest thing I had ever seen.

A housekeeper with a French accent spoke with Blake at the door, then he took the tray from her and brought it in. He placed it on the bedside table, and the sweet smells of vanilla coffee and strawberry jam made me sit up in bed, alert with hunger.

We shared the steaming carafe of coffee, basket of croissants, crusty bread, and fruit-filled pastries. I didn't care about crumbs in the bed or how much butter and jam I slathered over each bite. I savored every mouthful.

"You've got something on your chin," Blake said.

My heart stopped. Lurched painfully. Tears burned in my eyes.

Black slugs churned inside me.

No. No. No.

He reached over, and with a thumb, wiped away a spot of strawberry jam.

I could only stare at it, confused.

"Wait, there's still a bit more."

I sat there, frozen, waiting for my body to be torn apart by darkness.

Blake took my coffee out of my hands and put it down, then crawled on top of me, kissing the jam softly off my chin.

"Are you okay?" he asked as he looked down at me, supporting himself with his arms.

I blinked a few times, bringing myself back to reality and dispelling the tears before they could fully form.

"Yeah. Yeah, I'm okay." *I'm okay.*

"Just okay?"

I giggled at Blake's exaggerated puppy face. "More than okay. Perfect. Deliriously content."

"Then why do you still have these damned clothes on?" he growled.

Blake stripped away my dress and tights. I responded

by relieving him of his clothing too. Shirts and underwear were flung all over the room, landing on leadlight lamps and velvet armchairs. When we were skin against skin, Blake threw the sheet over us. Sunlight shone through the white fabric, making a glowing private world for two.

He lay his body gently onto mine from toes to chest and brought his hands up into my short hair. He lifted my face to his, and his tongue touched mine then delved into a kiss so deep and heady that everything else spun away.

I ached with delight at every touch, and arched my back against the mattress, enjoying the hardness of his arousal pressed between us. He reached out of the sheets, fumbled with his wallet on the bedside table, and returned with a condom. I took it from him, carefully rolling it down over his long shaft, enjoying how he watched me touch him.

We shifted and rolled together between the sheets, and he pressed into me. My mouth opened in a cry he silenced with a kiss. My breath and his mingled, growing faster, as each leisurely thrust added to the slow burn of ecstasy building inside.

I lay there, rocking against him, wrapped in his warmth and his scent, in the sweet glow of joy that had crept over me. In that moment, we could have been in Paris, or back in my own bed, or on the moon. I could have imagined us anywhere, and at the same time it didn't matter where in the world we were. I only needed Blake. I could stay in one room, one bed, in his arms forever. He was all I needed.

Then we weren't in bed anymore. Blake lifted me out, carrying me by my thighs, my legs knotted around his waist as I moved up and down on him, refusing to break that connection, my arms around his shoulders and my kisses on his neck.

We moved like that into the bathroom, and he reached away to run the shower. My fingers toyed with the muscles of his chest as he turned back to me, lust smoldering in his eyes.

Once the water was steaming, he pulled us both under.

I gasped at his lips, drawing him closer as though I could consume him whole. The stream of the shower ran down between our mouths, hot water spilling around our tongues.

I fell back against the shower wall and he pressed me there, his chest to mine, his hands gripping tight under my thighs. The air was cool, making my nipples pucker and my skin rise into goosebumps, confused and excited by the contrasting splashes of hot water. Tremors ran through my body.

He thrust into me, driving me against that wall harder and harder, breaking me apart and making me whole again. Our cries sounded out over the gurgle and rush of the water. We both came within the very same moment, and I let tears of happiness and awe run down my cheeks, unseen under the fall of water surrounding us.

It was afternoon by the time Blake and I stepped out of our room. I could hear the low rumble of the falls, and they drew me to them, calling to a primal, wild part of my soul.

It was windy and a little cold, but we were only a couple of blocks away and we wandered down the streets, our hands linked, and smiles on our faces.

The viewing platforms were crowded with tourists, but in my eyes, only Blake, myself, and the falls existed. I stared out over them with my mouth open, the soft spray raining down onto us. The immensity of the falls, the sheer power and beauty, staggered my imagination. They were huge, bigger than I'd ever pictured based on photos I'd seen. My heart pounded with life and my blood sang a matching tune to the roar of water. I kept looking over at Blake, wondering if he was bored or if he thought I was being silly, but he wore the same smile as me.

We stayed there until it became dark, and the falls were lit up with brightly colored lights like something from a fantasy world. It was intensely magical, and it gave me an amazing gift—inspiration for my art. There were ideas I had never considered before flying around my head. Shapes of passionate bodies and passionate water, fusing, merging in splashes of color. I was desperate to get back to our room and the sketchbook I had there.

Blake had made all of this happen for me. He'd worked so hard for this, and for me, and I had no idea what would be next, what else he'd have to do for me from that childhood list. He'd told me we had a booking for dinner, and I wondered if that was from the list, or just something we were going to do. I had become confused as to where free will ended and the list started. And, in my darkest thoughts, I still wondered if Blake really wanted to do these things or if he felt somehow obligated.

By the time I turned away from the sight of the falls, my bubble had completely burst. On our way to dinner, the realistic part of me thought it was time I reminded myself I had the results of a cancer test waiting for me. I'd almost forgotten. I almost felt like I was living a life free of that. I couldn't forget though that getting that result was going to be painful.

And I wasn't sure I could survive the pain that would come from a fall as high as the one I was about to crash-land from.

Chapter Fifty

BLAKE

The restaurant looked like nothing from the front. It sat between a newsagent and a greengrocer in a small strip of shops by a highway. Old men sat in groups out the front, making themselves at home like they were regulars. The plain dirty white interior was filled with plastic tables and chairs, each with a red-and-white checkered tablecloth and a simple white vase holding a freshly cut rose bud. It was a recommendation from James, and at first sight I was disappointed. This was meant to be a special night, and this place didn't look special.

Then the smell of garlic, spices, and slow-cooking meat drifted out to us, exquisitely delicious. I followed it, and Georgina, inside. We found a quiet table in the back of the restaurant, in a small courtyard framed by rose bushes. *This is more like it.*

Nerves left me quiet, unable to say what I needed to. Georgina had become pale and drawn since we left the falls. Something raw and vulnerable stirred inside her. Looking at the shadows under her eyes, I wondered how long she'd been living with the thought that she was dying.

We all die. I knew that. It was the price we paid to get on the ride in the first place. But for most of us it was distant, easy to forget. But to believe it was imminent, just on the horizon—I couldn't imagine how that would feel. Would I manage to keep my head up, and keep going like Georgina did? Would I even be able to make it through a day without breaking down and crying my eyes out?

I could only hope the results gave us good news: that the lump was benign. And if it was bad news, if it was … *cancer?* The word hurt my heart. It was such an ugly sound. Cancer. Even the syllables sounded insidious, nasty, and evil. I could picture a blackness spreading through her body, and it hurt so bad.

Maybe that was why Georgina hadn't told anyone for so long. I wasn't sure I would want people looking at me and seeing only death.

Looking at Georgina now, I saw life. I saw love. I didn't give a shit if she was sick, if she was dying. If I only had her for a little while, I would take that. I knew it wouldn't be all sunshine and rainbows and pithy wisdom bestowed upon me like in the movies. She would be tired; she would be sick. She would be angry and sad and so would I, and we would suffer. I knew that. I understood it. I wanted to be with her anyway.

Stars twinkled above the open courtyard and the waitress brought some bread and took our order. Everything on the menu was overtly French, and Georgina smiled at my cringing when she ordered snails. She giggled, and for a second she looked about twelve years old. I wished I had known her then, before she got sick, before she became so afraid that people, life, and her own body would hurt her.

We sat, barely talking as we enjoyed each other's company and the delicious meal, the heartiness of the rich dishes and red wine keeping us warm. Georgina dipped torn pieces of sourdough bread into the garlic butter left behind under the snail shells, and popped them into her mouth. She ate like a cat, picking delicately and lapping up every morsel. The little pink triangle of her tongue came out and licked at her lower lip, like a tiny blooming flower. She had an unselfconscious delight about everything she did that turned me on.

I had to say something to her. But my voice kept

catching. Fear held me back, and I wished I was as brave as her.

We finished, and after paying I caught up with Georgina out the front. She was leaning against the wall, looking deep in thought and far too sexy from behind.

I put my arms around her. She turned in my embrace, and I kissed her three times lightly across her lips. We walked down the street, and although plenty of cabs passed by, we wandered together slowly, arms wrapped around each other, no real destination in mind.

Until Georgina said, "I want to see the falls again."

We returned to the highest lookout just as fireworks exploded in the sky above us. The sky turned purple to match, the color reflecting in the low clouds and mist surrounding the falls. Streaks of coral orange and bright pink burst in shimmering stars. Up on the lookout, it felt as though we were in the sky amongst them.

Rainbows sparkled from everywhere. Little drops of spray stuck in Georgina's dark hair, glittering like diamonds, and she was smiling in awe, pointing at the fireworks as they whizzed past us. I could see only her. Her head was back and her long creamy neck was exposed above the scarf she wore. The skirt of her dress swirled around her legs, and she looked like a painting come to life. I had never seen anything as alive and beautiful as she was.

I reached for her and she came into my arms, nestled

against my chest, and rested her forehead against my chin. She fit so perfectly into my body, into the curve of my own skin and bone. The world around us glittered like magic, and I knew it was the right time.

I breathed my fear out of me and it turned to crystals on the cold air.

Pulling the ring box out of my jacket pocket, I stepped back a little. The concrete was soaked, and the water went right through the fabric of my jeans as my knee went to the ground. Georgina paused, her eyes opening wider and her pretty mouth rounding into a tiny circle.

"Georgie, will you marry me?" I popped open the box.

The ring was a plain silver band with a modest diamond set within a pretty art deco design. From the small selection at the pawn shop that night, it had caught my eye, and I knew it was the right one. It was gorgeously unpretentious, and it was the perfect ring for Georgina.

Her mouth fell open. She stood there for what felt like eternity. Tourists up and down the lookout stopped and stared at us.

Georgina took a slow step back. I noticed the desolation in her eyes.

I should have known by now exactly what her response would be.

She ran.

Chapter Fifty-One

GEORGINA

Mist from the falls splattered in my eyes as I ran, merging with the tears and making it hard to see, hard to know where I was going. I didn't care where I went. Fear and grief drove my feet hard against the wet concrete to take me away from Blake. The roar of the falls couldn't cover the sound of sobs breaking through my chest.

Why would he do that?

Was this just another thing to tick off my childhood list? It had to be. *What was it? Receive a proposal? Get married? Have a family?*

Of course I would have included something like that. Why hadn't I seen this coming? I should never have agreed to this. He'd done all these outrageous and impossible and insane things, for me, for my lists, would he do this too? Never, never would someone like Blake want to marry someone as broken as me otherwise.

I don't even know how he'd forgiven me for what I'd done to him.

Maybe he hadn't. Maybe this was something much worse.

Was this revenge? Getting me back for making him go through my sexy bucket list, for using him and then abandoning him? Was he proposing, just for some list, so he could laugh and take it back and say it meant nothing?

I had trouble believing Blake could be so cruel.

But I could believe that I deserved that cruelty. And that I never deserved him.

I was down the stairs from the upper lookout and rounding the lower-level viewing area when Blake overtook me and blocked my path.

"Please, just stop," he said, panting. He reached for my arms and I backed away. The few other tourists braving the cold night watched with concern, and I backed off farther, ducking into the shadow of the staircase.

"Why did you ask me that? Was it on my list?"

Blake looked confused for a moment, and then laughed, almost relieved. "Your list? No, of course not."

"I don't believe you," I said, only because I couldn't accept the alternative.

Blake reached into an inside pocket of his jacket and pulled out his wallet. From it came a piece of purple paper, folded up small.

"Your list is finished. We've done everything. Niagara Falls was the last thing." He handed me the list. "I want to marry you because *I want to marry you*."

Flowers – From an anonymous admirer!

Be in a music video

Go to a carnival

Own a Unicorn

Go to the ocean

Date Magic Mark

Own a motorbike

Go to Niagara Falls

Make amazing memories that last forever!!!

I took the list from him with shaking fingers and stared at my handwriting, hearing my own voice from when I was fifteen.

I could hardly whisper, "You've done everything. You did everything for me."

"I've done a lot of crazy things for you, for love, or because I was told to." He held out the closed ring box between us. "But this is all me. This is my choice. I want this, and I want you."

I stared at the paper again, confused and awed. "What was the wafflewich about?"

"Just something I wanted to try." Blake chuckled. "Hey, I get to try things too."

Don't smile at me, please. I had let myself be with him now, but there's a huge difference between dating and forever. Especially when my forever had an expiration date—one that might come too soon. "Please leave me and live your life better without me."

"Georgina …"

"I watched my mom die." I wiped at my eyes with my damp scarf. "It was awful, but what was worse was seeing my dad watch her die. I don't want you to go through that."

The mist had soaked through Blake's hair and his eyelashes clung together, star-like, flashes of fireworks reflected on them. "It's my right to decide what I want to do, and what

I can handle. I love you—why can't you get that through your head? I know you've been trying to push me away because you think you should, but have you ever *wanted* to push me away? Has that ever been what you really wanted?"

My answer came out as a sob. "Never."

"Then be with me, love me, and let me love you, and we'll face any outcome together." Blake gathered me into his arms again, and I felt his lips press against my soaked hair.

I thought back to the lists we'd completed, lists of items I would have once thought impossible. With Blake by my side, I could do anything.

"We will," I said, and for the first time, I believed it.

Blake planted a series of kisses along my hairline. "Now, do you have any other lies or lists or dark secrets to tell me?"

A giggle of pure relief rattled from my lips. "No."

Blake dropped down to one knee and held out the ring again. He gave me his biggest grin. "Georgina Stone, you're the strongest and most amazing woman I've ever known, and I want to be with you for every moment of our lives, no matter what. Will you marry me?"

I could barely speak. I just smiled, and sobbed, and laughed, and nodded as I stared at the man I loved. He swept me up into a tight hug. A few bystanders who'd noticed the second proposal happening were applauding. Fireworks crackled and boomed in the sky behind us.

I kissed Blake, hard and long and deep, and more cheers came from the crowd. "I love you. I've loved you in a way that feels like it's always been a part of me, and always will be. It feels like forever."

Chapter Fifty-Two

GEORGINA

"I'm ready to go home. I'm ready to face my results."

They were my first words to Blake the next morning when he woke up to me running my fingers through his golden hair. He simply nodded, and we packed and were on a plane home by lunchtime.

For the whole flight, I couldn't stop looking at the ring on my finger. It was more beautiful and inspiring than the azure sky and toy-town world out the window. I looked at it, amazed in knowing it was really there. That Blake knew *everything*—and hadn't rejected me. That I had been brave enough to say yes, to admit my love, to accept being loved.

I still had fear. Lots of it. But I wasn't going to run away anymore.

I held my hand in front of my face, admiring that bright stone. "Do you ever look at a cut gem, like a perfect diamond, and think of how much surrounding gem was cut away and turned into waste to make this shape?"

Blake smiled at my musings. "I don't think I ever have."

"I think it has to be done, those brutal cuts, that loss, to show the beauty within. To make it shine like that."

He kissed my forehead and held my hand, and I knew that he understood me completely.

I placed my other palm over my breast and pressed softly, feeling that lump under the skin. I wanted to curse it, but I knew without it I wouldn't have had all these amazing experiences. I wouldn't have met Blake, or Kaley, or Priya.

Those silver linings could be so fucking ironic.

Without the lump, would Julie would still be alive? I held the weight of her death in my hands, and I held her in my heart. She wouldn't have been at that intersection if not for me, but I didn't make it rain. I didn't drive the truck that crashed into us. I didn't speed in that rain and lose control.

When I broke down all the moving parts I could almost believe it wasn't my fault she died. Life was so complex, a series of coincidences and luck, good decisions and bad decisions, and accidents and life-changing moments. Asking 'What if?' couldn't change anything. We had to work with what we had. If that accident hadn't happened, if Julie hadn't died, I might never have told Dad about the lump, never got tested. I might have continued down that self-destructive path.

Losing Julie was a tragedy, but I couldn't change it and I couldn't hate it because it was a part of my life.

I think I was starting to understand what Dad had meant about lemons now. I was learning to love the lemons, not just the lemonade.

Dad loved his fruit metaphors. He once said being a parent was like growing tomatoes. If you didn't tie the plant to a support, it became a sprawling mess, its fruit spoiling in the dirt. But you couldn't make the ties too tight, or they would break the fragile stems, and there would be no fruit at all.

Dad used to drive me nuts, always wanting to hang my art projects on the refrigerator, or telling every diner in his restaurant about his beautiful daughter. I had never stopped to wonder what it would have been like for me without his approval, without his sincere interest in me and the things I found fascinating, without his unflinching support and care throughout my treatment.

I remembered the time he had made me beetroot and ricotta sandwiches on warm focaccia bread at two a.m. because I had woken up sore, itchy from radiation burns, and with this incredible craving for beets and cheese.

He had always been there for me, not just my dad, but a good dad. The best.

I missed Mom, but it was an abstract emotion based on the feeling that a kid needed a mother. Dad had been everything I needed.

It was going to break his heart if I had cancer again. I didn't want him to come to hear the results with me. But I had to let him. I had to give him the respect owed such a good father, and I had to let him father me.

As soon as we got home, I called the hospital to make an appointment for the next morning. Then I called Dad, and spent an hour on the phone with him.

Being home again warmed my heart. I loved the potted geraniums and peeling paint. I loved my gigantic unicorn and its little narwhal friend. I loved my freezer filled with leftovers from Dad's restaurant. It was *home.* It was the place I lived, where my best friend had lived, where my new friends would live as long as they needed to.

Coming home to Priya and Kaley felt right, telling them what was happening in my life felt right. Their excitement at my engagement news felt awesome, and when they insisted on coming to the hospital with us the next day as well, it felt right to let them.

Blake stayed with me in my room that night, and

I realized we'd never shared my bed. I'd always run away to his place. It felt good welcoming him there, into my life, completely.

Chapter Fifty-Three

GEORGINA

When I was a little girl, I pretended to be a princess a lot of the time. I would wrap the long scarves my mother had worn over her head during chemo around my waist and shoulders, like they were my mantles and my wedding gowns. Those scarves had stayed with me during my own chemo.

They had all eventually fallen apart. The only one still left intact was made from filmy green silk printed with weirdly shaped, giant yellow birds. I asked Dad once where Mom had gotten it, thinking there must be a story there, but he said it was just something she had liked in a store.

As a kid, I'd made up my own stories for that scarf—how it reminded her of the tropical vacation she had taken and never told Dad about, or of the pet parrot she'd had when she was a kid living on a pirate ship. At this point in my life, I figured it had just struck her as quirky and when your life was at stake, you often needed something to smile at.

I wore that scarf when I walked into the Breast Cancer Care Center to get my results. So that Mom would be with me. Just like Dad was, and Blake, and Kaley, and Priya. I was guarded and loved on all sides.

We told the woman at reception I was there, then took our seats to wait. Dad and Blake sat either side of me, and Kaley and Priya sat opposite us. I unwound the scarf from my neck and laid it across my lap, petting it like a cat.

"I never liked that scarf," Dad grumbled, staring at it. "Used to make me think of flying mucus." He reached over and patted it as well. "Now it just makes me think of your mom. She'd be so proud of you."

That was when he saw the ring on my finger.

I hadn't told him on the phone. I'd meant to announce it as soon as I saw him this morning but got distracted. Impending results from a cancer test were a bit distracting.

"Blake proposed at Niagara," I confirmed nervously. I was worried what he'd say—that we were too young or it was too soon or that it was a reaction to intense circumstances. And maybe it was all those things, but it was also our choice.

"Spontaneous indeed." He muttered something about tomatoes and then put his arm around my shoulders. "Congratulations. I think it's beautiful." Tears filled his eyes as he looked from me to Blake. "You're both beautiful together."

I wrapped my arms around Dad's neck and let his bushy eyebrows tickle my cheeks.

Blake put his hand on my knee, and I could feel his fingers shaking. Across the narrow floor, Kaley's knees jittered the way they had when I'd first met her and she was getting tested herself. Priya chewed on a fingernail.

I felt still, and calm. Not hard like a stone or locked into invisible armor. This was different. It was acceptance.

I had woken in my bed that morning in Blake's arms, surrounded by a giant rainbow unicorn and a cute plushy narwhal, with a smile on my face. We were almost late for the appointment because I didn't want to get out of that bed. Not from fear. From losing track of time with me in Blake's arms and him inside me.

I still felt that warmth spreading through me.

The lemon-yellow waiting room had large vases of fake sunflowers in every corner, and the Breast Cancer Care Center logo was etched into the windows and painted large on the wall above the reception counter. It was a simplified bust of Botticelli's *Venus*. I nodded at her sure, accepting smile.

"You look like her," Kaley said. "I don't know how you do it. Babe, I was curled up on the floor crying when I came in for my results, and that was *after* I got the all clear."

"She's not kidding," Priya said.

"I'm sure it will be fine though. You'll be fine. It will be fine. This is going to be fine."

I smiled at Kaley's rambling and just shrugged.

When I was fifteen I had searched for signs and portents. I had stared at the receptionist, tried to read the expressions on the faces of nurse's or doctor's, thinking a frown thrown my way would mean the worst, or that a secret smile meant good news awaited me.

Not anymore. I was ready to accept either outcome. We all lived. We all died. Our whole galaxy would someday be nothing but stardust, and it was terrible and awe-inspiring.

Could I be fine with that?

"Everything dies. Everything changes. In the greater scheme of things, does any of this matter?"

Blake stared down at me, silent. Then he asked, "How do you feel, right now?"

I looked around at my entourage, so scared for me, caring so much for me. "Loved. Happy. Alive."

"Then that matters."

Kaley awed and Priya hugged her. She whispered, "We matter."

It might be easier if everything didn't matter. Nihilism had its upsides. But mattering made it all *worth it.*

I would make every moment of my life matter.

Images of a wedding day filled my mind along with the realization that *holy shit,* I'd agreed to get married. Being with Blake forever was one thing, a sort of inevitable truth, but the realization that there would be a wedding had just caught up to me. Regardless of what happened next, with my results, there might be a wedding, there might be me moving in with Blake or him with me, or finding a new home together. There might be us, having a family. There were so many what-ifs and maybes and hopes ahead of me.

I thought I was done with lists, but my mind was filled with the future. I pulled a pen and my black journal from my bag and started to draft one final list. The last list I'd need for the rest of my life.

Be strong, and allow others to be strong for me

Be brave, brave enough to tell the truth and ask for help

Accept fear, but don't let it rule me

Love fully, love myself, and believe others can love me

Be okay with my life, my body, and with what makes me human

Be okay with life when it's terrible. Be okay with death

Remember that lemons are always worth it

Next to those words, I sketched a little bald lion.

"Georgina? Georgina Stone?" A young female doctor looked up from her clipboard, seeking a response from the nervous crowd in the waiting room. Dad still had his arm over my shoulders and Blake had his arm around my waist. They both squeezed their love into me.

I am Georgina Stone. I am strong—stronger than I ever knew. I am loved. I am brave. It will be okay.

Whatever came next. Whatever life threw at me.

I was ready.

Be strong, and allow others to be strong for me

Be brave, brave enough to tell the truth and ask for help

Accept fear, but don't let it rule me

Love fully, love myself, and believe others can love me

Be okay with my life, my body,
and with what makes me human

Be okay with life when it's terrible.

Be okay with death

Remember that lemons are

always

worth it.

EPILOGUE

GEORGINA

"Georgina Stone?" The doctor called out again, peering from above her horn-rimmed glasses. I confirmed my presence with a wave, but my legs didn't want to move.

The young doctor had a smile that strained her lips when I made her wait a full minute before standing and gathering myself, my things, and my family. Blake and Dad both came with me; Priya and Kaley wished me good luck and waited behind.

I'd never seen this doctor before. But that wasn't strange. While I was officially still under Doctor Kefford's care, really that meant I could be seen by any of the larger team of doctors who she worked with. You only get to see the lead doctor if it wasn't a routine checkup.

The doctor led us down the hall—not to a normal examination room, but to Doctor Kefford's private office.

It felt a bit like being sent to the principal's office. Was this where they sent patients to tell them they only had weeks left to live? Had I waited too long, my own fear and stubbornness costing me the chance to live? Fear clutched at my heart and squeezed, so I took the hands of the two men I loved into mine and squeezed them just as tight. They held my hands back firmly, and I took a deep breath.

"It will just be a moment. Take a seat."

The office had a giant wooden desk with piles of papers threatening to slide off one side. Behind it was a huge corkboard filled with photographs of people. Most of them were bald or wearing wigs, and all of them were grinning despite looking barely alive. I wondered if those were all the patients Kefford had ever treated. I wondered how many had lived. I caught sight of my fifteen-year-old face up there and gave myself a small nod of respect.

If you made it, then so can I.

When Doctor Kefford walked in, she seemed flustered, and a man in a business suit followed her. I shook her hospi-tal-cold hand when she extended it to me, as clean and soft as I remembered it. Everything about her seemed soft, from the flouncy floral blouse under her white coat to her wispy blond hair.

The man was a contrast in hardness, and stood to the side of the room like some kind of bodyguard as Kefford sat down on a chair right in front of me, looking me in the eyes. Her hands reached out just inches from mine. She looked at me the same way she always did, her head tilted to the side and a squinty smile that oozed sympathy.

"Georgie, how are you feeling today?" Doctor Kefford spoke in long, sweet, hushed tones, smiling, as though soothing a newborn.

Her voice took me back to a place I didn't want to go, to the cold sterile rooms and the whir of the drip machine pumping even colder poisons through my veins. To the memory of long nights spent vomiting, watching my hair falling off my head, and endless needles and pain.

I made a noncommittal sound.

"It's been a while since I've seen you. You've grown into a woman. How's college?"

"Good. How's your … baby?" I remembered her being pregnant during my first round of treatment. She'd always been so kind to me, but I had hated her at the time because she was the one who gave me hard news, prescribed me pills that made me sick, and had to explain my chances in cold, hard numbers.

Doctor Kefford just smiled and tilted her head even

more in response. She knew this wasn't about her, and that I wasn't here for small talk.

She looked back to the man in the corner, and he nodded to her again. Down to business then.

"This is Mr. Harris, the hospital's attorney." She gestured across to the man.

Dad frowned. "Why do we need an attorney here?"

"It's nothing to worry about—just standard bureaucracy for events like this."

The attorney stepped forward and his voice was monotonous, as though reading a pre-prepared script. "Georgina Stone's pathology was done using brand-new testing equipment. The equipment is cutting edge, but it is susceptible to a small margin of error if it isn't properly calibrated, or staff are not properly trained. This hospital does not take responsibility for any technical issues causing false results and has done its utmost to provide accurate testing."

I blinked. "What?"

Doctor Kefford put a hand up, warding the man back to his corner. "We had to re-run Georgie's test a couple of times. Both due to errors in the equipment, and because I wanted to be absolutely sure, for you."

"Damned right you want to be sure," Dad grumbled.

"Tom, we're sure. That's why it took so long. Luckily, we had enough sample to retest."

I felt as if I'd been holding my breath since she came in. I couldn't wait any longer. "And?"

I heard the doctor's next words, but they didn't register at first.

The roaring in my ears sounded a lot like the ocean, the ocean on the day that Blake had taken me out to play in the waves. My chest felt like it contracted to the size of a pea, and my breath squeezed out of my lungs, which had become too small and too narrow for it.

"I am sorry, could you repeat that?"

Kefford swallowed visibly and smiled. "Georgie, the lump isn't cancerous. I'm sorry you've had to go so long thinking the worst."

Her words felt like setting my whole body out under the sun after a long, cold winter and letting the warmth and the light sink down all the way into my bones. My heart started pumping fast, and I drew a huge breath into my lungs, tasting the sweetness of the air.

"I don't have cancer," I whispered. A shudder in my throat brought tears to my eyes, and I started laughing.

I put a hand on my dad's arm and with one look at me, he grabbed me into a hug and spun me around in circles. I only had my feet on the floor a second before Blake lifted me off my feet in an embrace.

Kefford smiled at us, and I leaned over and kissed her

on the cheek, causing her to whimper and put a hand over her sniffling nose and smiling mouth.

Dad gave me that smile, the same one he gave when I was a kid and he'd let me eat ice cream for breakfast. "You two get out of here. You've spent more than enough time in hospitals. I'll stay and wrap things up."

"Thank you, Dad."

Blake and I ran out of the office, laughing and shouting like little kids.

Kaley and Priya saw us coming, saw the looks on our faces.

"OMIGOD OMIGOD!" Kaley jumped in the air as if she'd won a car, and then crash-tackled me. Priya helped us both back up again. The receptionist shushed us through her huge grin. I'm sure she saw too many people leaving after receiving bad news, and despite the commotion we were causing, everyone in that waiting room seemed happy for us.

We all jogged out into the corridor outside, giggling in the unstoppable way that came from pure relief.

"Massive party at your place tonight!" Kaley called.

"*Our* place."

"I'm so fregging happy you're okay."

"She won't be okay after all the junk food we're going to eat," Priya said. "Even with the good news, all this drama has given me the intense needs for junk food."

Kaley nodded. "Chicky Choco-Cakes. Gummy Whirls. Burrito-flavored chips. Oh, and those cocktails with champagne and butterscotch and ice cream."

"And marshmallows. We'll make a little campfire in the backyard. I've been wanting roasted marshmallows for a while," I added. "Not pumpkin flavored ones."

They told me they would sort it all out, and left Blake and me alone in the hospital corridor.

He picked me up, swung me around, and kissed me. The diamond in my ring flashed, and his eyes sparkled brighter. "So, Georgie, what do you want to do with the rest of your life?"

"I want to learn how to ride that bike you built for me. I want to make art. I want to swim in the ocean again and see rain falling on Paris streets. I want to make love and dance and taste foods I have never tasted." I kissed his cheeks and mouth and hands. "I want to love you forever, and I want to see you dance at that strip club again."

Blake let out a hearty laugh. "Imagine what our next year will be like."

I had to laugh too. These last few weeks had been insane. I'd had so many adventures and awakenings. I had fallen in love. I'd been arrested and made love under the stars. I'd come to terms with how much I missed my mom, and lost a friend. I had hurt more, laughed more, felt more, wanted more, and cried more than I ever had in my life.

"We can do any of those things, or none of them. I don't want to live a list; I just want to live. With you," I said.

Somewhere along the journey of doing my lists, I'd learned how beautiful life could be. I found out that sex could be just as silly, funny, awful, sad, passionate, and fun as life itself. All the bad things that had happened mixed in with the good, and made this big colorful pattern that hurt my heart in all the best ways.

When I wrote my first bucket list at fifteen, my childish ideas of romance were colored by my lack of experience and the hope for a happily-ever-after that I'd been sure would never come. But here I was, basking in my happily-ever-after with my prince by my side.

I stopped in the hospital corridor and looked up at Blake. "I know you once said that I shouldn't add new things to my bucket list, but I was wondering if you'd be happy to make an exception now?"

Blake looked suspicious. "Is this the two men thing again? Because I'll have to go all caveman on you."

I laughed, the idea of him tying me up driving my confidence and lust-filled thoughts. I grabbed Blake by the collar of his shirt and dragged him toward the open door of a vacant examination room.

"Actually, I had something different in mind. Making love on a hospital bed, maybe? Do you think that's something you could arrange?" I asked innocently. "And maybe a little caveman is okay too."

Blake growled, threw me over his shoulder, and locked the door behind us.

It was the best sex we'd ever had, but somehow I knew it was only going to keep getting better.

A Note From the Author

Georgina's story is very special to me. It's about life, and every moment, up and down. It's about all the moments in the beautiful, terrible, rapturous, and tragic, miracle of life.

Many authors say to 'write what you know', and this is that story for me. I've had cancer at a young age. I still suffer the fear and medical anxiety it left me with. Many of the moments in this story are based on my direct personal experiences. And other moments are purely wild fantasy. It's up to you to guess which is which.

I hope that Georgina's story has meaning to you and your journey through this crazy thing called life.

Now here's your Public Service Announcement section—I was twenty-six when I was diagnosed with breast cancer, completely out of the blue. I was healthy in all other ways, with no family history. Cancer doesn't discriminate. It can happen to anybody at any time. Self-check, get screened, if in doubt talk to your doctor. You and your life are valuable and miraculous. Savor every moment. Make it last.

Love the lemons, not just the lemonade.

About the Author

Lena Fox is a pen name of Selina Fenech. Professional daydreamer, Selina Fenech writes "adorably dark" Epic and Urban Fantasy for teens and adults. Filled with sweet and quirky characters, laugh out loud moments, and breath-taking adventures, her unique worlds are perfect for readers who love thrilling twists paired with happily ever afters.

Artist, mother, and cancer survivor, Selina is determined to live life to the fullest, and loves escape rooms, gardening, and all forms of food and geekery.

Selina also applies her distinctive take on magical realms as a world-renown fantasy artist and has published many illustrated books, oracle decks, and colouring books.

Official Website www.selinafenech.com

Find More Books by Lena Fox

Discover urban fantasy, paranormal romance, contemporary romance, young adult, epic fantasy, fairy tale retellings and more from Lena Fox and Selina Fenech.

Visit www.selinafenech.com
to sign up for a free sampler library!

www.ingramcontent.com/pod-product-compliance
Lightning Source LLC
Chambersburg PA
CBHW011922190726
48283CB00009BA/2846